DEAD END

BARRY FRIEDMAN

DEAD END. Copyright © 1995 by Barry Friedman. All rights reserved.
Printed in the United States of America. No part of this book may be used or reproduced in any manner whatsoever without written permission except in the case of brief quotations embodied in critical articles or reviews. For information address
Forward Press, P.O. Box 288082, San Diego, CA 92128

Cover design by Carolyn Yabe

Library of Congress Catalog Card Number 94-78432
ISBN 1-885591-17-9

Forward Press
P.O. Box 288082
San Diego, CA 92128

Printed in the USA by

Morris Publishing
3212 E. Hwy 30
Kearney, NE 68847
800-650-7888

ACKNOWLEDGEMENTS

The characters and events in this book are fictional.

Lieutenant Robert Vega of the Canton, Ohio Police Department and Harold Hand, former Los Angles Police Department Homicide Detective, gave me valuable technical advice concerning police procedures.

I gratefully acknowledge the help and encouragement given me by Bruno Leone of Greenhaven Press, and Evelyn Bruyere. I am deeply indebted to Shirley Allen, Judith Hand, Phyllis Humphrey, Henry Johnson and Suzanne Middleton for their thoughtul reviews and constructive criticisms of the.manuscript.

Brenda Griffing did a masterful job of brushing away the lint and clipping the loose threads.

Finally, but not least, Florence Feiler has my everlasting appreciation for her unflagging faith in my literary endevours.

This one's for Sue

ONE

ALMOST SIX-THIRTY. The parking lot, dimly lit by a single spotlight suspended high on a pole. As he trudged to his Buick station wagon, Gibson glanced at his wrist watch again. The calendar on the face of the watch read April 7. Tomorrow would be Harriet's birthday, her thirty-sixth. He debated whether to stop and pick up the silver bracelet he had bought at Potter and Lemon. The engraving he had ordered would be finished. The store remained open until seven, but the hell with it. He'd do it tomorrow. This evening he was too tired. Just wanted to get home, have a drink and relax before dinner.

At the thought of food, his stomach growled and he remembered that he'd had no lunch. Nothing new. Half the time he went without eating from breakfast until he arrived home at seven or later.

When he turned the key to unlock the station wagon door, he discovered he had just locked it instead. Probably had forgotten to lock up in his hurry to get to the office. Wouldn't be the first time.

He unlocked the door, tossed his briefcase on the front passenger's seat and sank into the driver's seat. He'd relax for a moment. He closed his eyes for ten seconds, then put the key in the ignition.

While he was buckling his seat belt he felt sudden pressure against his neck. A bug? He reached behind to slap it. His fingers came into contact with metal. Startled, he glanced toward the rearview mirror, but it was tilted up so he was seeing only a dim reflection of light from the car roof. Gibson started to turn.

"Don't turn around!"

"What the hell do you want?"

"Shut up and drive!"

It surprised him that he wasn't frightened. He'd thought about being held up and wondered what he would do. Now he knew. He reached for his wallet. "Look, take what you want and get out. I won't—"

"Keep your fucking hands on the wheel!" The metal he'd felt now pressed firmly into his neck. A gun barrel. "Get this car moving!"

Gibson started the car.

"Left out of the driveway."

The evening rush hour traffic had thinned out. Only a few cars passed in the opposite direction, there were no cars in front of his, no pedestrians in this part of the city at this time of day.

As he drove, Gibson prayed he'd come across a cruising police car. Ram it and duck down in the front seat. He dropped that idea quickly. He'd give the guy his money, watch, credit cards, whatever he wanted. He wasn't ready to be a hero and die.

Now they were traveling south on Dueber, past Prairie College Road and were out of the city. At Fohl, a red, white and blue shield-shaped sign pointed to southbound Interstate 77. The gun barrel was pushed more firmly into his neck. "Get on the interstate here."

Interstate? Who the hell was this guy and where was he taking him? He felt sweat pouring down the sides of his chest from his armpits. His throat tightened, he could hardly breath. Despite his grip on the wheel his hands began to shake. This had to be more than robbery. Gibson hadn't spoken since offering the guy his wallet. But now he had to make another try. "For crissake, take the car. Let me out. There's no one around. It'll take me half an hour to get —"

"Shut up and drive!"

On the interstate, Gibson drove slowly in the right-hand lane hoping someone in another vehicle would look into his car, see what was happening.

The voice from the backseat ordered him to set the cruise control to fifty-five. Gibson did as he was told. His eyes moved side to side frantically, looking for something, anything. He pleaded, "Look, I've got a wife and two small kids. Jesus Christ, I'll give you anything, I'll do anyth—"

"Shut up and drive!"

Gibson's mind was racing. *This fucking madman is going to kill me.* "Please. PLEASE. PLEASE." Half sob, half scream. The only response was increased pressure of the gun into his neck Suddenly, fear turned to rage. *Why me? WHY ME?* Gibson's jaws clenched. His hands squeezed the steering wheel so tightly his fingernails dug into the soft flesh of his palms. He wasn't about to wait until the bastard decided where he was going to stop and do whatever he wanted to do. Even if the carjacker, or whatever the hell he was, was crazy, he wouldn't shoot him while he had the wheel, barreling down the highway. Gibson floored the accelerator, the Buick shot ahead. The pressure of the gun was no longer on his neck. He flicked a glance back. The gunman, thrown off balance, had fallen backward into the rear seat. *I'm gonna make it. I'm gonna make it.* Gibson jerked the steering wheel sharply to the right and the car skidded off the paved portion of the road, onto the berm, throwing up a shower of gravel and dirt. Momentarily the car balanced on its two left tires. He leaned his body left, trying to make the car roll over. It teetered, then, still speeding ahead, righted itself, fell back on to all four wheels and bounced against the guard rail for 100 yards. Steel ground against steel. Sparks flew. He strained, trying to swing the steering wheel in the opposite direction, still hoping to make the car roll over, but the violent maneuvering caused the motor to stall. With the power steering mechanism off, he could barely turn the wheel. As the car slowed, Gibson reached for the door handle. Before he could depress it, from the edge of his vision he saw the gun butt come crashing down on his skull. As darkness closed in he turned, saw a face he recognized.

* * *

CANTON MAN FATALLY SHOT

CANTON. A 40-year-old Canton businessman was found dead in his car early this morning. The body of Henry Gibson, 3946 Gramercy Ave. was discovered between State Route 20 and Interstate 77. on a little-used dirt road that leads to the farm of Herman Schuler. Schuler found the car at 5:30 AM with Gibson's body on the front seat.

Stark County Sheriff's Office spokesperson, Deputy Sheriff Karen Vandergrift said that preliminary reports by the medical examiner indicate that Gibson had suffered gunshot wounds and a probable skull fracture. He is believed to have died yesterday evening. Vandergrift stated that Gibson apparently had been robbed. A wallet empty of cash and credit cards was found in the car. Papers in a briefcase left in the car confirmed the identification. Vandergrift stated that investigators have no suspects and are working on the theory that Gibson had picked up a hitchhiker who robbed and killed him. An investigation by the sheriff's office with the help of technicians from the Stark County Crime Laboratory in Canton, is underway.

A longtime Canton resident, Gibson had been assistant sales manager of Sterling Wholesale Hardware Company. He is survived by his wife, the former Harriet Remington and two children: Henry Jr., age 10 and Heather, age 7.

In what may be a related incident, Theodore Lambert, 36, of Sherryville, reported to the Ohio Highway Patrol that he had seen a station wagon, described as similar to Gibson's, swerve off the pavement of I-77 at approximately 7 PM yesterday. The station wagon struck a guard rail and appeared to have stalled. Lambert, driving south on I-77 stopped to render assistance, but before he could reach the vehicle, it was driven away headed south. The incident occurred three miles north of the off ramp to U.S. Route 250 and approximately twelve miles from where the Gibson vehicle was found. Lambert could not see how many people were in the station wagon, nor could he see the driver.

* * *

Dr. Harry Hanson, medical examiner for Stark County, pulled up his rubber gloves as he walked to the autopsy slab and inspected the body. A photographer from the crime lab had already taken a number of pictures of the body from various angles. Phil Moore, the technician seated on a tall lab stool, cleaned his fingernails with the point of a nail file.

Hanson stood at the side of the autopsy table snugging his fingers into the gloves, peering down at the body of a man wearing a light blue blazer and gray slacks. The top button of the man's striped shirt was open, the knot of his dark blue tie was pulled down. The dead man's black shoes were highly polished, his hands were encased in clear plastic bags held with rubber bands at the wrists. The body lay on its right side, knees drawn up and the upper half bent forward in the fetal position. In other surroundings it could have been a man taking a midday nap on his office couch.

Hanson stepped on the foot-pedal switch of the dictating machine, his voice echoing off the cement walls and floor as he talked into the microphone suspended over the autopsy table.

"The body is that of a Caucasian male. . ." He described the corpse's dress and position, then turned to Moore. "Okay, Phil, off your ass. Help turn him over."

The men flipped the body onto its left side. Hanson bent to inspect two small round holes, one in the skin just below the man's open shirt collar, the other about six inches lower, in the midline seam of the jacket. A circlet of black surrounded each hole.

"Tattooing around the bullet holes indicates near-discharge of the gun muzzle to the victim."

He measured the diameter and position of each hole, reading his measurements into the microphone. Pushing a metal probe into each of the bullet holes, he recorded their depths and angles. He stepped back while the photographer moved in and took several close-ups.

Hanson said, "What do you think, Phil? A twenty-two?"

"Uh-huh. Either that or a twenty-five."

With some effort, they straightened the dead man's legs to undress him. Rigor mortis, Hanson knew, came on about five hours after death and lasted about thirty-six hours. He estimated that the man wearing a toe-tag that read "Henry Gibson," had been killed around seven the night before. It was now four o'clock the following afternoon, the body rigid as a board. The technician kept pressure on the dead man's knees to prevent them from returning to their flexed position.

The skin over the entire front of the body was a mottled purple, that over the back was lemon yellow. "Was he on his face in the car when you found him?" Hanson asked.

"Yeah, he was squeezed down between the dashboard and the front seat on the passenger's side, resting on his elbows and his knees. When we got there he had already stiffened in that position. We had a hell of a job wedging him out of the door."

Hanson then directed his attention to the head. He parted the thinning, dark brown hair and ran his gloved fingers over the scalp. With a hand lens, he carefully inspected the hair and underlying scalp. He snipped a few strands of hair with a scissors, placed them in a small plastic envelope. From another part of the head, he pulled a few hairs loose and deposited them separately into another envelope. Then he resumed dictating. "Over the center of the occipito-parietal junction there is a hematoma measuring. . ." He gazed up at the ceiling while he pressed on the hematoma and felt in its depths a depression in the skull. The bony edges of the depressed area were sharp. "Depressed skull fracture," he mused. "The size of the scalp hematoma suggests that there was an interval of at least fifteen minutes between the infliction of the depressed skull fracture and death."

When he finished the autopsy, he stripped off his rubber gloves while he dictated his summary. "I conclude that death was due to penetrating bullet wounds with entry through the seventh cervical vertebra, and through the disk space between the seventh and eighth thoracic vertebrae. The cervical wound transected the spinal cord and extended through the esophagus and trachea. The bullet causing this wound was lodged in subcutaneous tissues of the neck, anterior to the trachea.

"The thoracic wound transected the spinal cord at that level and perforated the left ventricle of the heart. This bullet passed through the sternum and was found in the subcutaneous tissues of the anterior chest wall.

"Either bullet wound could have been the proximate cause of death.

"The depressed skull fracture and the underlying laceration of the parietal lobe of the brain were not necessarily fatal."

He gazed at the two bullet fragments in the palm of his hand for a few seconds, then dropped each into a small cotton-lined cardboard box which he handed to Moore. The lab tech had accumulated a carton full of material including the victim's clothing, fingerprints and scrapings, a jar containing samples of his stomach contents and several vials of blood. He placed the carton on a small carrier. As he wheeled it out, he raised a hand. "So long, I've got enough work here to keep me off the streets for a while."

* * *

GIBSON RITES HELD; MURDER STILL UNSOLVED

CANTON. Funeral services were held in First Presbyterian Church yesterday for Henry Gibson, 40-year-old salesman, who was robbed and slain on April 7. The eulogy was given by the Reverend Lloyd R. Eaton. Burial was at Plymouth Cemetery.

Gibson's body was discovered early Wednesday in his station wagon on a dirt road near Interstate 77. He had been shot and assaulted with a blunt instrument.

Investigation by Stark County Sheriff Office personnel has so far turned up few clues. Ballistics tests on the bullets recovered from Gibson's body have not matched those from other recent shootings in the area. The only fingerprints found in the murder vehicle were those of the victim. Authorities declined to comment on additional laboratory studies that were reported to be in progress.

Deputy Sheriff Karen Vandergrift revealed that Gibson had left his office in the Sterling Building, 3990 4th St. here, at about 6:30 PM. Tuesday, April 7, after phoning his wife Harriet that he was on his way home. Since his usual route passed by the West Tuscarawas ramp to I-77, Vandergrift said, "We are working on the assumption that he picked up a hitchhiker near the ramp. The assailant appears to have forced the victim at gunpoint to drive south on the interstate. There is evidence that Mr. Gibson tried to take control by maneuvering the car at high speed. The assailant apparently subdued him by striking him on the head, fracturing his skull. While Mr. Gibson lay unconscious, the assailant seems to have driven the car to the spot where the murder and robbery occurred."

Vandergrift said that K-9 Corps dogs had traced the killer's tracks from the station wagon. Several potentially important pieces of evidence were found, but the sheriff's spokesperson would not elaborate. She said the killer probably walked back to State Route 20 and hitchhiked along that road. Since a hitchhiker on the interstate would be picked up by highway patrol, it was less likely that the interstate would be used as the escape route. A plea was issued for information from any witnesses who may have driven by the area during the evening of Tuesday, April 7.

Henry Gibson is survived by his widow the former Harriet Remington. . .

TWO

ONE MONTH LATER.

Al Maharos watched with distaste as Frank Fiala licked the fingertips of his left hand while he held the steering wheel with the other.

"Trouble with this shit," said Fiala, "it gets everything sticky."

Maharos gave him a look of contempt. "'This shit,' you crude bastard, is *baklava*, a delicacy in the civilized world. Anybody else would die for it. You just passed it."

"Passed what?"

"The building where we're going. It's 433, right?"

Fiala jammed on the brakes and made a U-turn, narrowly missing a truck. The truck driver yelled something and Fiala gave him the finger as he pulled in to a loading zone marked No Parking. He flipped down the sun visor with the PD seal.

Fiala squeezed his five-eight, two-twenty body out from behind the wheel. His bushy black hair came down to within an inch of eyebrows so thick that they almost hid his eyes. His nose had been fist-flattened against his face a dozen times during his forty-three years. As he got out of the car, he yanked both trouser legs down from where they had crept up on his thick thighs.

Another warm day, warmer than usual even for May. Maharos thought about leaving his hat in the car, but even after all these years he felt self-conscious about his baldness. He wiped the sweat from the liner and from his head and put the hat back on. At least the black hat didn't show sweat stains.

On the building directory they found the listing: Bost, Frankel and Horner, Attorneys-at-Law,...Suite 507.

In the elevator Fiala said, "Is that all he did, work comp?"

"Yeah."

"Who'd want to kill a work comp lawyer?"

Maharos said everybody.

The receptionist looked from one to the other as they walked into the waiting room. "Can I help you?"

Maharos flipped open his shield case. "I'm Youngstown PD homicide detective Al Maharos. This is my partner, Frank Fiala. We need to get some information on Mr. Horner."

"Let me call Mr. Bost. He's the senior partner. I think he's been expecting you. Have a seat."

They stood while she talked into the phone. When she hung up she said, "He'll be right out."

Harrison Bost looked to be in his late sixties. Dark-framed glasses, suspended from the earpieces by a black cord, bounced on his chest as he approached the two detectives. He extended his hand and introduced himself.

"Come into my office." He shook his head as he led them to a spacious, panel-walled room at the end of the corridor. "I can't tell you what a shock this is. George Horner was like a son to me. I paid his law school tuition. Such a bright young man. What a waste!" He sat behind a large, polished mahogany desk and waved to a pair of leather-covered easy chairs. "Do you have any idea who killed him?"

"No," Maharos said. "We've just started the investigation, We're trying to find out as much as we can."

"Have you talked to Sally yet?"

"The wife?"

Bost nodded.

"No, we plan to question her next."

Bost said, "You know, she called me last night to see if I knew where George was. I figured he had been working late, he often did. This morning your office called to tell me what had happened. Then I went right over to see Sally. The poor girl was absolutely devastated, of course. The doctor came, gave her a shot to quiet her down."

Maharos said, "Yeah. We heard that she had been heavily sedated. That's why we waited to talk to her."

"Can you tell me what you've learned so far?"

"Well, as I said, we've just started to investigate. All I can tell you is that Mr. Horner was found shot dead in his car. The car was parked on a dirt road near Portage Lakes, a short way off I-77. Some kids who were hiking in the area saw the body in the car. We just came from the scene."

Maharos left it at that. His job was to get information. He wasn't giving any more than the bare facts, although he knew that technicians from the mobile crime lab had gone over the scene for clues. With the help of the K-9 Corps, they had found what they believed were the killer's footprints. Casts had been made and sent to the lab to identify the type of footwear and to estimate the size and weight of the wearer. The techs had taken the car in and were dusting it for fingerprints, vacuuming it for fibers.

Bost said, "Have you any idea when he was killed?"

"The medical examiner estimates it happened between six and ten last night."

Bost spread his hands. "What would you like me to tell you?"

"How long had Mr. Horner been with your law firm?"

"Since he got out of law school—what's that?—six years now. He specialized in workers' compensation law, you know. One of the best—maybe *the* best in this part of the state."

"When did you last see him?"

Bost thought for a moment. "Yesterday morning around ten, before he left the office for an arbitration hearing."

Fiala took notes in a spiral notebook. In his lap he had a minirecorder to tape the conversation. "That'd be Thursday, May seventh, right?"

Bost gave him a cold-fish stare. "If that was yesterday's date, the answer is yes."

Fiala glanced at Maharos sidelong, without raising his head from the notebook in which he'd been writing, then slowly looked up at Bost. He spoke softly. "I hope we're not having no attitude problem here. You do want to help us find whoever killed your partner, don't you?"

Bost raised his eyebrows. "What? Why naturally. Of course."

"Just wanted to make sure."

Bost scratched his chin and a little smile crept into the corners of his mouth. "I'm sorry. I didn't mean to—. You'll have to forgive me, officers. This thing has upset me more than I can tell you."

Fiala said, "Sure. You were saying—"

"Yes. I saw George yesterday before he went to a hearing."

Maharos said, "Did he actually go to the hearing?"

"Oh, yes. I know he did."

Bost explained that an urgent call, concerning another matter, had come in for Horner while he was at the Arbitration Center. His secretary had called Horner out of the hearing to give him the message.

Maharos said, "Do you know who called?"

"Oh, I'm sure it had nothing to do with George's—" He appeared unable to bring himself to say "death." Bost stopped for a moment before continuing. "The call came from the office of the Industrial Commission, in Columbus, about another case he'd been handling."

After learning of Horner's death, Bost had spoken to the arbitration referee in an effort to trace the victim's movements. According to the referee, after the usual preliminaries, the hearing had begun at around eleven, with the participants breaking for lunch at twelve-thirty.

Maharos asked, "Do you know where Horner had lunch and with whom?"

"I don't know for sure, but the attorneys who attend these hearings usually eat at the Oak Tavern, it's on—"

Maharos nodded, "I know the place."

"I'm almost certain he ate with the man he represented. It's his usual practice with an out-of-town client like this one."

At one-thirty Horner had returned to the hearing, which had ended at four o'clock. Then he'd come back to the office to finish some paperwork. "I was busy when he returned and I left the office for the day before he did, so I actually saw

George for the last time yesterday morning. I—I just can't believe I'll never see him again—" Bost's voice broke and he shook out a large handkerchief and blew his nose.

Maharos said, "I know this is hard for you, Mr. Bost, but—"

The lawyer waved his hand. "No, no. Don't mind me."

"Who is the last person who had contact with him?"

"Nancy, I believe. His secretary."

The phone on Bost's desk buzzed. He spoke into it briefly and glanced at his watch. When he hung up, Maharos said, "I'm sure you have many things to do and I don't want to keep you. But if we stand any chance of finding out who did this, we've got to do it before the trail gets cold."

Bost waved a hand, "Detective, *nothing* is more important to me now than helping you find the person who killed George Horner."

"Okay. There are a couple of questions I have to ask you, then we'll call it quits, for now."

Bost leaned forward, waiting.

"There's another member of your firm, isn't there?"

"Yes. Irving Frankel. He's on vacation in Italy. I've tried to reach him, but he's between cities."

"How did he get along with Mr. Horner?"

"They were very close. Irv is a few years older than George but they were like brothers."

"This may sound indelicate, Mr. Bost, but I've got to ask. Do you know if Mr. Horner was having—how shall I put it—"

"Did George have a woman on the side?"

Maharos nodded.

"Emphatically no! He and Sally were happily married with four beautiful children. I don't know a more devoted husband and father."

Maharos knew plenty of guys, each a devoted husband and father who'd been making it with some other guy's devoted wife and mother. He said, "Of course."

Fiala said, "Did he have any unhappy customers? Maybe some nut who might have been pis— didn't like the way he represented him?"

DEAD END 15

Bost turned his palms up. "Look, in this business the clients are *never* happy. You get them five thousand, they complain they should have gotten *twenty*-five. George, like all of us, has had clients saying they were going to sue for malpractice. Few of them actually do. But threats against his life? I don't know of any. You can check with Nancy, but I'm sure George would have told me if he had gotten even one."

Maharos said, "We'd like to look around Mr. Horner's office."

"Certainly. Nancy will help you with anything you'd like to see." He led them down the hall.

George Horner's office stood at the other end of the corridor, close to the waiting room. From the size and location of the office, it was clear that Horner'd been the junior member of the firm. His secretary shared an office, a wallboard-partitioned section in an adjacent room, with two typists.

Nancy, a petite brunette with a good figure, and in her early thirties, slouched with her elbows on the desk, smoke curling from a cigarette that dangled between two nicotine-stained fingers. The woman was probably quite attractive, Maharos thought, when her eyes weren't swollen and red. A half-empty Kleenex box stood on a corner of the secretary's desk. She snuffed out the cigarette in an ashtray overflowing with butts, waved away the smoke that clouded the room, and stood up. She extended her right hand to Maharos when Bost introduced them. He glanced at her other hand, saw no wedding band.

Bost said, "And now, if you'll excuse me. If you need me for anything—*anything*—I'll be in my office." He turned to Nancy. "The detectives would like to look around George's office. Let them do anything and see anything they'd like."

Maharos wondered if Nancy also called her boss by his first name. He said, "My sympathies, Miss— I'm sorry, I don't know your last name."

She forced a smile. "It's *Mrs.* Taylor. Call me Nancy, everyone does."

Mrs. plus naked fourth finger left hand. Maharos said, "We'd like the name and address of the client Mr. Horner represented at the arbitration yesterday. We'll have to question him."

Nancy took a file folder from her desk top. "I've got it right here." Fiala copied the information into his notebook.

"Could we see your boss's appointment book, please?"

She handed it to Maharos, he leafed through several pages. The only notation for May 7 read, "Lawton arbitration hearing." A large X through the rest of the page probably meant that Horner had expected the hearing to last most of the day. The pages for May 5 and 6 listed a few names. Nancy explained that these were office appointments for clients who had been in to discuss their cases. Fiala asked her to photocopy the pages from May 1 to May 8, as well as the papers in the Lawton folder.

While the secretary ran the copy machine, Fiala followed Maharos into Horner's small office. A gray steel table-type desk with a single top drawer took up most of the space. Three chairs against the wall faced the desk. A picture frame on the desk held a photograph of a seated, smiling, light-haired woman who appeared to be in her thirties. On one side of her stood two girls, one about eight years old, the other maybe six. On the other side posed a solemn-faced boy who looked to be about four. On her lap the woman held a boy about two years of age.

A low two-drawer file case sat alongside the desk. Fiala tried the handle, found the case locked.

Nancy returned while Fiala was trying to yank open the file case. "Mr. Horner kept his personal papers in that cabinet. I don't have a key."

Fiala said, "Mind if we look for it?"

Nancy shrugged. "Mr. Bost said you could see anything that would be helpful. I guess it's all right. Certainly he won't be needing—" She didn't finish the sentence and dabbed her eyes with a tissue as she walked back to her office.

The key lay in the first place Fiala looked: the desk drawer, in the middle of a pile of paper clips. The files held copies of Horner's will, a trust deed of which he and his wife were grantors, several brokerage statements and a folder of letters. Maharos flipped through the letters, using the end of his ball-point pen to turn them. Several were handwritten, most were typed. He handed the folder to Fiala. "Let's take these. We'll look at them later."

A loose-leaf calendar lay on the desk, opened to yesterday's date. The page opposite the date was noted, "Lawton."

Maharos leafed through several of the preceding pages. The handwritten notes on each were, for the most part illegible. Many appeared to be doodles. He called to Nancy through the open door. "I'd like to take this calendar and go over it in my office"

An empty white plastic bag lined the wastebasket next to Horner's desk. Fiala looked under the bag, found nothing else in the basket. He said, "Good cleaning service they got here."

The single desk drawer held, in addition to the assortment of paper clips, a few blank labels and a checkbook. The stubs were made out to people whose names meant nothing to Maharos, but he told Nancy he would take the book along for further examination. Fiala wrote out a receipt for the items they removed.

Maharos asked Nancy to come into Horner's office. He leaned back in the chair behind Horner's desk, beckoned her to sit in one of the chairs opposite. Fiala sat in one of the other chairs, the notebook on his knee.

Maharos asked, "How long have you been working here, Nancy?"

"A little over three years."

"Have you been Mr. Horner's secretary all that time?"

"No." She gestured with her chin to the two girls who were typing in the adjacent area. "I'd been in the steno pool for about six months. Then, when Mary—Mr. Horner's secretary at the time—left, I took over."

"What time did you last see Mr. Horner?"

"At about five-fifteen yesterday afternoon. He was sitting right here at his desk reading a file when I popped my head in and said goodnight."

"Do you know what file he'd been reading?"

"I'm not sure, but I think Mr. Lawton's file."

"The arbitration?"

She nodded.

"Did he expect someone to come in after you left?"

"No. He had no appointments scheduled."

"Would he have scheduled someone without your knowledge?"

"I doubt it. He never made appointments himself—at least without notifying me."

Maharos said, "Was it usual for him to stay after you left?"

She nodded. "Mr. Horner was a hard worker, often the last one to leave."

Fiala said, "Where did he usually park?"

Nancy pointed to the parking lot, visible through the window. "That's the parking lot for the building. He always left his car there."

Maharos walked to the window and looked out. More than thirty cars were in the marked spaces. "Did he have a special space?"

Nancy Taylor walked to the window and pointed to a place at the far left. "That's the space reserved for his car—when someone else didn't grab it."

"Did that happen often?"

She smiled. "I can't tell you how many times he'd walk in here steaming,. He'd yell like Papa Bear, 'Who's in my space?'"

"What about yesterday?"

She thought for a moment. Shrugged. "I'm afraid I don't know."

Maharos nodded to Fiala, watched as he made a note to question the other building occupants. Find out if anyone saw Horner leave. Check if he'd been alone.

Maharos said, "Was anyone else in the office when you left?"

She thought for a moment. "No, the other secretaries actually left a few minutes earlier. Mr. Bost had gone home at around four-thirty."

Maharos said, "Do you open all your boss's mail?"

"Yes."

"Have you at any time seen anything that might be considered a threatening letter?"

She shook her head. "No, not *life*-threatening. He's had several letters from clients who were unhappy about one thing or another."

"For example?"

"Well, two or three wrote that they thought his fee seemed too high for the settlement they received. He wrote back or called each one and explained that the state Industrial Commission prescribes the amount."

"Do you remember who they were?"

"Not off the top of my head. But I can look through the files and get the names for you."

"I'd appreciate it. Any other unhappy people?"

She thought for a few moments. "I recall one man who sounded angry, complaining about the small settlement. He accused Mr. Horner of not pleading his case hard enough. I can get the correspondence out, but I know Mr. Horner got the maximum allowable in that case."

"Can you get his file for me?"

"Yes, but it won't be much help. The man died. He had black lung disease. I guess even the maximum isn't enough for something like that."

Maharos nodded.

"Nancy, do you know anything about Mr. Horner's social life?"

She slipped a cigarette from a pack she held, lit it and shook her head as she exhaled a cloud of smoke. Uh-oh. She needed time. "Very little. He handled any social calls himself. Mrs. Horner kept their social calendar."

"How well do you know Mrs. Horner?"

"She'd come down here once in a while. I guess four little children kept her pretty busy at home."

"Did you and your husband have any social relationship with the Horners?"

"*Ex*-husband. No, I never saw the Horners socially."

"Or Mr. Horner alone?"

She frowned. "Mr. Horner was a married man, Detective."

"You understand why I have to ask these questions, even though I know they may be embarrassing. The only way we're going to find out who killed Mr. Horner is to know as much as possible about the man. In a homicide investigation, sometimes people try to hide things from us because the truth may be painful. But sooner or later we find out, and it saves time to know from the start."

She nodded. "Oh, of course, I understand."

"So, do you want to answer my last question?"

"Did I go out with Mr. Horner? No, our relationship was entirely professional." She blew a cloud of smoke and jabbed out the cigarette in an ashtray.

Maharos stood up. "Thank you. I may be calling on you again in the next few days if anything comes up, if I need answers to any other questions."

"Certainly, any time."

Nancy Taylor led the way out of the office.

In the blue Chevy, Fiala took a plastic envelope out of the glove compartment. He removed his suit jacket and, from one of its side pockets, shook into the envelope Nancy's cigarette butt.

Maharos watched, grinning. "You didn't believe her either?"

Fiala shrugged. "Like you always say, take no chances."

THREE

THE HORNERS' WHITE clapboard, two-story home was in an upper middle-class neighborhood. Bikes, toy autos, and skateboards lay scattered on the lawns, basketball hoops projected above many of the garage doors.

When Maharos and Fiala drove up and parked in the driveway, a clutch of onlookers on the sidewalk were gaping at the house A man in his late thirties, wearing a gray business suit, opened the door partway. Maharos had his shield case in his hand. "I'm Detective Al Maharos. This is my partner, Frank Fiala."

"I'm Tom Hendricks, Sally's brother. Come on in."

In the small living room, an attractive brunette sat in the middle of the couch, an arm around each of the little girls they'd seen in the photograph on Horner's desk a few hours earlier. The girls' eyes were red and swollen, their lower lips trembled.

Hendricks said, "This is my wife Sue, and Toni and Karen Horner. Sally's upstairs. I'll get her."

Maharos said, "Listen, if she's still resting, don't disturb her."

"She's awake now," said Sue Hendricks. She smoothed the hair of the younger girl. "The boys are staying over at my sister's."

Hendricks went upstairs and a minute later came down supporting his sister on his arm. Sally Horner wore a long blue robe. Strands of light brown hair stood out from her head like quills. She wore no makeup, and her eyes had a glazed, far-away stare.

Sue Hendricks got up from the couch. "I'll be in the kitchen with the girls, dear."

Hendricks said, "I'll stay here with Sally, in case she needs me."

Maharos and Fiala stood until Hendricks had eased Mrs. Horner down on a sectional chair. He dragged a chair to her side and sat with an arm draped across the back of her easy chair.

Maharos said, "I can't tell you how sorry we are about your husband, Mrs. Horner. We hated to bother you, but it's important that we move along with our investigation as fast as possible."

She nodded but remained silent.

Maharos didn't expect to get much useful information. "I'm not going to ask you too many questions," he said. "But the most important is: Did your husband have any enemies, anyone who might have threatened him?"

Sally Horner continued to stare off into space. Finally, in a barely audible voice, she said, "Nancy Taylor."

Maharos and Fiala exchanged looks.

Maharos said, "His secretary?"

She nodded.

"What makes you think she's an enemy?"

Her eyes narrowed. "They were—he wanted to fire her."

"When did he tell you this?"

"Two days ago. The day before he—" She covered her face with her hands. Her shoulders shook, her sobs silent.

"Why was he firing her?"

Sally Horner slid her hands from her face and stared at the floor without answering.

Maharos waited. Finally he said, "Mrs. Horner, was anything going on between your husband and Mrs. Taylor?"

A small nod.

"How did you find out?"

"He—he told me."

"When?"

"Last week." Her voice grew stronger. "About a week ago George looked—I don't know, depressed when he came home. I asked him if he'd had a bad day. He told me about firing Nancy Taylor. I asked why. He told me about—you know, sleeping with her." She paused, gazed at the window.

Maharos waited for her to continue. "He said it happened only once, knew he'd made a mistake. She kept inviting him to her place. He refused. Finally, he told her if she didn't stop pestering him, he'd fire her. She said if he did, she'd tell me about their 'affair.' He knew the story would come out eventually, and said he wanted it to come from him."

"Did your husband say she'd threatened him? Threatened to *kill* him?"

"No. But who else would have done it?"

"Mrs. Horner, before he told you, did you have any idea that your husband and Mrs. Taylor had—been together?"

She snugged her robe close to her body. "I don't know. One time, a couple of months ago, I thought maybe they'd had an affair. She's attractive, divorced. Well, you know how men are. But I passed it off. Told myself I'd been concerned about nothing. Never gave it much thought again—until—"

"When did you talk to your husband last?"

She gazed at the carpet, her lips trembling. When she looked up her eyes were brimming. She took a tissue from her pocket and dabbed her eyes. "Yesterday morning, at breakfast."

"Did he say anything about his plans for the day?"

She shook her head. "He rarely told me anything about his business."

"Did he say anything about coming home late for dinner—or anything like that?"

"No, but he frequently worked late."

She told them that around eight-thirty she'd phoned the office and listened to the after-hours recording. She hung on hoping that George was screening calls, so at the beep she identified herself but got no reply. She called Harrison Bost at his home. He said he had no idea where Horner had gone but assured her he'd turn up, "I thought George might have stopped off somewhere on his way home."

"At Mrs. Taylor's?"

Her glance dropped to the floor. She spoke softly. "It crossed my mind."

"Did you call there?"

"Nancy Taylor's home?"

Maharos nodded.

"No. I guess. . . I didn't really want to know."

Hendricks stood up, leaned across Mrs. Horner. He gently placed his arm across her shoulders. "You okay, honey?"

She patted his hand, smiled feebly.

"Mrs. Horner," said Maharos, "I know this will be painful for you, but it's important that we know. When did your husband and Mrs. Taylor—become intimate?"

Sally Horner's eyelids drooped, as though she was about to drop off to sleep. When she spoke, her voice was low. Maharos leaned forward to hear. "In February, George had to go court in Cleveland. He told me it was a longshoreman case and I guess they try those in Federal court." The case was continued to the next day, Mrs. Horner said. He called to tell her that because of the icy roads he'd stay at a Cleveland hotel.

Maharos said, "Was Mrs. Taylor with him?"

Mrs. Horner nodded. "I didn't know until just recently, as I said. They had dinner and a few drinks and then's when it happened."

"The only time?"

She shrugged. "That's what George told me."

"What did you say after he told you?"

Sally Horner's lips quivered. "I guess I became a little hysterical. At first I told George that I couldn't go on living with him. I'd get a divorce. He kept on telling me that it happened one time, a one-night thing. Never happened before, would never happen again.

"For a few days I. . ." She shook her head. "Finally, I got hold of myself. Realized he'd always been a good, affectionate, thoughtful husband. With four young children, it wouldn't be easy for me if I had to get along without him. So I told him I couldn't forgive him, I could never forget it, but I'd stay with him for the children's sake. He promised he would get rid of that. . ."

A practical woman, Maharos thought. "A little while ago, when I asked if you thought your husband might be at Mrs. Taylor's house when he hadn't come home, you said, 'It crossed my mind.' Did you worry that he might have changed his mind about firing her?"

Sally Horner took a deep breath before she answered. "I didn't know *what* to think. My world had fallen apart. I—I just lost any feeling of security. Before, I never had any reason to mistrust him. Afterward—after he told me about himself and Nancy Taylor, I wondered if I could believe anything he told me."

"Just a few more questions, Mrs. Horner," said Maharos. "I know you called in to the Youngstown Police Department around ten."

"Uh-huh. They said it was too soon to start a missing person search, but I gave the officer who took the call a description of my husband anyway. I spent the rest of the night sitting here in this chair, praying. A lot of good it did."

"Do you know any reason for your husband being at Portage Lakes? Do you know anyone there?"

"That's where they found him, isn't it?"

Maharos nodded.

"No, I don't know anyone who lives there—or even nearby."

Maharos took a deep breath, let it out. Now came the tough part. "Mrs. Horner, who was home with you last evening?"

She drew her brows together. "Just the children. Is that what you mean?"

"Uh-huh. What time did you eat?"

Mrs. Horner's head came up. She glared at Maharos, the glaze in her eyes replaced by fire. "Look, I don't know what you're driving at. I don't remember what time we ate. Five-thirty, six. What difference does it make?"

Tom Hendricks had been sitting on the arm of Sally's easy chair. He stood, his jaw jutting, color gone from his face. "What are you trying to do, Detective. Hasn't this poor girl been through enough?"

Maharos held up his hand. He spoke quietly. "Take it easy, both of you. There are certain things we've got to find out. I know this is a difficult time for all of you. Mrs. Horner, I'm just trying to establish where you spent last evening between six and ten."

Mrs. Horner shouted the answer. "Right here. Cooking dinner for my family. Feeding my four children. Wondering where my husband had gone. Worrying because he hadn't come home. *That's* where I was."

Maharos had expected the reaction. Like a dental drill burrowing into a tooth, he had exposed a sensitive nerve, the part of every inquiry he disliked most. But he had to do it. Sally Horner was a suspect. She had a motive. Whether she had the desire or the means to murder her husband, *or have him murdered*, remained to be seen.

Maharos and Fiala stood up. They'd learn nothing more that day from Mrs. Horner. Maharos said, "I appreciate your talking to us, Mrs. Horner. We may want to talk to you again later on."

Sally Horner said nothing. Head bowed, she silently sobbed into a tissue. Hendricks, seated on the arm of her chair, gently massaged her shoulder.

At the door, Fiala turned around. "By the way, Mrs. Horner, do you smoke?"

She raised her head and slowly shook her head, her voice now subdued. "Not for years, why?"

"Just curious."

In the car, Maharos said, "Well, let's talk to that secretary again. This time we'll take her downtown." He nudged Fiala with his elbow. "I'm glad you remembered about the tech's report."

They had seen a preliminary report from the crime lab. Cigarette butts had been found in the ashtray of Horner's car. The butts were stained with lipstick.

FOUR

NANCY TAYLOR SAT at the scarred table in the interrogation room across from Maharos. She leaned back, chain-smoking, slim legs crossed, a shoe dangling from a toe. Quite a change in her attitude. Self-assured, no longer weepy. A portable tape recorder on the table made a faint hissing sound.

Maharos had read the *Miranda* rights. She said she did not need the advice of a lawyer, nor did she want one present. She had done nothing wrong. Yes, she admitted, she and Horner had spent the night together in a Cleveland hotel. That was the only time they had been intimate, she didn't consider that an "affair."

She lived alone in an apartment.

Maharos said, "Did you ask Mr. Horner to your home any time after that night you spent together?"

"No."

"Did you tell him you would tell his wife about what had happened in Cleveland if he fired you?"

"Never! And he never said anything about firing me. I did my work. He liked what I did. In fact, we never talked about that night in Cleveland."

Maharos asked her about her former marriage. She had been married seven years. Had no children. Her ex-husband, an alcoholic, had beaten her several times while drunk, and she had divorced him four years ago. The last she knew, he was somewhere on the West Coast. She wasn't going steady with anyone but had dates once or twice a week. Maharos jotted down the names of her male friends.

"When was the last time you were in Mr. Horner's car?"

Her brow furrowed. "In his car? I don't know, maybe a week or two ago."

"Where did you go?"

"Probably to court. Yes, we went to court."

"Did you often accompany him to court?"

"I wouldn't say 'often.' But when there were a lot of files he had to take with him, I'd go along to help. Many times, during a trial, he'd have me find things in a file while he questioned a witness."

"And you'd go to court in his car?"

"Certainly. The courthouse is a mile away. Do you expect me to walk there?"

Maharos placed his palms on the table, leaned forward, aware of her musty, sexy perfume. "Mrs. Taylor, when I spoke to you in your office I asked you to be frank and open. I told you that if you'd try to hide anything, we'd find out eventually. Remember?"

"Yes."

"And when I asked you whether anything had gone on between the two of you, you denied it, right?"

Her eyes blinked rapidly. "I just got through telling you, I didn't consider that one night as being a big deal."

"Yeah. Well, I'm asking you now: Did you have anything to do with Mr. Horner's death?"

She started to speak but he held up a hand. "Before you say anything, let me point out if you did have anything, *anything*, to do with Mr. Horner's death we're gonna find out about it. I mean, it may have been accidental, maybe even justifiable. Even if you didn't pull the trigger on the gun that killed him, if you know anything about it, now is the time to say it."

Again, Nancy Taylor's mouth opened and he silenced her with a gesture. "Look, Nancy, we're all human. We all make mistakes. It only gets worse if we—"

She broke in, "Listen, Detective, I had nothing to do with George Horner's death. If you want me to take a lie detector test, fine. Let's do it. But I'm not going to sit here and let you make accusations. Maybe I *do* need a lawyer."

Maharos stood up. "That's up to you. One thing, we'd like to do is examine your hands. It's a test that can tell us if you've fired a gun recently."

Nancy threw her head back and laughed. "Oh, really now!"

"Do you have any objections?"

"Of course not!"

This was one cool cat. Maharos had used the gunpowder residue test as an excuse to see her reaction. Nearly twenty-four hours had elapsed since Horner had been shot. By now the chances of finding such evidence were negligible, even with the most sensitive techniques. Although he did not believe everything she told him, she probably had nothing to do with Horner's death.

* * *

Lieutenant Ed Bragg squared the corners of the sheaf of papers he held and placed them in a file folder labeled "Horner." He handed the folder to Maharos seated opposite his desk. "Looks like you got shit so far."

Bragg, four years from retirement, counted every day—when he wasn't eating, which was most of the time. The men and women in the squad room made bets on which would go first, the spring on the lieutenant's swivel chair or his thirty years.

Bragg said, "Nothing in his personal letters?"

"No. Fiala went through them and came up empty," said Maharos.

"That secretary is clean?"

He wobbled a hand. "A little hanky-panky, but nothing on her we can use."

"Ballistics?"

"Nothing."

"Prints?"

"Horner's."

"I see the lab found nothing."

"Well, not exactly *nothing*. They got some navy blue fibers from the carpet in front of the back seat. They think they're from a sweater, but they don't match anything in Horner's clothes closet. They're still working on it."

Bragg flipped his hand. "S-u-r-e. Probably turn out to be a May Company lot of fifty thousand."

Maharos said, "Did you read the ME's report?"

"Yeah he's a big help too. He says the guy was shot in the back. Twice. And his head was bashed in. We coulda got as much from one of the Boy Scouts who found the body."

"Frank spent a week on Horner's case files. He picked up a few leads. None of them panned out."

"You mean we got here a lawyer nobody hates enough to kill him?"

"No. It's just that the list of haters is too big."

"What about our snitches?"

"Frank put the word out on the street. None of the gangs had anything working with Horner."

"All right, you been on this for three weeks now. Where do you go from here?"

Maharos shrugged. "Got any ideas, Ed?"

"Nope. Probably some crazy. We're just runnin' in place. I'm afraid we're gonna end up puttin' this one on the shelf."

FIVE

MAHAROS SAT in the squad room, his feet on his desk. He was thinking about the Horner investigation but couldn't come up with any fresh ideas. Besides, Lieutenant Ed Bragg, his superior, had more or less told him to drop it. The phone rang.

"Maharos."

"Hi, Daddy."

"Annie, sweetheart. I was just thinking about you."

"I bet!"

"Are you home?"

"Uh-huh. Where were you last Sunday? I was expecting you."

Maharos' feet hit the floor. Jesus. He had promised Annie he'd take her to lunch and a movie. He had gotten so wrapped up in the Horner thing, as well as two other investigations that were still open, he had forgotten it was Sunday. "Annie, you want the truth?"

" 'Course."

"I was so busy I forgot it was Sunday. Honest. Look, if it's okay with Mom, how about I pick you up Saturday morning and we spend the weekend together. Lunch at McDonald's, a movie or whatever you want. Sunday we can drive out somewhere and picnic, just the two of us. How about it?"

He pictured the long-legged twelve-year-old, running her fingers through her long silky hair, auburn like her mother's, chewing on a strand while she talked. Scratching the tip of her small, upturned nose by running her palm up and down over it. He thanked God she had inherited the looks of the O'Learys. From Maharos all she got was love.

"Wellll."

"Want me to ask your Mom?"

"Yeah. Maybe you'd better. Only she's not home now."

"Okay, I'll call back later."

"Don't forget. Today is Thursday already.

"Don't worry, I won't. Bye, honey."

Four years since the divorce. The fifteen-year marriage had been great for him, lousy for Marcie. The same tired story he'd heard from every other divorced police officer: come home to change clothes, leave the dirty laundry and go. Often his ex had said she wished it had been another woman instead of The Job. Another woman she could compete with.

"Quit the force," she'd pleaded.

He'd said, "Don't ask me to do that, it's the only thing I know. The only thing I'm good at."

"You could be good at anything you wanted. You could be a concert violinist if you devoted as much time to that as you do to being a cop."

Maharos smiled thinking about it now. He couldn't carry a tune on a kazoo.

Annie. It had taken seven years, half a dozen fertility tests and three miscarriages before Marcie, with labor pains coming every three minutes, had to call a black and white patrol car to take her to the hospital. Maharos was staked out in a fleabag hotel, in the room next door to the girlfriend of a murder suspect, hadn't shown up at the hospital until an hour after Annie, covered with slimy meconium, had been welcomed by the obstetrician with a slap on the ass.

Looking back on it, that's when Marcie changed. She began carping at him about raising her daughter as a single parent. Not that she didn't have a legitimate beef, but in the few hours Maharos was home he didn't want to hear complaints. At first he just tuned her out. Then came the spats. They weren't quite in the plate-throwing, fuck-you-and-your-family category. Not quite. But when Marcie's Irish temper flared it could rock the civilization that had been born in Greece centuries before.

One day Maharos pointed out that the wives of Greek men raised the children. The husband worked and drank *ouzo* with his buddies. That's the way it was gonna be. Furthermore, he was taking a week of vacation time starting the day after next, to go fishing on Georgian Bay with two of his detective buddies. Marcie had reminded him that her name had started with an O-apostrophe before they were married, hadn't always ended with -os, and she suggested what he could do with his Greek customs. When Maharos returned a week later with two walleye that barely made the legal size, Marcie and Annie had been replaced by a note.

Now Marcie was remarried. He'd known she wouldn't be on the open market very long. Sam Hudson was a comfortable, unexciting widower who owned an insurance agency. At fifty-eight, sixteen years older than Marcie, he had two grown and married children. Most important to Maharos, the guy adored Annie.

Maharos scratched a note on the appointment page of a spiral calendar that lay open at the current date, Thursday, June 4. "Call Marcie—weekend with Annie."

SIX

INTERSTATE 77 starts at Cleveland's west side and threads its way south, down the eastern third of the state. It crosses the Ohio River at Marietta and continues through West Virginia, ending at Columbia, South Carolina.

Once you get past Canton, where you could wave at the Pro Football Hall of Fame and the Hoover and Timkin plants as you drive by, the landscape on both sides of the interstate consists of trees and gently rolling hills. About twenty-five miles south of Canton, New Philadelphia and Dover sit side by side just off the highway.

If your farm was, say, off State Route 39 or 416, and you needed feed for your livestock, you'd probably load your pickup at Noah Hamberger's Feed and Hay in New Philly. Hamberger's a surly son of a bitch, but people buy from him because his DoubleX Hybrid is good quality for the money. Besides, his is the only feed store for miles around.

Of course, if it were Sunday, Hamberger wouldn't be at the store. He'd be home, a white frame three-story house off Rainbow Lane, surrounded by some rye grass and two acres of tall elms, sturdy oaks, buckeyes, some maples and a few pine trees. He'd probably be tinkering in the barn with his 1984 Buick Century, his 1973 Ford pickup, or the International Harvester riding tractor.

In fact, that's exactly where he was at ten-thirty, the morning of June 7. Under the Buick, draining the oil. He was on his back, lying on a flat wooden platform fitted with roller wheels so he could scoot himself under the car. It was a squeeze, and he had to suck in his big belly to make it under the car frame. Martha Hamberger always said that at his age, fifty-seven, he ought to take it over to Pete Fisher's Shell Station and let Pete do the job, rather than strain himself. But Noah was a hard-headed, tightfisted Dutchman who wasn't going to part with $14.85, oil and labor, for a simple job. Besides, Martha wasn't home to object. On summer Sundays she stayed on at the Grace Lutheran Church after services, to help the other ladies of the auxiliary arrange tables for the afternoon outdoor social.

Couldn't ask for a better day for the outdoor social. Even now, midmorning, it was sunny with just enough of a breeze to blow the humidity away. The thick stand of trees that almost surrounded the house gave enough shade to keep it cool.

The shadows cast by the trees were good cover for Ephraim Rankins who had been standing, hidden behind the thick trunk of an oak, waiting for Hamberger just as he'd done on each of the past three Sundays. At eight that morning, he'd parked his Dodge van on a dirt road that ran between a couple of fields about a quarter-mile past New Philadelphia's business district. He'd strolled the three-quarters of a mile to Hamberger's house and had been there, behind the oak, when Hamberger returned from church and parked the Buick in the barn. He waited while Hamberger walked back to the house, changed out of his Sunday suit to overalls and came back to work on the machines.

Rankins watched as Hamberger rolled himself on his back under the Buick. Then he crept to the barn door, careful not to step on gravel or loose stones that would crunch underfoot. He grabbed the shovel he'd leaned against the wall just outside the barn while he was waiting for Hamberger to return from church.. Now he was in the barn, three feet from where the top of Hamberger's head poked out under the car frame.

He listened to the musical sound the oil made as it dripped into the metal basin Hamberger balanced on his chest. When the oil stream stopped, Hamberger turned the cock, closing the oil drainage valve. He steadied the basin of waste oil and, using his heels to push against the barn floor, began propelling himself backward, from under the car. He kept his eyes on the basin, making sure it stayed level so the oil wouldn't spill. His head, neck and upper chest had cleared the car frame when his backward progress was stopped. Rankins' feet were blocking the wheels of the roller platform. Hamberger shifted his gaze from the basin and looked straight up into Rankins' face.

Hamberger sucked in his breath. He squinted like he was trying to recognize the face. He said, "Who is it?"

Rankins just smiled.

Again Hamberger said, "Who is it?"

Rankins' answer was to swing the shovel with both hands, like a baseball bat, and smash it down into Hamberger's face.

He watched for a moment, the shovel poised to strike again. Hamberger's arms and legs twitched a few times, then he lay still, blood pouring out of his nose and mouth. Funny how they all twitched like that for a few seconds.

Rankins dropped the shovel and pushed Hamberger, still on the crawler, to the pickup. A large canvas tarp covered the truck bed. It was secured by a piece of clothesline that ran through grommets along the tarp's free edges. He pulled about six feet of line free of the grommets, took a knife from his pocket and cut it off from the rest of the line, then cut that in half. He used one half to tie Hamberger's hands behind his back. With the other half he tied his feet together at the ankles.

Hamberger was a stocky son of a bitch; unconscious, he was dead weight. It took most of Rankins' strength to stand him up and prop him against the tailgate. By bending Hamberger backwards and boosting him, he was able to get the big bastard's upper body well into the truck bed so he wouldn't slip off to the barn floor. Then he climbed into the truck, pulled Hamberger to the center of the truck bed, and covered him with the tarp.

Rankins stood, stretched and pressed his fists into his aching back for a moment. Rubbing where the scar was helped ease the pain. He climbed down from the truck bed, took a pair of rubber gloves from his pocket and pulled them on. With a handkerchief, he wiped the handle of the shovel he'd just used. In the cab of the truck, the key was in the ignition. He started the motor, backed out of the barn and headed out of the driveway on to Rainbow Lane. It was a quiet, peaceful, sunny morning in early June. Couldn't ask for better weather for the church social that afternoon. Too bad Noah Hamberger wouldn't make it.

SEVEN

THE WATER IN the pool at Firestone Park, south of Akron, was still cold even though the air temperature was 82. It would be mid-July before the water would be warm enough to stay in longer than a few minutes. Annie Maharos' lips were blue and she shivered as she shook her hair out of her bathing cap while she jogged to where Al Maharos sat on a blanket spread out on the spacious lawn surrounding the public pool. She flopped down on the blanket next to him. His plaid shorts had gone out of style ten years ago, but the hell with it. Why spring for a new pair, then wear them once a year? A floppy hat kept his scalp from burning. A picnic basket next to the blanket was filled with ham and egg salad sandwiches and cans of Coke and two cans of beer for him. He and Annie had made the sandwiches in his apartment that morning before taking off for the park.

Maharos looked up at the sun. "Getting hungry yet?"

"I guess I could eat," said Annie.

She reached into the basket and handed him one of the ham sandwiches. She unwrapped an egg salad sandwich for herself and popped open a can of Coke.

"What a day," said Maharos. He hadn't felt this much at ease for months. A lump filled his throat as he gazed at Annie. She wore a flowered bikini that covered almost nothing of her thin body. He noticed that she was starting to bud breasts. She'll have nice boobs like Marcie, he thought.

"Going out much?"

Annie looked at him through the hair that covered part of her face. "You mean am I dating?"

"Uh-huh."

She shrugged. "Tommy Ames took me to the May dance at school. His Mom drove us. After, we went to The Liberty for ice cream. I went to the movies with him last week too"

"What, are you going steady with Tommy?"

"Oh *Daddy*!"

"Just asking."

She shoved his shoulder and grinned. "What is this going to be, a lecture on the birds and bees?"

"Yeah. Maybe you're ready."

"Oh, *Daddy*!"

Maharos was a little embarrassed talking to his daughter about sex, but he didn't know how much she already knew. "Hey, I see kids your age get in all kinds of trouble. I want to be sure you aren't one of them."

"Oh, *Daddy*. Don't be such an old fud. Next you'll be asking me if I'm on the pill."

Jesus. "You know about the pill already." It was a statement, not a question.

" 'Course. Anyway, don't worry. I know how to take care of myself—and I'm *not* on the pill."

The kids today, he thought. He'd have to have a talk with Marcie. Find out what Annie knew and didn't know.

Annie was taking small nibbles of her egg salad sandwich. She looked at Maharos out of the corners of her eyes. "Wanna hear something? Janie? You know, Janie Boyd? Well she started her periods. We went to see *Ghostbusters II* and just when it got exciting, Janie pokes me and goes, 'I got a terrible cramp.' I go, 'Oh no!' And she goes, 'I gotta go to the bathroom. Please come with me.' These guys we know from school are sitting in back of us? And when they see us get up they start whistling and stuff. So we go to the ladies room and her panties are *soaked* with blood. Yuck! Well, they had one of those machines, you know, like Coke machines—"

"Vending machines."

"What?"

"They're called vending machines. You put a quarter or a half a dollar in them and you get a sanitary napkin."

"Only you had to put *three* quarters in these. Seventy-five cents! For one little pad! Anyway, we both only had dollar bills. So I had to run out to the cashier and get change..."

Annie was waving her arms telling the story.

Maharos sat on the grass grinning. He half-listened to what she was saying. He loved to hear her talk with such animation and enthusiasm.

"—so can we go to Sea World later this afternoon?"

She caught him by surprise. He hadn't realized that she had finished telling about Janie's period.

"Way over to Geauga Lake Park? That's a good half-hour drive."

She wiped her mouth with the back of her hand. "You said we could have the whole day together."

Maharos shrugged a shoulder. "Okay. I guess I owe you one anyway, for last weekend."

Annie jumped up, threw her arms around his neck and planted a wet kiss mixed with egg salad on his cheek. "You're fun to be with, Daddy. I wish it wasn't only on Sundays."

"Hey, let's not get into *that* again."

They finished eating, and while Annie went into the ladies locker room to change into a sun suit, Maharos folded the blanket and packed up the picnic basket.

It was six o'clock and they were in Maharos' Ford, driving back to Youngstown. Annie was still chattering about the acts by the dolphins and Shamu at Sea World. Maharos was peacefully quiet, wearing a faint grin. He was content to listen, occasionally making a comment. The pager on his belt beeped.

He instinctively glanced from one side of the highway to the other, looking for a phone. He found a public pay phone outside a fast-food restaurant at the next exit and dialed Youngstown police headquarters. The call was from Joe Byers, the duty officer in the detective squad room.

"Hate to bother you on a Sunday, Al. Something came in over the wire that Fiala said you'd be interested in."

"Yeah?"

"New Philly reported a homicide and Frank thought the MO was something like the one you were working on. The one where that lawyer got iced?"

"Horner?"

"That's the one. Anyway, the guy in New Philly was found with his head bashed in and shot in the back.."

Sounded promising.

"When did the New Philly homicide take place?"

"The doc thinks it was around noon today."

Maharos glanced to the car where Annie was resting her chin on the sill of the car window. Her eyes were closed, she'd had a busy day. "Okay. I'm over near Akron. I've got to take my daughter home. I'll be in the office in about an hour. You can fill me in then."

EIGHT

MAHAROS YAWNED, STRETCHED and said, "Want me to drive?"

Frank Fiala glanced over to the passenger's seat. "Have a nice snooze?"

Maharos had been dozing in the seat next to Fiala during the ninety-mile drive from Youngstown to New Philadelphia. It was Monday morning.

He asked, "Tired driving?"

"Nah, we're almost there. Know where the sheriff's office is?"

"Yeah, I'll give you directions when we get into town."

Twenty minutes later, Fiala pulled the blue Chevrolet into the parking lot next to the gray limestone Tuscarawas County Administration Building. He parked in a space marked "Reserved for Sheriff Vehicles."

The receptionist pointed down the corridor. "Sheriff Anderson's office is 208. You can go right on down."

Grunting, Sheriff Thomas Anderson pushed himself up from his desk chair. A broad smile on his beefy face, he extended a hand the size of a catcher's mitt. He was a giant, six feet six, weighing almost three hundred pounds. His upper arms bulged the seams of his sweat-stained, short-sleeved uniform shirt. "Glad to be of help. How was your trip down from the big city?"

Maharos said, "Thanks for seeing us, Sheriff. The big city? Listen, it's been a few years since I've been down here. This place has grown. You're not too much smaller than Youngstown." He was thinking that Anderson himself wasn't a hell of a lot smaller than Youngstown. Enough small talk. "What have you got so far on that homicide?"

"Hamberger? Noah was a hay and feed dealer here in New Philly. Everybody around here knew the guy. Tough businessman but honest, hard worker." He shook his head, "Sorry to see old Noah go. The son of a bitch that killed him oughta fry. But these fuckin' liberal courts. Prob'ly get away with a manslaughter conviction. Guy never had a job in his life, sat around all day suckin' wine out of a bottle."

Maharos and Fiala looked at each other. Maharos said, "You mean you got a collar?"

Anderson's eyebrows went up. "You didn't get the word? Oh yeah, you been on the road. We pulled in this drifter early this morning. He'd been hangin' around town for about a week with two other bums. They were sleepin' in an empty shack about a mile out of town. Come in every day to buy cheap wine and some grub. Our deputies'd kick 'em out of the shack but they'd go back. We'da pulled 'em in before all this happened but our jail space is so fuckin' crowded. The last thing we needed was more smelly bodies."

Maharos said, "You think this guy you got was the one that killed Hamberger?"

Anderson leaned back, creaking the springs on his chair. "Oh he's the one, all right. Had Noah's wallet in his sack."

"Was he still in the shack when you found him?"

"Nah. Bastard was on the road, State Route 39, tryin' to hitch a ride. The other two took off. We've got a huntin' party out. We'll pick 'em up. Meanwhile, we're runnin' a NCIC check on the guy. Should have it on the computer in a little while. Anderson sat forward and leaned his elbows on the desk. He peered intently at Maharos. "On the phone last night you said somethin' about a connection between this case and one you're workin' on?"

Maharos shrugged. "Well, before you told us about your suspect, we thought the MO in this case sounded something like a case we're running. Now I'm not so sure."

Fiala said. "Can we see your collar?"

"Sure. He's upstairs in the lockup. We've got an interrogation room there. I'll send one of the deputies up with you."

Maharos said, "Has he got a lawyer yet?"

Anderson waved his hand, "Shit yes. We ran this by the book. The public defender is a young squirt just out of law school. I'll get him down here. Want some coffee?"

"That would be nice, thanks. By the way, did you get a gunpowder residue test on your suspect?"

Anderson jutted out his jaw. "Hey, we may be country cousins, but we know all about that scientific shit—just like you big city boys. Yeah, the tech from the mobile lab is runnin' the test. Don't have the results yet though."

Maharos said nothing. The sheriff was obviously touchy about the city detectives questioning his handling of the case. Time to back off. Might need the guy's cooperation.

Maharos and Fiala were drinking coffee in the reception area outside the sheriff's office. A young man in a suit, with tousled, sandy hair, came through the door and strode up to them. A wide grin on his freckled face gave him a Tom Sawyer-like appearance. "Hi. You the Youngstown detectives?"

Maharos nodded.

"I'm Harry Robinson, the public defender. I understand you want to talk to my client."

"If it's okay with you—and him."

"Want to tell me what it's about?"

"We're working a homicide by an unknown perpetrator, happened just outside Youngstown. A lawyer named Horner. Maybe you heard about it. We got word about Mr. Hamberger's murder. Some features resemble what we saw with Horner. We'd like to talk to your man."

Robinson sat without speaking for ten seconds. Then he said, "Do you *really* think there's any connection between the two?"

Maharos said, "Frankly, we don't know what to think. We didn't even know anybody had been pulled in on the Hamberger case until we got here a few minutes ago. We came down to get what information we could, check out the scene, that sort of thing. But, as long as we're here and the sheriff has a suspect in custody, we'd like to ask him a few questions."

"I can't see where it can do any harm," said Robinson. "I'll have to ask my client, of course."

In the elevator with Robinson and a deputy sheriff, Maharos and Fiala were quiet. Robinson said, "Mind if I ask, what's the resemblance between this case and yours?"

Maharos said, "No problem. Both were gunned from behind, two small caliber hits each, heads bashed in, too, and both were left in their vehicles on dirt roads close to I-77. One of the things we wanted to check out was the ballistics from the Hamberger case to see if we've got a match."

Robinson asked, "Where near I-77?"

"Portage Lakes."

"Where's that?"

"Between Akron and Canton."

"That's a long way from here."

Maharos shrugged.

Robinson said, "When was your guy killed?"

"About a month ago. In fact, *just* a month ago."

"Any prints in your case?"

Maharos shook his head.

"Any suspects?"

"Nope."

"Was the guy robbed?"

"Uh-huh."

The elevator door opened and the four men got out. The deputy walked ahead. Robinson turned and faced Maharos and Fiala. "Wait, let me get this straight. There are two homicides, both of which were caused by shots from behind, both had head injuries. The bodies were found near I-77 about fifty miles apart, both were robbed and you think there's a similarity?"

Maharos smiled.

Robinson went on. "How many homicides were there in Ohio the past month? How many were shot? How many people travel down I-77?"

"When you put it *that* way, it's pretty far-fetched."

Robinson rolled his eyes. "Boy! Still want to talk to my man?"

Fiala said, "Well, we're here. What've we got to lose."

"Listen, the best thing I could wish for is that both these murders were committed by the same person—and it turned out to be someone other than the guy in here."

They were standing outside the cell block door. The deputy spoke into a wall phone and the steel-barred door was unlocked by another uniformed officer. He ushered them into the cell block and clanged the door shut behind them, then led the way down a narrow cement corridor. On either side were two barred cells. Maharos thought four cells was a little bit of overkill for this farming community. Still, each small cell held two prisoners who watched in silence from their double-decker bunks. The confined space smelled like the dregs of a wine barrel and urine. At the end of the corridor was a windowless interrogation room furnished with a wooden table and four chairs. The detectives and the young public defender waited while the deputy went to get the prisoner.

Fiala placed a small portable tape recorder on the table, pressed the "record" button and ran a sound test.

Maharos said, "What's your client's name?"

"Roy Young," said Robinson.

A moment later, the deputy returned, leading a tall, thin-faced man wearing a prison gray coverall stenciled on the front with large black letters that read "Property of Tuscarawas County." On the back, in even larger letters was the word "PRISONER." Young had a lock of dark brown hair that hung over one eye. A stubble beard covered the lower half of his face. His hands were manacled behind his back and his gaze was fixed to the floor. When he was seated, the deputy unlocked the handcuffs and remained standing alongside him.

Maharos said, "You can leave him with us. We'll yell for you when we're through."

The deputy nodded and left.

Fiala talked to the tape recorder. "Today is June 8. It is 11:45 AM and we are in the Tuscarawas County Administration Building. Present are: Homicide Detectives Al Maharos and Frank Fiala, Youngstown PD; Harry Robinson, Tuscarawas County Public Defender; and Roy Young, suspect being held in the county jail.

Robinson turned to the prisoner. "Roy, these detectives from Youngstown are working on a case up there and want to ask you some questions. Is that okay with you?"

Young looked up for the first time. Creases appeared between his brows. "Youngstown?"

Maharos asked, "Ever been there?"

"I don't even know where it is." His accent was an Appalachian drawl.

Robinson held up a hand. "For the record, Roy, are you willing to answer their questions?"

"Uh-huh."

"Say 'yes' or 'no.'"

"Yes."

Robinson nodded at Maharos. "All right, Detective Maharos. You may proceed."

Maharos fixed his gaze on the young attorney for five seconds. He thought, kid's just out of law school, already he's a judge. He turned to the prisoner. "Mr. Young, do you have an address?"

"Shit no."

"How long have you been in New Philadelphia?"

Young shrugged a shoulder, "I don't know, coupla weeks."

"Where were you before you came here?"

He looked at the ceiling. "Let's see, I think in Wheeling. Yeah, Wheeling."

"That's West Virginia, isn't it?"

"Yeah, I guess so."

"Have you ever been north of New Philadelphia?"

"Where's north?"

Maharos glanced at Fiala who was slowly shaking his head.

"How old are you?"

"Twenty-four."

"Where were you born?"

"Kentucky."

"*Where* in Kentucky?"

"Doylesville. Real little town outside Lexington."

"When was the last time you had a job?"

Young looked at Robinson. "Do I have to answer these chickenshit questions?"

The lawyer said, "Only if you want to."

Maharos decided he was wasting his time. "Look, Young, the sheriff told me they picked you up on suspicion of murder."

Young for the first time came out of his sullen stance. He leaned forward, placing his palms on the table. His eyes blazed. "You tell the sheriff he's fulla shit! I didn't kill nobody."

Maharos went on quietly, "Sheriff Anderson told me the wallet belonging to the murdered man was found in your possession."

Young sat back. "Okay, I took the guy's wallet. He's layin' in the back of the truck, right? I thought he was drunk and figured to roll him. I grabbed the wallet and ran. I swear, I didn't know the guy was dead until the deputy picked me up and brung me here. I thought he was pullin' me in for vagrancy. Figured I'd get a few meals off the county. I shoulda took the fifteen fuckin' bucks and thrown the fuckin' wallet and the credit cards away. I never killed nobody."

Maharos had questioned many people in twenty years as a police officer. He had learned to know when they were lying and when they were not. Young was a bum, a drunk, a vagrant, a petty thief. He may have killed in a drunken brawl, but he was telling the truth now. He turned to Fiala. "Want to ask anything more, Frank?"

Fiala said, "Done any time, Roy?"

Young shrugged, "A little. County joints. No hard time."

"Where?"

"Kentucky, West Virginia."

"Ohio?"

"Nuh-uh. I only been in Ohio a few weeks."

Maharos decided they'd had enough. He got up and rapped on the door while Fiala turned off the recorder and tucked it under his arm. The deputy returned, led the prisoner back to his cell, then escorted the three men to the cell block entrance and let them out. Maharos and Fiala let Robinson guide them back to the sheriff's office.

Sheriff Anderson had left for lunch, but the secretary in his office handed Maharos a sheet of computer paper. He recognized it as a report from the National Crime Information Center in Washington, D.C. "Sheriff Anderson said you could look at this. He said he'd be back in an hour, if you want to wait."

Maharos and Fiala glanced at the paper. It stated that Roy Young had not been arrested for any serious crime. Stapled to the NCIC report was a record that had been obtained from the Kentucky Bureau of Criminal Information. It listed Young's previous arrests and convictions. There were half a dozen, all for vagrancy, public intoxication, assault and battery. His incarcerations had been in city and county jails, as he had told them.

Maharos handed the paper back to the secretary. She said, "Sheriff Anderson said if you wanted to view the murder scene he'd have one of the deputies take you out there."

"We'd like that," said Maharos. "Is there somewhere nearby to grab a bite?"

"Uh-huh. There's a cafeteria one floor up—if you don't mind the food."

Maharos and Fiala were finishing their overcooked hamburgers when a very young deputy sheriff came to the table where they sat. He had pink cheeks and light brown hair, and his uniform looked as though it had just come out of a box. His name tag read "L. Raymond."

"You Detective Maharos?"

Maharos nodded.

"I'm Larry Raymond. Whenever you folks are ready I'll drive you out to where they found Mr. Hamberger's body."

"We're ready."

Raymond took them to a black and white Dodge with a large star decal on each side door. He drove about a mile to the entrance ramp to Interstate 77. While he drove, he told them that Hamberger's body had been found in the bed of his old Ford pickup. A farmer who lives off the dirt road where the truck was parked phoned in yesterday. Raymond said, "I took the call and remained at the scene until the coroner's assistant pronounced old Noah dead, looked over the body and took it off to the county morgue." A mobile unit from the Stark County crime lab in Canton had been called in to go over the scene. The technicians had dusted the truck for latent prints. No weapon had been found.

About three miles north of New Philadelphia on I-77, Raymond took an exit marked "Dover" and "State Route 39." He drove for a mile on the state road, then turned right on a narrow dirt road. A quarter of a mile further on he pulled to the side of the road.

"Here we are," he said.

The road was bordered on both sides by a pine woods. Yellow plastic tape strips partially covered by dust, lay in the road and hung limply from the surrounding bushes, the remnants of the sheriff's cordon.

Maharos looked around. "Did the crime lab techs find anything?"

Raymond said that casts had been made of several footprints in the dirt around the truck, but nothing else had turned up.

Leaving Raymond and Fiala talking by the side of the patrol car, Maharos walked down the road in the direction they had come, looking to either side. About a hundred yards from where they had parked, he noticed a single tire track in the dirt by the side of the road. He traced it with his eyes, saw that it led through a shallow ditch to a dense clump of bushes, a yard from the side of the road. One bush was flattened, its twigs bent, as though pressed down by a heavy object.

He called to Fiala and Raymond, who trotted to the site. Maharos pointed to the tire track and the partly crushed bush. "Looks like some kind of vehicle was driven in here."

Fiala said, "Single track. What are you thinking, motorcycle?"

"Maybe. Sheriff Raymond, was this segment cordoned off?"

Raymond looked up and down the road as though trying to jog his memory. "I don't think so."

"Were there many gawkers?"

"Yeah. It didn't take long for the word to get out. A lot of the locals came over to see what happened to Noah Hamberger. I'm sure there were a lot of people right here, especially kids, you know, young guys from the farms around. Especially since it was Sunday, they had nothing else to do.

DEAD END   51

They couldn't come close to where the truck was parked because we had the area cordoned. So they looked on from here and from the road beyond where the truck was parked."

Maharos scratched his chin. "Well, it wouldn't do any harm to take a cast of this tire track and also take a closer look at the bush. See if there is anything there that might be helpful."

Raymond started toward the ditch but Fiala put his arm out restraining him. "Hold it. This is a job for the lab techs. How long do you think it would take the mobile unit to get back here?"

Raymond shook his head. "We waited a couple of hours yesterday. They come from Canton, you know."

Maharos said, "I think they need to come again."

Raymond hesitated and kept his eyes on the ground.

Fiala said, "Is there a problem?"

"Well, I'll have to run this by my boss."

"Anderson?"

"Uh-huh."

Fiala said, "Well, go ahead. Get him on the horn."

They started walking back toward the patrol car. Raymond shuffled along behind, obviously not anxious to make the request to Sheriff Anderson. "I'll put the call through, but will one of you ask him, you know, about getting the mobile unit back here?"

Maharos said, "I'll ask him." Raymond was apparently a new kid on the block. Maybe he had gotten his fingers burned dealing with Anderson before. Anderson thought he had the case locked up with the vagrant he had in custody. Maharos was just as sure he had the wrong man.

Raymond spoke briefly into his radio and handed the unit to Maharos while the call was patched through to Anderson. Maharos explained what they had found and finished saying, "What do you think, Sheriff, about getting the mobile crime lab back here to take a closer look at those bushes, maybe take casts of that tire track?" His language was as diplomatic as he could make it.

The sheriff's voice came blasting out of the little radio. "Shit no, we don't need the lab unit back here! I ain't gonna waste their time and the county's money. Do you know how many people's been tramplin' down ever' bush up and down the goddam road? There was kids on bicycles, ATCs, mopeds. Shit, there was even a couple on skateboards, for chrissake. Skateboards on a dirt road! Besides, we got the guy already. Lemme talk to Raymond."

Maharos handed the phone back to the deputy and watched his face turn to scarlet before he said a demure, "Yessir," and hung up.

Raymond climbed into the driver's seat. "He wants I should bring you back now."

They made the return trip in silence.

At the county office building, Maharos and Fiala retrieved their car and left without stopping in at the sheriff's office.

NINE

EARLY JUNE IN Ohio. While Fiala drove from New Philadelphia back to Youngstown, Maharos sat alongside gazing at the landscape. The gently rolling hills were green with freshly sprouting alfalfa, hay and corn. Every few miles they passed a farmer riding a tractor in his fields, right next to the interstate highway. Traffic on I-77 was light, just a few cars and trucks. In cars or RV's they passed, kids pressed their noses against the windows or waved at the detectives. School was out and families were on the road, towing their cars or boats behind the tall RVs.

Maharos watched the shield-shaped signs flash by. On top, the red background with white letters that said, "Interstate." Below, a blue background and white numbers, "77."

Near Youngstown, a lawyer had been shot dead and left in his car on a side road off Interstate 77. Near New Philadelphia, a hay and feed dealer had been shot dead and left in the bed of his pickup truck on a side road off Interstate 77. A month apart. *Exactly* a month apart.

Logikos. Maharos could hear the deep voice of his father, a man who'd had less than a fifth grade education in the old country. Who knew π was the sixteenth letter of his alphabet, knew nothing of its mathematical significance, yet knew his plow made a circular furrow roughly three times longer than the distance across the center of the same circle. Think. Reason. These you don't learn from books, Alexander, he would say. My testicles, he would say, gave you what my father and his father got from their great-great-great grandfathers. Men named Socrates and Aristotle. *Logikos.* Coincidence is a lazy man's way of explaining. There had to be a connection between the two events that appeared to be separated in time and space.

Fiala glanced at Maharos out of the corner of his eye. "When you don't say nothing for half an hour, you're either asleep or thinking. You ain't asleep."

"I'm thinking."

"I know. You're thinking the same thing I'm thinking."

His eyes half-closed, Maharos nodded. "Uh-huh. Maybe the Youngstown PD could get rid of one of us and save a salary. No sense duplicating."

"Better be you. I need the dough."

Maharos said, "When we get back, call the crime lab and ask them to send us copies of their findings in the New Philly case. I want to compare their ballistics with ours on Horner. I also want to see the autopsy report on Hamberger."

"You want me to call Sheriff King Kong and ask him for it?"

"I guess we'll have to go through him, much as I hate to."

Fiala said, "Want to send the mobile techs down to cast that tire track, take a closer look at the bush?"

"You mean on our own? Forget about Anderson?"

"Yeah."

Maharos shook his head. "Nah. You know who'll be getting the bill, don't you?"

"The city."

"Damn right. Ed Bragg's over budget now. He's not gonna sit still for *that*. Maybe Anderson is right. So many people went through that dirt road, there's no way to know who made the tracks."

Lieutenant Bragg wiped flecks of Danish muffin icing from his mouth. "So what did you guys find out?"

Maharos was seated across from Bragg. He knew the lieutenant liked to get to the bottom line with as little detail as possible. "Fiala's writing up his report now. The main thing is, they've got a collar in their lockup who's the wrong guy. We're waiting for the lab and autopsy reports, but I've got a hunch whoever killed the guy in New Philly also killed Horner."

"What makes you think the guy they picked up is the wrong one?"

Maharos related briefly the interrogation of Roy Young. Bragg nodded idly. He said, "I'm going to have to take Fiala off the case. Last night we caught a jewelry store robbery where the owner was shot dead. I've got Hassler on it and I need Frank to help him. You'll have to work the Horner case alone."

"Okay."

"And Al, I'm getting some heat from the bar association. They don't like losing members. They want to know why we haven't figured it out yet."

Maharos shrugged. "I'll try harder."

Karen Hennessy a civilian employee in Records, held at arms length the request form Maharos handed her, as though it had dangerous germs on it. She said, "You want me to punch up *all* the homicides in Ohio that occurred on the seventh of the month?"

Maharos said, "You read it right."

"The seventh of *each* month?"

"Uh-huh."

"Starting when?"

"You can start with last November."

"Last *November*? This is *June*."

"I know how to read a calendar."

"And you want to know *where* each one occurred?"

He counted to five, slowly. Finally, "Why is it every time I hand you a request you go through a major interrogation? It's written there in plain English."

She put up her hands defensively. "Okay, okay."

"I need it by tomorrow afternoon."

As he walked toward the door, he saw Hennessy's reflection in the glassed segment. Without turning around, he said, "And put your tongue back in your mouth."

He heard her mutter, "How does he *do* that?"

At his desk, Maharos read through the report from the Stark County crime lab.

Casts taken of footprints in Hamberger's barn were of two types. One matched the work shoes Hamberger had been wearing, the other a size three Adidas. The approximate weight of the person who wore the gym shoes was 125 to 130 pounds. A similar set of footprints had been found near the pickup truck where Hamberger's body lay.

A woman?

He read on. The back of the shovel found on the floor of the barn was covered with blood that matched Hamberger's. No, not likely a woman. There were no latent fingerprints on the shovel. *No* prints? Hamberger must have used the tool. The absence of any prints probably meant that the killer had used the shovel to bash in the victim's face, then wiped the handle clean. Why didn't the killer simply shoot him rather than knock him out first and shoot him later?

Another thing: Hamberger had been described as being a husky man. There were no signs of a struggle. Maharos was trying to picture someone as small as the footprints seemed to indicate, smashing a guy as big as Hamberger. Although he hadn't gotten the autopsy findings yet, he'd be willing to bet that Hamberger, like Horner, had suffered a cerebral concussion before he had been shot dead.

Maharos pieced together the information. The bloody shovel in the barn told him that Hamberger had been clobbered there. A crawler found at the scene was blood stained. If Hamberger had been lying on it when his face was bashed in, the David versus Goliath question could be explained. Blood in the bed of the pickup where the body was discovered, indicated that the victim had been driven, probably unconscious, to the dirt road where he was shot and left to die. Why not finish him off in the barn?

The lab had found no latent prints, except those belonging to Hamberger, anywhere in the truck .

The bullets had been sent to the crime lab from the medical examiner's office They were identified as having come from a twenty-five caliber handgun, probably a Colt. Spent shells found on the floor of the truck cab verified that the gun was a semi-automatic. The ballistics specialist found that the bullets did not match those that had killed Horner, nor did they match any others on file.

Hair and fiber analysis from the victim's clothing and the truck seat showed mainly an assortment of vegetable fibers. One sentence in the report leaped out at Maharos: "Several fibers removed from the back of the driver's seat, were of a navy blue wool." Wool? On a warm day in June? Were these fibers the same type found in the vacuumed material from the carpeting of Horner's car? Hamberger had not been wearing anything made of wool. Probably the wool fibers came from the clothes of the killer. They had adhered to the seat because that person had driven from the barn to the spot where the body had been found.

Maharos was becoming more and more convinced that the two murders were committed by the same person. Since most serial killers selected their victims at random, there probably was no connection between the two victims—*if* there were only two. And *if* they were both killed by the same person.

The computer printouts that Maharos had picked up from Karen Hennessy were still fan-folded. He tore the four sheets apart at their perforations before starting to read them.

The data were listed in four columns. The first column consisted of the names of the victims; the second, the jurisdiction charged with investigation of the crime; the third, the type of homicide; and the fourth column, the status of the case —whether closed by a conviction, trial pending, or open, meaning unsolved.

He started with November 7.

Homicide Victim........Jurisdiction....Type...Status

November 7

Benson, Carl Alfred....Cincinnati PD...MV....Conviction
White, Thomas R........Cleveland PD...St......Conviction
DeAngelo, Anthony J..Columbus PD...GS....Awaiting Trial

December 7

Bannister James J......Fairfax Sheriff...MV....Conviction
Carson, Edward, N.....Dayton PD.......MV....Conviction
Masson, Herbert........Cincinnati PD....MV....Conviction
Thompson, Evan T.....Cleveland PD....GS......Closed
Thompson, Abdul-K...Cleveland PD....GS......Closed
Thompson, Emily........Cleveland PD....GS......Closed

January 7

Borden, Isaiah............Cincinnati PD....St........Awaiting Trial
Burnstein, Frank F.....Canton PD........GS......Open
Lancaster, Victor D...Toledo PD........MV.....Conviction. . .

 Maharos fished a yellow, lined pad from his desk drawer and examined the list of November 7 homicides. Benson was a motor vehicular death, undoubtedly hit and killed by a drunk driver. Not interested. He put a line through the name. Thomas White was a stabbing victim in Cleveland. A little out of the territory, and stabbing was not the MO he was looking for. He placed a question mark next to the name. DeAngelo had been killed by gunshot and his murder was being investigated by police in Columbus. Although a suspect had been apprehended and was awaiting trial, Maharos knew from experience that the wrong person could have been arrested: case in point, *Young, vs. Tuscarawas County*. He circled the name.
 The December list contained no likely candidates for further study. He recalled the Thompson case in Cleveland from reports he had read at the time. All members of the same family. One had killed the other two and turned the gun on himself.
 The suspect who had gunned down Frank Burnstein in or near Canton in January, was waiting to be tried. Here it was June. What had happened to his constitutional right to a speedy trial? Canton was in the right vicinity for his investigation. Maharos drew a circle around "Burnstein."

He went through the list eliminating the vehicular homicides. The stabbing victims he separated from those who had been killed by gunshot. He subdivided the list into geographic categories. When he had finished, he had the names of thirteen people—in addition to George Horner and Noah Hamberger—who were possible gunshot victims of a serial killer.

Now came the legwork.

TEN

DETECTIVE LIEUTENANT CHARLES Birtcher of the Canton Police Department peered over the tops of his half-glasses. "Is that the Greek Adonis I see invading our territory? Or maybe Kojak?"

Al Maharos had just walked through the door of Birtcher's office. "Hello, Charlie," he said.

"Has Ed Bragg sent you over to spy? See how a department *should* be run?"

Maharos ran a finger over the top of Birtcher's desk and examined the tip of his finger.

"Actually, we're trying to recruit someone to do our office cleaning. But I don't think you've got what we want." He extended his hand. "You're looking good, Charlie."

Birtcher looked at the top of Maharos' head. "Hey, I think you've grown a hair since I saw you last."

"Yeah. In my nose."

It was worth a chuckle from Birtcher. "What's up, Al?"

Maharos sank into an easy chair in front of Birtcher's desk.

"You've got a guy I'm interested in talking to." He glanced at a sheet of paper in his hand. "Lance Harwood—the Burnstein case."

Birtcher gave him a sideways leer. "This your day for boys? You're no longer interested in girls?"

"What have you got on Harwood?"

"He's a fag. He and his lover had a spat. It got past the biting and scratching stage. Harwood put him away with a twenty-five, or maybe it was a twenty-two, I forget. Anyway, Lancie-baby's in the lockup. I think his trial is on the books for next week. What's your interest in the case?"

Maharos said he was investigating George Horner's death and looking at all the comparable recent homicides for a possible lead. He asked, "Do you have a confession from Harwood?"

Birtcher shook his head. "No. He claims he's clean. Says he loved the guy too much to even think of killing him. But we had picked him up twice for assault with a deadly weapon, a knife. Both times he had cut up his roommate, Flossie Burnstein."

"Flossie?"

"Not what you think. Flossie is—was—Frank. He was a nurse at Mercy Hospital. We should have put Harwood away before, but Burnstein refused to press charges. They kissed and made up. This time, Harwood *really* kissed him off."

Maharos asked, "Where was Burnstein killed?"

"We found him in his car out near Hurford Run, know where that is?"

"It's a little south of here, isn't it?"

"Yeah. It's a creek, just off I-77 . Want to look at the file?"

"I'd like that."

Birtcher buzzed his secretary and had a thick file folder brought in. He handed it to Maharos. "I'm not sure what you expect to find. Didn't you say your homicide occurred in May? Harwood was locked up at the time."

Maharos knew that Birtcher would laugh him right out of his office if he told him that he was investigating all the homicides by gunshot that had occurred on the seventh of each month. He shrugged. "Obviously Harwood's not a suspect in Horner's death. It's just that there are some similarities. Maybe we've got a copycat."

Birtcher furrowed his brow but said nothing. Maharos took the file into the squad room and sat at an unoccupied desk to leaf through it.

Burnstein and Harwood had been roommates and lovers for three years. They lived in a fancy condo in an upper-middle-class neighborhood. Lance Harwood was a decorator who worked for a large furniture store. His work was highly regarded, but he had a reputation for being temperamental. Other employees found him difficult to work with.

Frank Burnstein was pleasant, placid and friendly. He made friends *too* easily to suit Harwood, whose jealous rages tended to result in shouting that had been reported to police by neighbors on three separate occasions. Twice, as Lieutenant Birtcher had told Maharos, Harwood had attacked Burnstein with a knife. Both times the wounds had been superficial, although they required suturing in a hospital emergency room. Police had been notified by ER personnel as required by law, but Burnstein did not press charges. Harwood's last knife attack had occurred two days before Burnstein was killed.

The last time Burnstein had been seen alive was when he went off duty from his three-to-eleven PM shift at Mercy Hospital. The night security guard saw him walking to his car in the hospital parking lot. Harwood contended that Burnstein never arrived home. He did not report Burnstein missing, claimed it was not unusual for him to cover for one of the nurses on the night shift. The following day Burnstein's body was discovered in his car by the side of a county road.

Following Burstein's death, police, in a routine check with the local gundealers, discovered a Firearms Transaction Record Harwood had filled out four years before. He admitted to having bought a twenty-five caliber handgun. He said he purchased it for protection because he had to go to the homes of clients at night. When Harwood had been asked to produce the gun, he was unable to find it.

By the end of an hour's reading, Maharos had learned two things that convinced him that Burnstein and Horner and possibly Hamberger as well, had been killed by the same person: First, Burnstein had been shot twice from behind. One bullet had entered at the base of the neck and the second between the shoulder blades. *These entry sites were identical to those of the bullets that had killed Horner.* Maharos hadn't received the autopsy report on Hamberger yet. Second, vacuumed material from the carpet in the back of Burnstein's car included blue wool fibers. He made a note to check if they had been compared to those found in Horner's car carpet and in Hamberger's truck.

Maharos closed the file and stared at its cover. What significance was there in the location of the bullet entry sites? It *had* to be more than coincidence that the two bullet holes in each case were identically placed. One notable difference was that Horner and Hamberger had sustained severe head injuries as well. Burnstein had been spared that. He had been described as a passive individual. Was it that he didn't resist like the other two?

Another thing: here are two gays living together. Violence between homosexuals is not uncommon, but, as a rule, these fights erupt in a moment of passion and in the home. If Harwood *did* shoot his lover wouldn't he have done it in the apartment they shared? Would Burnstein have willingly gone with an angered man who had a history of attacking him? There's also the question of how would Harwood get back home from a remote road? The file had described the suspect as fastidious and debonair. Somehow Maharos couldn't picture the decorator trudging down a dusty road at night, or hitchhiking, as he theorized Horner's killer and possibly Hamberger's as well, might have done in leaving.

He shook his head to clear it, and took the file back to Birtcher's office.

The lieutenant greeted him, "Well, detective, did you get any ideas?"

Maharos was not ready to tell Birtcher what he suspected, what he *knew*. For one thing, he was not sure Birtcher would agree with him. The Canton police had what they considered to be a credible suspect. The district attorney, relying on the circumstantial evidence, had presented a convincing case to the grand jury and Harwood had been arraigned for murder one. Because it was a capital case, Harwood had been imprisoned without bail for five months. Maharos knew the repercussions would be horrendous if he blew away the case against Harwood at this time. Besides, it could drive the killer underground for a time, only to surface with a new rash of killings. Maharos said, "Can I talk to Harwood?"

Birtcher said, "Come on, Al. If you've got something I want to know about it. Don't give me any 'copycat' shit."

"How solid do you think your case is?"

Birtcher gestured to the file that Maharos had returned to his desk. "You read it. You tell *me.*"

Maharos knew he would get no cooperation from Birtcher unless he leveled with him. "Okay, Charlie, here are the similarities. Horner was found dead in his car. So was Burnstein. Both on side roads. Horner was shot twice with a twenty-two, once at the base of the neck, the second time between the shoulder blades. Burnstein was shot in the same places, although with a twenty-five. Either wound could have been fatal. Why hit these guys twice? Here's another thing: the techs vacuumed some blue wool fibers from the carpet in the back of Horner's car. I see in their report they found some in Burnstein's car. We ought to have someone run a comparison, if it hasn't already been done."

Birtcher fixed his gaze on Maharos without speaking. He stood up from his chair and walked to the window, looking out with his hands clasped behind his back. "You realize, Maharos, you're knocking my case into a shit heap—not to mention inviting a lawsuit for false arrest and wrongful imprisonment."

Maharos could feel the tension rising in Birtcher. He knew what must be going through his mind and tried to offer consolation. "Assuming there's a connection between the two homicides—which so far is based on conjecture."

Birtcher turned to face him. There was no humor in his expression now. "You want to talk to Harwood, right?"

Maharos nodded.

"Okay. Let me contact his lawyer. If Foaming Homer says it's all right, you got it."

Homer Lavant had been the leading criminal lawyer in Canton for more than twenty-five years. His flamboyant dress and courtroom histrionics were distracting enough to draw attention away from the most odious client. His behavior, calculated to be obnoxious, often influenced juries to react sympathetically toward the poor bastard who had him for a lawyer. Maharos was glad he'd have a chance to fortify himself with lunch before facing Stark County's answer to William Kunstler.

Lavant bounced into the waiting room outside Lieutenant Birtcher's office where Maharos had been waiting. Five foot-five, weighing 200 pounds, he looked like Santa without the beard. His flowing white mane brought emphasis to the pinkness of his skin. His smile exposed a row of evenly-capped white teeth as he greeted Maharos. "Sorry you had to wait, Detective. My deposition this morning ran overtime."

Maharos nodded. "I understand. I think Lieutenant Birtcher told you that I want to talk to your client, Lance Harwood."

"That's *all* he told me. Obviously, I want to know why."

"I'm investigating the homicide of a Youngstown resident, an attorney named Horner—you may have known him."

Lavant nodded. "Not personally, but I know of the case. What possible connection is there to the murder that my client is accused of?"

"All I can tell you at this time is that there are some similarities in the two. I can't go into it in any more detail, but I can assure you that Harwood is not a suspect in the case I'm investigating. In fact, Harwood was in jail when Horner was killed."

Lavant gazed at him without speaking for a few seconds. Maharos could sense the man's wheels turning. The lawyer wanted more information. Perhaps he could wheedle it by threatening to refuse the interview with his client. Finally, he shook his head. "I'm afraid that won't do, Mr. Maharos. I need to know why I should allow Mr. Harwood to be interrogated at this late stage. You know, of course, that his trial is coming up. *Voir dire* begins next week."

"I realize that. All I can say is that any information I can get from talking to Harwood is more likely to help him than hurt him."

Again Lavant shook his head. "Too vague, Maharos. I won't do business with you under those restrictions."

Maharos rose from his seat. "Then I'm afraid it's no go. If you change your mind let me know." He held out his hand to the lawyer.

Lavant put up his palm like a traffic cop and smiled. "Okay. You're a good poker player, Maharos. But I'll be there with you when you question him, of course."

"Of course."

Even though he wore ill-fitting, gray prison clothing, Lance Harwood made Maharos feel poorly dressed. He sat erect, opposite the detective at a round table in the interrogation room, with his arms folded defiantly across his chest. His blonde hair was swept back from a broad forehead, his light blue eyes slightly hooded. Alongside Harwood sat Homer Lavant.

Maharos asked, "Mr. Harwood—may I call you Lance?"

Harwood nodded.

"Your attorney has probably told you that I want to talk to you in connection with a homicide that has some similarities to Frank Burnstein's murder. Let me say at the outset that you are not suspected of being involved in the case I'm investigating. Is that clear?"

Harwood nodded again. Lips tightly compressed.

"Does the name George Horner mean anything to you?"

Harwood looked at Lavant who said, "Go ahead and answer."

Harwood opened his mouth to speak but Maharos held up a hand. "Hold it Lance. Before you answer, I want to be sure you're doing it of your own free will, and not because your lawyer suggested it." Maharos was making sure he was not cutting a hole in the prison wall for the guy to slip through on a legal technicality. A stunt like that was vintage Lavant.

Harwood nodded and said, "I understand, I'll answer. Wasn't he the Youngstown lawyer who was killed?"

"Right. Did you know him or have any connection to him in any way?"

"No. The only thing I know about him is what I read in the papers."

"How about Noah Hamberger?"

Lavant held up a hand. "Wait a minute. What are you trying to pull? Who is Hamberger?"

Maharos said, "Why don't you let the man answer? I'm not trying to 'pull' anything. Either he knows or doesn't know."

Lavant thought a moment then said, "Okay, Lance."

Harwood said, "Never heard of the person."

"Your file says that you had owned a twenty-two caliber pistol.. What happened to it?"

Lavant broke in. "Wait a minute. Come on, Maharos, you know better than to ask about a pending case."

Harwood waved him aside. "I don't mind answering. I've already explained about that gun to the detective who arrested me after Frank's death. I had bought the gun a few years ago because I often go—went—to people's homes to help them in decorating. Also, I often went in the evening. This city is getting so you can't walk around at night even in the *good* neighborhoods. Know what I mean?"

Maharos' head bobbed once.

Harwood went on. "For a few months I carried the gun, but it was bulky and, frankly, it *destroyed* the lines of my suits. I stopped carrying it and stuck it away in a drawer. And then, a year ago the apartment that Frank and I shared was robbed. When I reported to the police what was missing, I was more upset about the Rolex and two valuable rings that were stolen, than I was about that silly gun. I thought I told them about the gun after the robbery, but when they questioned me about Frank's death they asked where it was. Said I hadn't reported it missing. They found out about it, because I filled out some papers at the gun shop when I bought it.. I'm sure it was stolen in the robbery. But, of course, the stupid police wouldn't believe *my* story."

Maharos said, "Lance, I know that you and Frank Burnstein had quarreled, and the record shows that you had attacked him. Can you tell me what your fights were about?"

Lavant jumped in immediately. "Now I'm *really* going to put my foot down. Lance, I *forbid* you to answer. Maharos, I think I've been patient enough with you. I'm terminating this interview."

Maharos had learned from the file that Harwood claimed to have been at home, reading and watching television the night Burnstein was killed. He had read the interrogation transcript after Harwood had been picked up. He recalled the questioning:

DET. SUMMERS: What did you two fight about?
HARWOOD: Oh, it was so awfully SILLY. I'm ashamed to talk about it. The first time, we had been to a party and Frank spent the evening talking to this young man, a poet. Well, to make it brief, I'd had a few drinks and when we got home I

accused Frank of making a pass at the boy. Frank laughed it off, I flew into a RAGE and, well, you know what happened.

The second time, I think it was just a few days before he was—before he died. Frank didn't come home from the hospital until almost midnight. He always called when he was going to be late, but this time I didn't hear from him until he walked in the door. I was FURIOUS. He told me he had taken one of the nurses out for a drink after work. A girl! I flipped, of course. It was ridiculous. Anyway, one thing led to another and I—well, it was only a teeny cut on his hand. They made a big thing of it in the ER. Put STITCHES in it, for God sakes. All it needed was a Band-Aid.

Now that Lavant had signaled the end of his interview with Harwood, Maharos got up to leave.

Harwood dropped his chin to his chest and slowly shook his head. When he raised it to gaze squarely at Maharos, his eyes were misty. His voice broke as he answered. "Frank was the dearest, sweetest, kindest soul I ever met. He never harmed *anyone*. I can't conceive of someone wanting him dead."

Maybe someone who was insanely jealous, Maharos thought. He rose, extended his hand and said, "Thank you. You have been most cooperative."

Harwood touched his little finger to a corner of an eye and asked brightly, "Is any of this information going to help clear me?"

Maharos smiled and shrugged. He thought that Harwood had made a remarkable recovery from his grief.

ELEVEN

ALTHOUGH MAHAROS' DESK was in the back corner of the squad room, he spotted the note propped up on it as soon as he walked in the door, "SEE ED BRAGG!!" From the size of the paper and the huge capital letters, a rookie cop, much less a detective first grade, could have figured out that Lieutenant Bragg was unhappy about something.

In the three days since he had spoken to Lance Harwood in Canton, Maharos had questioned three other homicide suspects on the list Karen Hennessy had prepared for him. He had interviewed the families of two additional murder victims and spoken to police and sheriffs in neighboring Akron, Wooster and Alliance. So far, the only case in any way related to the Horner and Hamberger killings was that of Frank Burnstein. In that one, as in the others, Maharos had reached a dead end. From Burnstein's coworkers at Mercy Hospital he had learned only that "Flossie" was the last person in the world anyone would want to kill. Obviously, someone (and he doubted it was Harwood) hadn't gotten the word.

The growl that came from Lieutenant Bragg's office in response to his knock confirmed Maharos' suspicion that he was in trouble.

Bragg's eyes were almost obscured by his scowling brows. The downturned corners of his mouth reached his chin. "Come in and close the door," he ordered.

Maharos remained standing and Bragg did not offer him a chair.

"What the hell are you trying to do to us, Maharos?"

"Sir?"

"Don't give me any of that 'sir' shit." He pointed to the phone on his desk. "That thing has been ringin' like a three-alarm fire for the past two days. My ass has been tore ragged by everyone in the state from the Canton DA to the Chief Justice of the Ohio Supreme Court in Columbus. They all want to know why my department is torpedoing a case they've been building for the past five months that's going to court in a week! And they want to know what right one of my men has to talk to prospective witnesses in a trial that's out of our jurisdiction."

Maharos decided to buy time. Quietly, he said, "Mind if I sit down?"

Bragg thundered, "I don't give a shit whether you sit, stand or flip on your side. I want you to explain to me what the fuck is goin' on."

Patiently and softly, Maharos related where his investigation of Horner's murder had taken him. Bragg listened while impatiently tapping the edge of his desk with a pen and staring intently at him. Maharos concluded, "Look, we want to find out who the killer or killers are. We sure as hell don't want to see an innocent person convicted."

"Oh? Now we can forget about the principal of a trial by jury? Now, we can save the time and expense of courts and trials? Now all we need is some smart-ass detective who sticks a wet finger in the breeze and tells us who did what to who? Come on, Maharos, I don't need a sermon from you about convicting an innocent person."

Maharos shrugged. "Want me off the Horner case?"

Bragg pursed his lips and let the thought sink in before he answered. "Okay. I'll tell you what I want: I want you to stay on the case. I'll give you another two weeks to come up with something."

"Three."

"All right, three. But that's it. And I want a report on my desk every time you sneeze. I want to be on top of this thing minute by minute. Understood?"

"Yes sir."

* * *

The list showed no homicides on February 7 that fit the pattern. In fact, there had been only two homicides in the state on that date, one in Toledo and one in a small community outside Springfield. A hit-and-run driver had been apprehended, convicted and sentenced in the first, and a drunk driver was serving a jail term for the second.

The March 7 list contained the name of Marlon Graves, a resident of Tallmadge, a small town on the eastern outskirts of Akron. Graves had been shot to death and his murder was still under investigation by the Summit County Sheriff's Office.

A phone call put Maharos in touch with Deputy Sheriff Norton Kohler, who was in charge of the investigation. Kohler said that Graves had been a men's wear salesman in Tallmadge and had been found shot to death in his car on a dirt road near Barberton, a few miles southwest of Akron, and just off I-77.

Kohler told him, "We found out that Graves was a pretty heavy gambler. Probably not a very *good* gambler, which is why he sold suits for a living. Anyway, on the evening he was killed, he called his wife from the clothing store in Akron where he worked and told her that he planned to drive to Richfield for a Cavaliers game after work. He said she should go ahead and eat dinner by herself, he'd grab a bite at a stand at the game. He mentioned to one of his coworkers that he planned to stop off at the home of a bookie on his way to the game, and place a bet."

Maharos said, "Did he meet with the bookie?"

"No. We know the guy, Tony D'Allesandro, and we questioned him.. He said Graves had called before he left the store, but never showed up."

"What kind of bets did Graves usually make?"

"Anywhere from one to five hundred, occasionally as much as a grand."

Maharos whistled. "That's heavy. Do you think it's possible he had a winning bet and the bookie paid him off with lead."

"No. Tony's a successful. businessman He's not gonna knock off anyone for that kind of dough. He can take a two-, three-grand loss without any sweat. He collected over four K on other bets just that night. Besides, he told us that Graves was a regular customer, and over the course of a year the guy would drop a bundle on track and football bets. He was sure he'd get back whatever he might have lost—if Graves had lived.

"There's another reason we're sure Tony didn't do Graves. He had a rock solid alibi for his whereabouts most of the evening."

Maharos thought he wouldn't trust a bookie's alibi regardless how solid it seemed. "What's 'rock solid'?"

"Shortly after he spoke to Graves, the Akron police picked him up for soliciting bets and booked him into their jail overnight."

That's rock solid, Maharos agreed, unless the bookie had a hit man working for him. "Did he operate with someone else or a syndicate?"

"Tony D'Allesandro's a loner, but he's honest—and in this case, clean."

"Did Graves have the money he planned to bet when they found him?

"Nope. No money, no wallet."

"Any idea if he made it to the game?"

Kohler said. "We have no way of knowing. We showed his picture around to the ticket sellers, ushers, vendors. Got nothin' but laughs. They're too busy with the crowds to remember one face from another. I personally don't think he got to the game."

"Why not?"

"We found him in his car right outside Barberton. That's the opposite direction from Richfield, where the game was."

"Any other leads?"

"Nope. And the case is cold now. By the way, what's your interest in this?"

Maharos briefly told him that he was investigating any cases that fit the MO of Horner's murder. "I'll stop by this afternoon and have a look at your file on Graves, if it's all right with you," he said.

"Sure," said Kohler.

Maharos sat in the file room of the Summit County Sheriff's office with papers spread out on the table before him. Before he was halfway through, he knew he had found a match to go with the Horner, Hamberger, Burnstein murders. The autopsy report showed the same pattern of gunshot wounds, although the bullets recovered were from a thirty-two caliber Smith and Wesson revolver, different from the weapons used in the other three cases. The guy must have an arsenal, thought Maharos. Ballistics studies did not match any other cases on file. All the latent fingerprints recovered were those of the victim. Fiber analysis of the vacuumed material from the car and the victim's clothing gave no clues. Unlike the other three cases, there were no navy blue wool fibers reported.

One curious finding turned up in the chemical analysis of dirt particles found in the floor carpeting of the car. A substance in trace amounts was identified as glutaraldehyde. It was not present on the soles of Graves' shoes, and could have been tracked in by the killer. Maharos had no idea what glutaraldehyde was. He picked up the phone on the desk in the file room and asked to be connected with the Summit County crime lab. He asked for the chief technician. The operator said, "That will be Jerry Schwartz."

When Schwartz came on the line, Maharos explained that he'd been reviewing the lab report of Marlon Graves. "The report says you found glutaraldehyde traces in the car carpet sweepings. What's that?"

"Glutaraldehyde? That's a tissue fixative. You've heard of formaldehyde, also known as formalin, haven't you?"

"Yeah."

"Well, glutaraldehyde is a close cousin of formaldehyde."

"What's it used for?"

"I just told you. It's a tissue fixative. It's used to keep tissue —skin, organs and like that—from decomposing. We use it in the lab for processing tissue for microscopic examination. Formaldehyde works a little faster so we use that for routine stuff. Glutaraldehyde is a little better preservative. We use it mainly when we process tissue for electron microscopy. Glutaraldehyde is also a constituent of embalming fluid."

Maharos mulled that one over. He knew they hadn't found Graves already embalmed. "Any idea where it might have come from in Graves' case?"

"Have no idea. Maybe the guy who killed Graves."

"Or maybe one of your techs picked it up on his shoes from the lab and tracked it in to Graves' car?"

"Possible."

"Thanks." He hung up.

Bonnie Graves, Marlon's widow, was a thirty-five-year-old Dolly Parton-type blonde. Maharos had called from the sheriff's office and tracked her down at Angels' Hair, the beauty shop where she worked as a manicurist. Late in the afternoon, he sat self-consciously in the small waiting area flipping through *Bazaar*, while she finished working on a customer. In his reflection on the wall mirror next to his chair he could see the beads of sweat glistening on his hairless head.

Bonnie dried her hands on a towel and greeted Maharos with a broad smile when she completed her last manicure of the day. She said, "You want to talk about Marlon?"

Maharos explained that he was conducting an investigation of several homicides, Marlon Graves' among them. He looked around the small shop. Several women were under driers, others were having their hair cut. "Is there some place we can talk privately?" he said, and was relieved when Bonnie suggested a bar down the street.

The bartender at Harry's Place waved his towel and yelled, "Hi, Bonnie!" over the crowd noise of a wrestling match that blared from the overhead TV screen. Bonnie squeezed into a bench in one of the booths along a wall and Maharos sat facing her.

The waitress came over and said, "What'll it be, Bonnie?"

"Vodka and tonic, please, Trish." Maharos ordered a light beer.

When the drinks arrived, Bonnie said, "What's the sudden interest in Marlon's death? I thought they'd given up any hope of finding the person that did it."

DEAD END

Maharos explained that his interest was really in another unsolved case, in the Youngstown vicinity. "But if we can find a pattern, we may be able to tell if the same person has committed more than one murder."

"Gee, you mean there's a serial murderer loose?"

"Well, we don't know that for a fact. But it's one of the things we want to find out. What I'm trying to find out right now is whether there's a connection between any of the murder victims. You see, Bonnie, if one person *is* responsible for several of these deaths, is he or she just picking victims at random or is there some tie between them?"

"That's a lot of 'ifs'."

Maharos smiled. This gal wasn't one of your airbrain blonde types.

He showed her the names of the fifteen victims he had culled from the list of homicides that had occurred on the seventh of each of the past eight months. He had omitted any reference to the dates or locations of the murders. He asked her if she knew the names of the other people on his list. Bonnie took a pair of large-framed spectacles from her purse and carefully read through the list. When she came to the name of George Horner, she pointed to it with a long, vivid lavender fingernail. "That name looks familiar." Maharos' heart rate leaped. Then she continued, "Didn't I recently read about it in the newspapers?"

"You don't know if your husband knew him, do you?"

She shook her head slowly, "No, I'm sure he didn't."

Bonnie Graves confirmed that her late husband had been a compulsive gambler. She'd tried to get him into a rehab program but he was convinced that he would hit it big someday and denied having a problem. She was pretty sure he had paid his gambling debts. In fact, he would often clean out their bank account to avoid being blacklisted by the bookies he dealt with. "He saw other guys with busted kneecaps, so he was careful about paying up front when he made a bet."

Bonnie did not know of anyone with a reason to kill her husband.

She became teary-eyed after her second drink. For all his faults, Marlon was a loving, faithful husband. They had been married for twelve years, their first marriage for both. Graves had no insurance, so Bonnie had to keep the job she had held all during their marriage. They had no children.

Maharos was toying with the idea of asking Bonnie if she was busy that evening, when she brightened and coyly revealed that she was dating a guy who seemed serious about marrying her "as soon as his wife gives him a divorce." Uh-huh, he thought, that's the kind of gamble that kept her late husband broke.

Maharos gave her his card and told her to call if she thought of anything further.

On the drive back to Youngstown, the picture of Bonnie Graves fresh in his mind, Maharos recalled that it had been more than a month since he had gone out (or stayed in) with a woman. He was beginning to hate the mating dance each time he took out someone new: the posturing, the casual touch of hands, the tentative invitation "your place or mine?" the fumbling with clothing. Afterward, he would debate whether to continue a "relationship" or terminate it causing as little hurt as possible. Often enough, the decision to end it was not his.

Sure, they'd tell him he was fun to be with. Even exciting. His stories about his life with the sleaze kept their attention. He neither exaggerated nor minimized the danger. The truth was, he did most of his work with his head. Only once had he fired a shot at a person—but missed.

It'd be easy if he had an eight-to-five job. But he couldn't count the times when the promise of an evening of fun and excitement, had been broken by the chirruping of the beeper on his belt.. It might be two, three days before he could get around to calling again. He'd promise to make it up to them, but the same thing could happen a second or third time. No lady will stand around by herself, all dressed up and reeking with something expensive from Chanel, twirling the stem of an empty cocktail glass, waiting. Not more than twice or three times if she's in her right mind. It doesn't matter *how* exciting he might be, if she's not sure he'll be there.

Now that he was getting close to fifty, he thought that the time had come for him to find someone with whom he could comfortably spend his leisure moments. In a few years he would be eligible for retirement. Then he could take his pension and supplement it with a cushy part-time job. Selling security systems, or something like that.

In the past, he had given some thought to moving to Florida or California where he would get a police job in a small town. The deterrent was Annie. He wanted to watch her grow, at least until she left home to go to college. He knew that once he left Youngstown, he would rarely see the child; she would forget her father.

When be got back to headquarters, he stopped at Frank Fiala's desk. Fiala was typing up a report.

Maharos said, "Frank, a few weeks ago, you said Henny had someone she wanted me to meet."

Henny was Frank's wife and the mother of their six children. She had fixed Maharos up with more than a dozen dates since his divorce. Each time, after some emergency had forced Maharos to call things off at the last moment, she vowed it would be the last. But there isn't a married woman alive who can stand to see a healthy, eligible male eating and sleeping by himself when there are healthy, eligible females around.

Fiala looked up from his typewriter. He winked. "Uh-huh. Horny again."

"Don't be crude, Fiala. Since I no longer have you around to listen to my brilliant conversation, I decided to share it with an appreciative person of the opposite sex."

Fiala fished in his desk drawer and came up with a slip of paper. "Speaking of sex, here's her name and phone number."

TWELVE

LIEUTENANT ED BRAGG leaned back in his swivel chair while he chewed on the remains of a pizza. He beamed at Al Maharos sprawled in the chair in front of his desk. *"Now* we're getting somewhere."

Maharos ignored the "we" reference. All the information he had, and was sharing with Bragg, he had gotten by relentlessly sniffing into every cranny that seemed promising. Now he sat with Bragg telling him that he had uncovered another homicide that fit the pattern of the murders of George Horner and Noah Hamberger. Also, he had finally received Hamberger's autopsy report. From it he learned, without surprise, death had been due to twenty-five caliber bullet wounds, one through the spinal cord at the level of the seventh cervical vertebra and another entering from the level of the seventh thoracic vertebra, passing through the heart. Both bullets had been recovered and examined for characteristic markings. He had called down to the medical examiner's office and asked that photomicrographs of the spent missiles be faxed to other ballistics laboratories in the state for comparison.

Any question that Hamberger had been the victim of the same killer who had murdered Horner and Graves, was now erased. Maharos could now account for murders on the seventh of January (Burnstein), March (Graves), May (Horner) and June (Hamberger). It looked as though initially the killer was selecting a victim on the seventh day of alternate months. Hamberger's death broke the pattern. Was he picking up his pace and was now on a monthly schedule?

Bragg said, "I got a call from that lawyer in Canton, the one who's defending the swishy decorator."

"Lavant?"

"That's the one. He got an extension on the trial date. He figures maybe you'll dig up some evidence that'll help his case."

"Meantime his guy sits around in jail."

"Better a little more now than a lot more later."

"*If* we can nail someone else for the job on Burnstein."

"Anyway, you can expect to be subpoenaed as a witness when the trial comes up," said Bragg.

"Do they have a new trial date set yet?"

Bragg rummaged through the pile of papers on his desk and came up with a memo note. "Yeah. Wednesday, July eighth."

Maharos jotted it down in his spiral notebook.

Bragg said, "Okay, Al, what's our next move?"

"Well, I'm not finished bird-dogging the list I've got. There may be more than just the three homicides we know about. I could use some help."

Bragg shook his head slowly. "I wish I could spare someone, but I can't at the moment. In another week you can probably have Fiala back. Meanwhile, you're doin' fantastic on your own. Keep at it."

A great cheerleader. At least he was finally out of Bragg's doghouse, something to be thankful for.

Bragg's phone rang. He listened for a moment. "A call for you, Al."

Maharos rose from his chair. "Thanks, Ed. I'll take it at my desk."

The woman's voice said, "Hi, this is Bonnie."

He thought for a moment. "Bonnie?"

"Bonnie Graves, remember?"

A picture of a well-built blonde sipping vodka and tonic flashed into his mind. *That* Bonnie. "Of course."

"You told me to call if I remembered anything?"

"Uh-huh."

"Well, when you showed me that list of names, I thought one looked a little familiar but I wasn't sure so I didn't say anything at the time. Wasn't there a Gibson on the list?"

Maharos sat up sharply and pressed the receiver to his ear. With his free hand, he reached behind to the pocket of his jacket hanging over the back of his chair and brought out the list of homicide victims. He had gone over the names so many times, he was sure he remembered them all. He wanted to be certain. Yes, there it was in the column of April 7 homicides. Henry Gibson; gunshot victim; jurisdiction, Stark County Sheriff's office.

Bonnie Graves was saying, "First I thought the name was familiar because I had read about it in the newspapers, you know, like that other guy whose name I told you looked familiar?"

"George Horner?"

"Yeah, Horner. But no, I hadn't read anything about Gibson. Then, after I got home, I looked through a list I had kept of people who sent me condolence letters after Marlon died last March. I meant to answer them and thank the people who wrote. I never did, but I kept the list. Anyway, there was one from this guy Hank Gibson. I don't even know how Marlon knew him. I thought he might be one of the guys Marlon worked with at the clothing store or maybe one of his bookies. I don't know if he's any relation to the Gibson you have on your list, but I thought maybe I should tell you."

Maharos said, "Do you have the letter?"

"No. I threw it away. I didn't want to keep those things. They just made me feel sad."

"Do you have Gibson's address?"

"Yeah, it's right here on the list. Sterling Wholesale Hardware Co., 2337 Henry Street, Canton, Ohio. Funny, I didn't know Marlon even knew anyone from Canton. Shows you how little you can know about people you spend most of your life with."

"I don't suppose you remember what the letter said? Like, how he knew Marlon?"

"No. I got a lot of letters from people who said they read about Marlon in the papers. Many of them were people I didn't know. Some said they had been Marlon's customers. Some were, you know, bookies. *They* really miss him."

Maharos said, "What's the name of the clothing store where Marlon worked? I may want to do some checking."

"Simpson's Menswear. It's on Market Street in Akron."

"Bonnie, do me a favor?"

"Sure, what is it?"

"Don't say anything to anyone about my investigation— either our conversation the other day or today. If the newspapers get hold of this they'll make a big story out of it. Whoever killed your husband probably thinks the police have given up looking. We want him or her to keep thinking that."

"I understand. I won't say a word," said Bonnie.

Maharos' first call was to the Stark County Sheriff's Office in Canton. Deputy Sheriff Karen Vandergrift told him that Henry Gibson's murder and robbery had not been solved. There were no suspects, they were open to suggestions from him, and he was welcome to look at their file. Gibson, she said, had been an executive with a wholesale hardware company in Canton. It *was* the same Gibson.

The forty-mile drive to Canton took an hour. Thirty minutes after sitting down with Henry Gibson's file, Maharos knew he had filled another gap in his hunt; he had located an April victim of the serial murderer who deposited his kill along isolated stretches of northeastern Ohio country roads.

Maharos now had an important new lead: Henry Gibson, one victim, had known Marlon Graves, another victim.. Although details of the link between the two murdered men was still unknown, it now appeared that the killings may not have been random. It opened up the possibility that *all* of the victims were in some way related to the killer.

The bad news was that if Gibson's murder was one of the series, the theory that until June the killer struck on alternate months, went out the window. Gibson had died on the seventh of April. Maharos now could account for similarly patterned slayings on the seventh of January (Frank Burnstein), March (Marlon Graves), April (Henry Gibson), May (George Horner) and June (Noah Hamberger). Was February 7 omitted for a reason, or had Maharos overlooked someone?

It was now June 17. What would happen on the seventh of July, and the seventh of August, and the next month? Each time the calendar clocked a "7", could he look forward to another corpse with bullet holes in the neck and between the shoulder blades, lying on a dirt road? More important, could he act promptly enough to prevent another death?

Maharos was staring at the ceiling when Karen Vandergrift came in the file room. Her tan, sharply-creased uniform slacks did not hide a good figure. She said, "What's up there, spiders?"

Maharos grinned. "Thinking. That's how I think."

"Think about any way to find out who killed Gibson? We sure haven't."

"Maybe. I'm not sure."

Vandergrift flattened her palms on the table, leaned forward, her face a foot away from his. "You serious?"

Her light blue eyes were wide open. Her honey-colored hair was cut short.

Maharos briefly told her where his inquiry had led, starting with Horner as his index case. When he had finished, Vandergrift said, "Sounds like you're onto something. I think we'd better talk this over with my boss."

Sheriff Sherman McAllister sat with his hands folded across his stomach as he listened, unsmiling, to Maharos. Wire-framed glasses, perched on a thin nose, gave him a professorial look. When Maharos finished, McAllister turned to Vandergrift. "Who did the autopsy on Gibson."

"Dr. Hanson, at the Stark County Medical Examiner's morgue."

He asked Maharos, "Where was the autopsy done on the male nurse?"

"Burnstein's autopsy was done by the Stark County medical examiner's office too." Maharos could see where McAllister's questions were leading. If the same medical examiner had performed the two autopsies, why hadn't the similarities in wound sites been recognized?

McAllister picked up the phone on his desk and spoke to his secretary. "Get me Dr. Harry Hanson in the Medical Examiner's office."

While they waited, McAllister asked Maharos, "Are you working this case by yourself?"

"Yeah. I had a partner, but we were short-handed and he was taken off for another investigation."

McAllister turned to Vandergrift. "You're not working anything special at the moment, are you?"

"No sir."

The phone on the sheriff's desk buzzed. He listened, then said, "Dr. Hanson, I'd like to know who performed an autopsy in your morgue, a homicide case. Name of Frank Burnstein. Around 8 January this year."

McAllister waited with the phone at his ear. His face remained totally impassive. This is a no-nonsense guy, thought Maharos. A few moments later, McAllister said, "I see. Did you go over Dr. Browning's autopsy report?. . .Uh-huh. . .Do it and get back to me. . .No, I won't tell you what I'm looking for, I don't want to influence your opinion. Goodbye."

He placed the phone back on the cradle and spoke to the other two. "Dr. Glen Browning did the Burnstein autopsy. He was working in the medical examiner's office while Hanson was on vacation. When he returned, Hanson went over all the cases Browning had done, but apparently not in detail. Says he was swamped with other work. We'll soon find out if the wounds were similar." To Maharos he said, "We're as interested in this as you are. I'm going to assign Deputy Vandergrift to work with you. Do you want to discuss this with your chief?"

Maharos nodded. "Can I use your phone?"

Ed Bragg was enthusiastic in his acceptance of the sheriff's offer. Maharos wondered if he would be as thrilled if he knew that Deputy Vandergrift was an attractive woman.

THIRTEEN

RANKINS DROVE THE Dodge van at a steady fifty-five from Massillon, Ohio to Pittsburgh. It was an easy two and one-half hour drive through pleasant countryside. The window on the driver's side was open, the warm breeze massaged his face.

He didn't need radio talk shows to occupy his thoughts. The voices coming from the back of the van kept him company. First, Willie Jackson sang in his rich baritone, "Sweeeeet Chariot, Comin' fo' to carry me home." The song gave him a lump the size of a golf ball in his throat. But the topper was when King David sang,

"The waves of death were all around me,
The waves of destruction rolled over me,
The danger of death was around me
And the grave set a trap for me.
In my trouble I called to the Lord,
I called to my God for help,
In his temple he heard my voice,
He listened to my cry for help."

Rankins felt the tears roll down his cheeks as he listened. With his eyes glued on the road ahead, he called back over his shoulder, "I hear you too, Dave. I'm coming with help. You wait and see. Just you wait and see."

Sure he'd help King David. Hadn't Dave helped him, spoken to him, for all those years. What was he, sixteen, when he first heard David's voice? The Child Protection Agency in Akron had placed him with the Greenes, his fourth or maybe it was his fifth, foster home. Ed Rankin (he wasn't Ephraim Rankins yet) and old Charlie Greene were up in the hayloft replacing a broken plank. Charlie had leaned over the edge, nailing a new plank to a two-by-four, nothing between him and the cement floor fourteen feet down. Rankin was standing behind Charlie when David shouted in his ear, "Push him!"

He jerked his head around, but, of course, King David didn't want to be seen, and at first Rankin thought maybe he hadn't heard anything. Charlie kept on hammering. *He* didn't hear David even when he yelled again, "PUSH HIM."

Later, Louise Greene shook her head like she didn't believe him when he told the sheriff that he didn't see Charlie fall, just heard the thud and when he looked down, there was Charlie, his head like a caved-in pumpkin, his neck all crooked.

At the outskirts of Pittsburgh, the traffic was heavier. When he reached the western end of the city, he turned off Route 30 and crept along behind an unbroken line of cars and buses. He had to close the window to keep out the stinking gas fumes and the heat that bounced up from the cement street. With the air conditioner on it wasn't too bad.

Rankins turned right to a street of old, gray two-story houses with patches of brown dirt and weeds for lawns and pickup trucks in the driveways. Two blocks further the houses were older and dingier, and there it was, the paint on the house looking like an alligator's hide. He parked in front,, got out of the van and stretched his back.

Climbing the wooden porch stairs, he had to step around several that were split. He rang the doorbell, saw the curtains in a downstairs window part. In a moment, the door was opened and Duane Jackson's height and bulk filled the doorway. The bare black skin of his shoulders, covered only by the thin shoulder straps of an orange tank top, glistened with sweat. Jackson gave Rankins a big, toothy smile. "Hey, m'man, c'mon in."

They walked through the unlit hallway back to the kitchen which always smelled of stale beer. Jackson gestured to a chair. "Somethin' to drink, Jock?"

Jock, for jockey, because he was so small. The name Duane's brother, Willie, gave him at Lima State. Rankins would get fired up if anybody else called him Jock. Of course, Willie could call anybody anything. Nobody'd tangle with a guy six-eight, two-eighty and all of it steel. But he was Willie's buddy—his asshole buddy. Willie didn't even care that Rankins was white.

When Rankins was getting out, Willie told him if he needed anything to see Duane. Well, he'd seen him before, was seeing him again.

"How 'bout it, somethin' wet?, " Duane repeated.

Rankins shook his head. "I got to get right back. What have you got for me?"

"I got a nice forty-five I can let you have for three-fifty. Or how about a three-fifty-seven magnum? Give you a good price on it."

"No. Something small."

"Another twenty-five?"

"That's about right."

"Wait here."

Jackson disappeared through a door leading to the basement and a minute later returned carrying a brown paper bag. From it he drew a black twenty-five caliber semi-automatic pistol. He held it under the light of the exposed bulb hanging from the ceiling, and turned it from one side to the other in his large palm. "A beauty, ain't she?"

Rankins took the gun, examined it closely, placing it in his own palm, testing it for size and weight. He nodded. "How much?"

"Two seventy-five. Good clean piece."

"Can I test it?"

"Sure." Jackson led the way to the basement. At the foot of the stairs a door opened to a long, narrow, windowless room, empty except for two mattresses standing upright, back to back, against the wall at the far end. On the surface of the mattress that faced the room, the outline of a life-sized human figure had been drawn crudely with a Magic Marker. The upper half of the figure was riddled with holes.

Jackson placed three bullets in the magazine, handed the piece to Rankins. Standing in the center of the room with his feet spread, arms outstretched toward the mattress target, holding the pistol with both hands, Rankins squeezed off the three rounds in rapid succession. An empty cartridge case arched out after each shot.

He looked down at the gun in his hand and hefted it. "Okay, I'll take it."

While Rankins counted out money from his wallet, Jackson put the gun back in the paper bag. "Was up to Lima to see brother Willie last week. He say he be missin' you."

Jock nodded silently and handed the bills to Jackson. They went back upstairs, Jackson continuing the conversation. "Hey, how that van runnin'?"

"Fine. Runs fine." Six months before, Jackson had sold Rankins the van. Too cold to ride his motorcycle in the winter, he had said. Jackson had patted the side of the van. "This an eighty-three. You won't have no problem with it."

"Will I have to get different license plates? These are Pennsylvania plates."

Jackson had laughed. "Nah. Don't you worry none 'bout them plates. Anybody ask, you tell 'em you got the van from a guy in Pennsylvania. Don't have to tell who. Y'understand what I'm sayin'.?"

"Don't I need registration papers?"

The big man had scratched his chin. Faint amusement in his eyes. "Registration papers. Yeah, right."

A few moments later he returned, and thumbed through a thick stack of tan papers held with a rubber band. "Let's see. What I say? Eighty-three Dodge? Here we is." He'd pulled out one sheet and handed it to Rankins. It was a Pennsylvania vehicle registration for a 1983 Dodge sedan. Of course, the one he sold him was a van. And the vehicle identification number on the certificate was that of a car that had long since been melted down. But it was close enough.

Now, as Jackson opened the front door, he said, "Hey, man, it none of my business but what you be doin' all them pieces? Startin' a collection?"

"Yeah, man. I'm a collector."

At the top of the porch stairs, Jackson watched Rankins walk to his van clutching the brown paper bag. Finally, he turned, went back inside the house shaking his head. Rankins could hear him mutter, "That white boy's spooky."

FOURTEEN

KAREN VANDERGRIFT drove and Maharos rode shotgun in her black and white patrol car, on their way to speak to Henry Gibson's widow. Maharos had never worked with a female partner. Although five percent of the Youngstown police officers were female, Detective Lieutenant Ed Bragg had resisted accepting women detectives until a year before. After threats by the mayor of Youngstown and the city council to slash his already tight budget, he'd broken down and accepted Lucy Gage as detective third grade. Now, four women candidates who had passed all the qualifying tests were waiting for openings. Bragg pulled excuses from nowhere to hold off their appointments until after his retirement. When one TV newscaster called him a chauvinist, he said to a select audience in his office, "I never shoved nobody—and I don't give a shit what the guy says."

Vandergrift pulled up in the driveway of the brick three-story house in a neighborhood of upper-middle-class homes. Harriet Gibson answered the door and escorted them to the living room. Maharos glanced around at the gold and black wallpaper, lots of mirrors, chrome and Lucite. Gibson had apparently made good money, leaving his widow well off.

Mrs. Gibson was dressed in beige slacks and a loosely-fitting flowered blouse. She was in her mid-thirties, her face unlined, light brown hair pulled back to form a pony tail held by a thin, black velvet ribbon.

Vandergrift introduced herself. "Thank you for seeing us on such short notice, Mrs. Gibson. .I hope we're not keeping you from anything important."

"Not really. I was supposed to go to a Little Theater Group meeting, but it can wait."

"Good. Detective Maharos here is from the Youngstown Police Department. He's investigating a homicide case in his district, and it appears that Mr. Gibson knew the other victim. Why don't you tell Mrs. Gibson about it, Al."

Maharos barely recalled having given Vandergrift his first name when he introduced himself at the sheriff's office. He was impressed that she remembered. He broke away from these thoughts and explained that a man named Marlon Graves had been killed in March, and his widow had received a condolence note from Henry Gibson. "Your husband, of course, was shot a month later and we wondered if you could tell us how he knew Mr. Graves."

Harriet Gibson stared at the carpet for the answer. Slowly, she shook her head. "I have no idea who this Graves person is. The only thing I can think of is that he might have been a customer of Henry's. My husband was assistant sales manager of a wholesale hardware company."

"Marlon Graves was a clothing salesman for Simpson's in Akron. I don't think he would have bought wholesale hardware. Is it possible that your husband was one of *his* customers?"

"No. Henry bought all his clothes here in Canton. In fact, I did most of the shopping for his clothing. He was so busy he didn't have much time to do it himself. If I saw something I thought would look good on him, I would either buy it and bring it home, or have him go in for a fitting."

Vandergrift said, "Do you have any recollection of him writing a condolence note?"

"No. He wouldn't have written it from home. Henry did all of his correspondence at the office. I was the only one who wrote letters at home, and I didn't write a condolence letter to anyone named Graves."

Maharos brought out the list of fifteen victims who had been killed on the seventh of a month. In addition to Graves, were the names of Hamberger, Horner and Burnstein. "Mrs. Gibson, please look at this list and see if any of these names are familiar."

She ran her eyes down the list. "Burnstein. It seems I've heard that name before. Here's another, George Horner, isn't that the lawyer—" she raised her head. "I'm sure I read about these people somewhere. I don't *know* any of them. What have they got to do with Henry?"

Maharos explained that they were all men who had been murdered and that law enforcement agencies were looking for any possible connection between them. All killings had been well publicized and he knew it was going to be hard to find anyone who had not heard about them.

He tried another tack. "Did your husband have any social connections that did not involve you?"

Harriet Gibson sat up rigidly. Her eyes bore through Maharos. "If you're suggesting that Henry might have been unfaithful—"

Maharos put up a hand. He smiled. "I'm sorry. That's not what I meant at all. Graves was a gambler—a heavy gambler. I don't know how to put this question to you more delicately, but was your husband involved in any activities that might have put him into contact with gamblers, bookies, you know, that crowd?"

Harriet Gibson relaxed a little, although her resentment was still apparent. "Emphatically no."

Maharos thought she was unduly steamed up. Vandergrift stepped in for the rescue. "Mrs. Gibson, I hope you understand that we're trying to find any clue that might lead us to your husband's murderer. The last thing we want to do is offend you."

The young widow's composure broke down. She dropped her head and put her hand to her eyes. "I've been so hurt already," she sobbed. "You have no idea how this has changed my life. Henry's been gone, how long is it? Three months? What have you found out about who did it? Nothing! Now you come in and ask all these stupid questions. How do you expect me to feel?" She continued to sob softly, her face in her hands.

Maharos stood up and gestured with his chin to Vandergrift. He could see they had reached the end of the line. "We're sorry to have upset you, Mrs. Gibson. Thank you for your time."

Vandergrift took a card from her pocket and placed it on the coffee table in front of the weeping woman. "Here's my card. If you think of anything that might be related to what we've been asking you, please call." She patted Mrs. Gibson's shoulder as they left.

Back in the patrol car, they drove in silence for a few minutes before Vandergrift said, "Shall we ask around at the place where he worked?"

Maharos shrugged. "I suppose so, but I'm not optimistic."

At the offices of Sterling Wholesale Hardware, Clarence Chambers, the sales manager checked the records of Gibson's customers, but found no one named Graves.

Maharos had a thought. He said, "Do you have copies of Gibson's business correspondence?"

Chambers said, "Yes, we've transferred his files to Clem Gilmore, the man who took over Henry's job. His office is two doors down on your left. I'll buzz, tell him you're coming."

Gilmore was out of the office, but he had inherited Gibson's secretary. Emma Spencer was a small, mousy woman in her fifties. She appeared a little nervous when the two police officers walked in.

Maharos smiled to relax her, introduced Vandergrift and himself before he went on to explain the reason for his visit. "Mr. Gibson had written a condolence note to a Mrs. Marlon Graves in Tallmadge. Do you remember such a letter?"

Emma thought for a moment. "I don't remember it specifically. But if there was a copy of any letter such as that it would be in his personal correspondence file. I bundled them up and asked Mrs. Gibson if she wanted them. She said she didn't, so I had them destroyed. Matter of fact, it was just about three days ago. I don't know why I kept them so long. He's been gone several months now." She looked dreamily toward the ceiling. Suddenly, she turned her head toward Maharos. "I *do* remember writing the letter. Wasn't it some man who had been shot?"

Maharos opened his mouth to speak, but before he could say a word, she jumped out of her chair and ran to the door, calling back over her shoulder, "I'll be right back."

Maharos and Vandergrift looked at each other. Vandergrift made a one-shoulder shrug. "Is that the affect you have on people? Either they start crying or they run for the hills."

"Now you see why I'm the only flunk-out of the Dale Carnegie course."

Emma returned in a few minutes carrying a thick manila file folder. She dropped it on the desk triumphantly. "The janitor hadn't gotten around to burning it yet. Good thing I thought of it." She looked from side to side and covered the corner of her mouth with a hand. "Half the time, he sits down in the basement with a bottle, doesn't hear *what* you tell him."

Vandergrift said, "If it helps us find what we want, we'll buy him a gallon of his favorite rotgut."

Emma riffled through the papers in the file. "Do you know when it would have been written?"

Vandergrift said, "Around the early part of March, this year."

The secretary pulled an onion skin copy out, glanced at it for a second and handed it to the deputy. "Here it is."

Vandergrift held the letter so Maharos could read it over her shoulder. He was exhilarated at the prospect of making some progress. But not so single-minded that he wasn't aware of the faint scent of perfume as he stood looking over the deputy's shoulder.

The letter was dated March 10.

Dear Mrs. Graves,
I want to express my sincere sympathy on the loss of your husband. Although it has been several years since I saw Marlon, whom I knew for only a short time, I was fond of him and was shocked to read of his tragic death. I recall that he spoke of you with great affection. I know what a loss this must be for you.
    Sincerely,
    Hank Gibson

Vandergrift said, "I was hoping the letter would tell us how he came to know Graves."

"At least we know that it was some time ago."

"Uh-huh, and 'for a very short time.' Wonder what *that* means."

Maharos asked the secretary, "Do you have any recollection of Mr. Gibson having mentioned *how* he knew Graves?"

"He may have said something at the time, but I can't recall if he did."

"How long had you been working for Gibson?"

"Two years. Ever since Mr. Gibson was promoted to assistant sales manager. Before that I was secretary for Mr. Chambers. He had the job and then was promoted to sales manager. They left *me* behind." She sniffed derisively.

She'd only been working for Gibson for two years. From the way the letter was worded, it sounded as though the meeting with Graves had occurred before that.

"Do you have any idea where or when your former boss might have met Marlon Graves?"

"I've been thinking about that ever since you asked about the letter. I'm afraid I don't know. Did you ask Mrs. Gibson whether he was a personal friend?"

Vandergrift told her they had spoken with Harriet Gibson.

"Well then it had to be more than two years ago, that is, before I started working for him. Otherwise I would know if it was someone he had business dealings with."

Maharos said, "How would you have gotten Mr. Graves' address?"

Emma thought for a moment. "Mr. Graves lived in Akron, didn't he?"

"Tallmadge."

"Well, that's a suburb of Akron. I have a faint recollection of looking it up in the Akron phone book."

She reached up to a shelf containing a number of telephone directories. She selected one marked "Akron," leafed through the pages and pointed to a line. "Here it is. Graves, Marlon. It gives the address in Tallmadge"

Maharos said, "We'd like to keep this letter. Is that all right?"

DEAD END

Emma said, "Certainly. I was about to have it destroyed anyway. Is that going to help you find whoever did that awful thing to Mr. Gibson? He was such a hard worker, and a wonderful boss."

"It's going to be a big help. Thanks."

On the way back to the sheriff's office, Vandergrift said, "This is the first solid lead we've had since we started working the case. Our office had just about written it off as a homicide-robbery by some transient we'd never see again. Well, we know it's been more than two years since our man met Graves. That's a start."

Maharos was slumped in the passenger's seat, his hat tipped forward over his eyes. "Yeah. Now all we have to do is go back year by year and find out everything Gibson did since he was a kid."

Vandergrift let it slide. "If Gibson knew Graves, maybe he knew the other three you're working on: Hamberger, Horner or Burnstein." Her voice had risen two decibels. She was now enthusiastically in the hunt.

"Okay. You check with Mrs. Hamberger and Burnstein's—wife. I'll work on the Horner end."

"You got it. Let me have your extension at Youngstown PD."

He gave her a card. "Keep in touch."

This was going to be the start of something, Maharos felt.

FIFTEEN

DETECTIVE LARRY WAGNER held his hand over the mouthpiece of the phone and yelled across the squad room. "Hey, Al. Some woman wants to talk to you. On three."

Maharos punched the illuminated button on his phone. "Maharos."

"Hi, Al. This is Karen Vandergrift."

Maharos' pulse rate zoomed. Since leaving her in Canton, three days ago, he had spent more idle minutes than he would admit to thinking about her. Cozy, sexy fantasies. He had tried to push them from his mind. Hell, she was probably happily married to some handsome hunk around her own age. He did some mental arithmetic but developed a block trying to subtract thirty-one or thirty-two from forty-six, his age.

He felt his voice tighten. "Hello. How're you coming along?"

"Let me give you an update. I talked to Lance Harwood in the Metro Detention Center. He never heard of Gibson. He's still peed off that they won't set bail for him. Hey, that lawyer, Lavant, is something out of a comic strip.

"Anyway, I just got back from New Philadelphia. Mrs. Hamberger didn't know anything about Gibson. So far two strikes, no hits."

Maharos said, "George Horner's widow didn't know Gibson —or any of the others. Strike three."

Vandergrift said, "Dr. Hanson has reviewed the autopsy reports of Burnstein and Gibson. He's coming in this afternoon to go over the whole thing with McAllister and me. One of the reasons I wanted to get in touch with you is to ask if you would fax us the autopsy reports and the pictures of the gunshot wounds in the cases you've been following. We'd like to compare them with what we've got."

"I'll do better than that. I'll bring them myself. What time's your meeting with the ME?"

"Three-thirty. Hey, that will be great!"

"See you."

Maharos was in the men's room adjoining the detective's locker room, removing his five o'clock shadow at one-thirty when Frank Fiala walked in. Maharos glanced at Fiala's reflection in the mirror and went on shaving.

"You never did that for me when *I* was your partner," said Fiala.

Maharos went on shaving.

Fiala said, "Let me guess: your Canton partner is gorgeous."

Maharos rinsed the razor.

Fiala said, ". . .Not only is she gorgeous, but she's crazy for bald-headed older men."

Maharos dried the razor.

". . .Especially if they are of the Greek persuasion."

Maharos dried his face and splashed Canoe on his freshly-shaven cheeks.

Fiala went on, "If I didn't have to take a leak, I'd kiss you myself."

Maharos slipped on his shirt and started walking out. He said, "Don't forget to wash your hands."

He was at his desk putting on his suit jacket, when he saw Ed Bragg beckoning to him through the glass partition that separated the lieutenant's office from the large squad room. He stood at the open door of Bragg's office. "Calling me, Ed?"

"Yeah. You in a hurry?" He sniffed the air. "Wha'ja do, raid Hattie's whorehouse again?"

Maharos rubbed his chin. "I didn't get a chance to shave before I came on duty." He glanced at his watch. "I've got a couple of minutes. I'm going to—" He noticed a figure slumped in the easy chair in front of Bragg's desk. "Oh. I didn't see you, Shelly. How are you?"

Sheldon Ehrlich covered the police beat for the *Youngstown Herald*. He was a good investigative reporter, which was to say he was a pain in the ass to the men and women at the Youngstown PD.

Ehrlich waved a hand in Maharos' direction.

Bragg said, "Shelly and I were just jawing about the Horner investigation." He gave Maharos a hard look. "I told him that you were handling it."

Maharos caught Bragg's signal. He turned to the reporter. "Yeah. Well, there's not much I can tell you. We're still tracking down leads."

"Can't or won't?"

"Huh?"

"You saying there's nothing to tell, or there's something but you can't talk about it?" He wasn't going to let Maharos off easily.

"Believe me, when there's something the public should know, you'll be the first to hear it."

"Who's going to be the judge of that, you or me?"

Bragg held up a hand, "Hey, Shelly, lay off the guy, for crissake. He's got a job to do."

Ehrlich sat up in the chair. "So do I. I've been hearing all kinds of stories that Maharos is running around the countryside asking people about homicide cases that are out of your jurisdiction."

Maharos scowled. "Where'd you get your information?"

"I've got sources. Am I warm?"

Maharos was trying to keep his investigation out of the headlines. He knew that public knowledge that a serial killer was working in the area, would only cause confusion. Every kook would climb out of the woodwork and claim responsibility for everything from the Lindbergh kidnapping to Judge Crater's disappearance. Yet, he could not tell an outright lie. When and if he finally caught up with whoever it was he was looking for, he wanted to maintain his credibility.

"Shelly, don't press me. You know police work well enough to know that we've got to have breathing room."

"Background?"

"That's all I'll say."

The reporter turned to the lieutenant. "Ed?"

Bragg shrugged and turned his palms up. His portrayal of innocence was Academy Award caliber.

The four of them were hunched over Sheriff McAllister's desk, peering down at the array of Polaroids. Dr. Harry Hanson squinted through a small hand lens. "There's no question. The placement of the wounds in all of these is identical. There are powder burns around all the neck wounds so the gun barrel must have been placed very close to the skin. The skin of the lower entry sites, that is, those between the shoulder blades, was protected by the clothing each of the victims wore."

Hanson went on to explain that the bullets took somewhat different paths once they had entered the bodies of the victims. The missiles were thrown off course when they hit bony structures, but the result was always the same: death.

Vandergrift said, "Dr. Hanson, how easy is it to place a bullet wound in exactly the same place, like it was done here?"

"Not easy at all. It takes someone with some knowledge of anatomy. There are landmarks, of course. But you have to know what to look for."

McAllister said, "You mean our suspect may be a doctor?"

"Well, sure, someone in the medical field would have this information. But I can think of others, too. For example, I've got a lab diener, a pathology assistant, who would know enough about anatomy to pick the right spots. And he's had no formal medical training."

Maharos said, "While I'm thinking of it, so far only seven people know about the signature wounds: the four of us, my former partner, my chief, and Lieutenant Birtcher of Canton PD Homicide Division. I don't have to tell you, Dr. Hanson, how important it is to protect that information. The press is already sniffing around. Just before I came down here I was dogged by a reporter who, I think, has an idea that we're looking at serial murders. I'm not sure how long we're going to be able to stonewall. Once the word is out, you can imagine how hard it's going to be to work this case."

Vandergrift turned to McAllister. "What do you make of the fact that each of these victims was shot with a different gun?"

"I don't know. Seems odd that the killer would go to the trouble of changing guns and at the same time leave his signature by the way he shoots them. Hell, he or she wasn't trying to hide the fact that the same person was killing all these people."

Vandergrift said, "Maybe the killer *wants* it known that one person is responsible."

"Or doesn't care one way or another," said Maharos.

McAllister glanced at his watch. The meeting was over.

Outside McAllister's office, Maharos said, "Where's a good place to eat? I think I'll have dinner here before I head back."

"If you like seafood, there's The Whaler. It's only about three blocks from here," said Vandergrift.

"Sounds good to me. What about you? Want to join me, or do you have a family to feed? I'll even spring for the meal."

Vandergrift grinned. "I thought you'd never ask. *I'm* my family. Sure I'll join you, but we'll go dutch—and you'll have to give me time to change out of this uniform."

"Okay, but I'll buy the wine."

I'm my family, she had said. Maharos' anticipation level was rising to the red zone.

They had reached the parking lot. Vandergrift said, "Follow my car, it's that dirty yellow Chevy. My place is only ten minutes away. I'm a quick change artist."

Maharos sat in an easy chair in the spotless living room of Karen Vandergrift's two-room, condominium while she went into the bedroom to change. He gazed around at the simple blonde furnishings and down at the beige shag carpeting, wondering how she kept everything so damned clean and neat while she worked at a full-time job. He got up to examine more closely a framed photograph on the mantle of the fireplace at one end of the living room. The woman could have been a smiling Karen in her mid-fifties. The husky, square-jawed man next to her looked about sixty. His gray hair was crew cut and he stood with a stiffly erect, military bearing, faint posed smile on his lips. Maharos looked around for evidence of a man in Karen's life, found none.

Vandergrift called from the bedroom, "Fix yourself a drink, if you'd like. The makings are in the wood cabinet. If you're any kind of detective you'll know where to find the ice."

The low cabinet held bottles of liquor, tonic and soda, and several cocktail glasses. "Can I get something for you?" he called.

"Okay. Fix me a vodka and tonic, easy on the vodka."

Maharos mixed two and carried one to the closed bedroom door. "Room service," he called, and handed the drink to Vandergrift when she stuck her bare arm through the slightly opened door.

When she walked out into the living room twenty minutes later, she was wearing an emerald green dress, a thin, gold link chain at her throat, large pearl earrings and high-heeled black pumps.

"Now, *that's* how a deputy sheriff should dress," he said.

"Bet you can't even tell where I carry my service revolver."

"Mind if I frisk you?"

"Not until you read me my rights—and see that I'm fed."

He wasn't sure if, with all the banter, she was saying, try again later. He let it pass.

The Whaler was a franchised seafood restaurant outfitted with the obligatory fishnet ceiling, starfish and mounted oars on the walls and tanks of tropical fish used as room partitions. Maharos' mesquite-broiled trout was well-filleted and tasty. Vandergrift had the Atlantic red snapper and pronounced it "delicious." They finished the remains of the bottle of a California Chardonnay while they sat staring into the flickering oil lamp in the center of the table and each learned who the other was.

Karen had been an "army brat." Her father was a Regular Army master sergeant and during a thirty year career, had moved the family from Fort Ord, where Karen was born, through posts from the Philippines to Germany. She had a brother who was a West Point graduate, now serving with NATO in Belgium. Karen had gone to Ohio State University while her father was stationed at Camp McKinley outside Dayton. In college she had taken prelaw courses, but after graduation decided against going on to law school. "I decided to become a housewife instead. Poor choice."

Maharos waited, saying nothing.

"Tom was in law school at Ohio State when we met. After we were married, I took a job at Lazarus' Department Store selling housewares, and hated every minute of it. I had taken some courses in criminology while I was in college, was fascinated with the subject, and, when Tom graduated, I applied for admission to the Franklin County Sheriffs Academy in Columbus." She smiled peering over the lamplight. "Dr. Freud would probably say I was trying to emulate my father—you know, the uniform.

"Well, to complete my long, boring story, Tom couldn't take my long on-duty shifts, and found some company to while way his loneliness—one of the secretaries in his office. It really didn't take very astute detective work on my part to find out about it. I just walked into the house, when I got off duty earlier than expected one day, and figured out that the spike heels, dress, bra, slip and panties strewn from the living room to the bedroom were probably not my husband's. I reasoned that any guy stupid enough to bring his toys home didn't deserve me. Just like magic, my husband turned into an ex-."

Maharos said, "What brought you to Canton?"

"Well, I had no ties to Columbus, so after my divorce I found that there was an opening here, applied and got the job. Hard to believe, it's been six years already."

Maharos' eyes scanned the fishnetted ceiling while he did some mental calculation. Vandergrift broke in. "Thirty-six."

He looked puzzled.

"If you're wondering, I'm thirty-six. I got a late start."

His eyebrows raised. "I would have guessed thirty, thirty-one at most."

"I like your numbers better. Want to try my weight?"

His eyes scanned up and down. "You have no worries there."

"That's 'cause it's covered."

"I've already removed your clothing—in my calculations."

She nodded slowly, a faint smile on her lips. "I think this conversation is getting a little out of hand. What about you? You haven't said word one about yourself."

"Want me to start with the Parthenon?"

She glanced at her watch. "I think they close this place up at one AM Maybe you could start somewhere after Alexander the Great"

He shook his head. "You mean skip over a hundred years of Greek history?"

"Well, maybe just take it from the battle at Syracuse."

His face showed his mild surprise. "I'm impressed. Actually, my father was born in the shadow of the Acropolis. My mother came from the island of Mykonos. They came to this country in 1939, just ahead of the war in Europe."

"How did they get to Ohio?"

"My father had a brother who had immigrated a few years earlier and lived in Youngstown. My folks ran a little grocery store in Youngstown until Pop died. I came along during World War II, had your standard all-American Greek childhood. After high school I went to Kent State and by the time I graduated, we were well along in the Vietnam War, so I joined the navy. I was a communications officer on a destroyer for about two years."

"In Vietnam?"

"Mostly just offshore. It was pure dullsville."

"My Dad was in Vietnam, but the army show was anything but dull."

He smiled and tapped his forehead. "Why do you think I joined the navy? It turned out I wasn't so smart after all. We had a shipboard explosion that knocked me on my keester. The good part was, it got me back to the States and a medical survey out of the service."

"Were you badly hurt?"

"Not so bad that I couldn't pass the physical to get into the Youngstown Police Academy. Let's see, that was 1967."

"I was fourteen."

"Don't rub it in. Anyway, three years later I made detective third grade and married Marcie."

She leaned forward on her elbows. "*Now* we're getting to the part I've been waiting for."

Maharos told her about Marcie and Annie and the rest of it. He glanced at his watch. "Well, that's my arithmetic trick for the evening—putting forty-six years into twenty minutes." He was a little disappointed that she didn't seem surprised at the "forty-six years" part.

Vandergrift pushed her chair back and stood up. "I've got a long shift tomorrow."

Maharos gave the waiter his credit card.

Vandergrift said, "Hey, we were going dutch, remember? And do you realize we haven't spoken about our mutual homicides?"

"Yeah. Well don't tell the Youngstown city auditor. I intend to put this on my expense account."

"Well, in that case thank the City of Youngstown for a delicious meal—and an enjoyable evening."

There was an awkward moment for Maharos as he escorted Vandergrift to the door of her condo. She solved his problem. Smiling, she held out her hand. "Well, you have a long ride back home so I won't ask you in for a nightcap. Thanks again. See you soon."

On the drive home, Maharos breathed deeply. The scent of her perfume lingered in the car, and his thoughts of her face and body and their conversation stirred him in a way he hadn't felt since he courted Marcie.

SIXTEEN

"THE LOOT WANTS to see you, Al."

That was Detective Jerry Weaver's greeting as Maharos walked into the squad room.

"Bragg?"

"How many lieutenants we got?"

Ed Bragg was in his usual posture, leaning over his desk on which was spread a paper sandwich wrapper. He was eating the BLT that had come inside it. He wiped his mouth with the back of his hand when Maharos came through the door, and tipped his head toward the chair while he swallowed the mouthful of food.

He sucked some food from between his teeth, swallowed again and said, "You plannin' to draw your check from Stark County?"

Maharos wrinkled his forehead.

Bragg went on. "I figure you've been in this office twenny minutes and in Canton the rest of the time over the past four days. Meantime, you've used up two of the three weeks I give you on the Horner thing. And also meantime, I got reporters crawlin' up my ass wanting to know what's happenin'."

"Chief, we're not sitting on our asses. We've already nailed down five homicides, including Horner, that fit the MO. We've got a definite link between two of them, and it's just a matter of time before we establish that *all* of them are connected. That's the angle we're working on now."

"Who's this 'we'?"

"Deputy Sheriff Vandergrift and me."

"This Vandergrift know shit from Shinola?"

"Yeah. Vandergrift is bright and a good worker."

"Why doesn't he come here instead of you going to Canton all the time?"

Maharos was putting off any discussion of gender as long as he could, although he knew the truth about Vandergrift would eventually come out. "Because two of the cases are from Canton. The one we're tracking now was a gay nurse. We're trying to find out if any of the other victims were homosexual. Maybe *that's* the thread that will lead us to a motive and to the killer." He paused five seconds. In a low, almost inaudible voice, added, "Besides, it's 'she' not 'he'."

"You mean the nurse was a dyke?"

"No, the sheriff is a 'she.'"

Bragg sat looking at his desk top. His bald head became pink, then red. When he raised his head he stared at Maharos. He seemed unsure how to proceed. Maharos sat with his hands in his lap, fingers intertwined tightly. He lay in a foxhole, seeing a grenade roll in, waiting for the explosion. When it came it wasn't loud. A corner of Bragg's mouth turned up. A smirk, not a smile. His voice was low. "You think you're one smart-assed dick—and I don't mean detective. Let me tell you something, Maharos. You're still workin' for me. I hear there's any dickin' around with this lady cop—sheriff, whatever the fuck she is—you're on suspension. Got that? Now get the hell outta here." He swept his arm in a broad wave.

Maharos remained seated. Inside, he seethed with resentment. This bull seated on a throne he occupied only because of seniority was acting like a prosecutor, judge and jury. Although he secretly wished Bragg's insinuation were true, he couldn't let it pass.

"How long have you known me, Ed? Almost twenty years? In that time have you ever seen or heard of me doing anything unprofessional? You know goddam well I've played by the book every minute of the time I've been on this police force. I've got a wall full of commendations to prove it. I didn't ask for this 'lady cop,' but I'll tell you this: she's got more brains than a lot of guys I've worked with." Maharos waited a moment glaring at the lieutenant, then went on. "If you can't trust me to handle this case, lady partner or no, I shouldn't be working for you."

Bragg took a deep breath. He pushed himself off his chair and walked to the window, looking out at the cars streaming down the sunlit street on a perfect June day. He spoke to the window. "Al, I've got more respect for you than anyone in my division. I guess the pressure got to me. Like I told you, I'm hearing it from the chief, the DA, the bar association, shit, you name it. Maybe I been around here too long. Forget what I said." He turned, faced Maharos with a weak smile and extended his hand.

Maharos shook his hand. "It's forgotten. I don't envy you your job, Ed." He started for the door.

Bragg said, "And Al, this lady sheriff—you wanna grab yourself a piece, be my guest." He chuckled.

Vandergrift was driving the black and white patrol car with the large star decal on both sides, Maharos in the shotgun seat, when they pulled up in the parking lot of Friar's Tavern on McKinley Avenue in Canton. Maharos had in his lap a brown manila envelope. Vandergrift said, "This is it."

Maharos said, "You mean Canton only has two gay-lesbian bars?"

She shrugged. "I'm surprised there are enough customers for two places. Canton's so straight you could roll a bowling ball down Tuscarawas Avenue from one end to the other and never touch a curb."

Maharos said, "I would have said the same thing about Youngstown until recently. Now the closet doors are opening a crack and you see married guys and women peeking out."

They walked to the front door under the swinging sign on which was painted a chubby, smiling man, top of his head shaved, wearing a brown monk's habit. It took half a minute for their eyes to adjust to the dimly-lit room. The rancid smell of stale wine, liquor and cigarette smoke hung in the air. At two-thirty in the afternoon there was only one customer in the place. A young man with very blonde hair, wearing cut-off jeans was seated on a stool in front of the bar, a cocktail glass in his hand.

Maharos followed Vandergrift to the far end of the bar and the bartender, who was polishing glasses, eyed Vandergrift's uniform. "What can I do for you, officers?"

Maharos took a dozen pictures out of the manila envelope and laid them on the counter. Mingled with photos of Horner, Gibson, Graves, Hamberger and Burnstein, were shots of several other men not connected with the investigation. "We're trying to locate several people. Recognize anyone in these photos?"

"You're looking for gays, right?"

"That's who your clientele is, isn't it?"

The bartender nodded, scanning each picture in turn. He hesitated when he came to Burnstein's photo, glanced through the others and came back to Burnstein. "Isn't this Flossie Burnstein?"

"You know him?"

"*Knew* him. He used to come in here with Lance Harwood before—"

"Recognize any of the others?"

The bartender shook his head while he squinted at the pictures once again. "Why the sudden interest in Burnstein's case? I thought you had Harwood nailed to the wall."

Vandergrift said, "Just checking. Thanks."

Maharos put the photos back in the manila envelope and followed Vandergrift into the bright sunlight. They had already gotten the same response at the Blue Heron, Canton's other gay bar.

"I suppose it wouldn't hurt to ask at that steam room," said Maharos.

Vandergrift drove north on McKinley to Second, then east to a street that consisted of residential buildings on one side, and a row of five stores on the other.

She stopped in front of the store with a sign that read "Interiors By Harold." In the showcase were two shiny black, plastic chairs that appeared suitable only for someone who was swaybacked, and a low Lucite table over which was draped a length of cloth, black with broad, diagonal white stripes. On the back wall hung two abstract paintings that carried out the black and white theme.

The store next to Harold's bore no identifying sign. A pleated beige curtain hung on a brass rod, extending the width of the window. Barely visible over the top of the curtain, a wall, painted white, shielded the interior of the store from the street. In a lower corner of the store window, a cardboard sign read "Parking In Rear." The glass door of the shop was covered by the same beige material as the curtain in the showcase. obscuring the interior..

Maharos said, "This is the steam room?"

"Uh-huh. Harold, the decorator that owns the shop next door, runs it. I'll wait in the car."

Maharos got out and walked to the front door. Finding it locked, he pushed the doorbell. There was no response from inside the store, so he rapped on the glass of the door. A half minute later, the door of the decorator's shop opened and a man's head poked out. "Can I help you?"

He was in his mid-thirties, six feet tall but weighed no more than 135 pounds. His face was as thin and gaunt as the rest of his body. His brown hair, drawn back from his face, was fastened by a rubber band in a short pony tail. A small gold ring dangled from his left earlobe. His white shirt was open at the neck exposing a gold chain.

Maharos held his gold shield up for the man to see. "Detective Maharos. Do you run this steam room?"

"The steam room doesn't open until after six."

"Are you connected with its operation?"

The thin man hesitated. "Well, in a way."

"Are you Harold?"

"No, I'm Troy Woodridge, Harold's partner."

"I'd like some information. Can you help me?"

"I'll try. What is it?"

"Can I come in and discuss it?"

Woodridge glanced to the street where Vandergrift sat in the patrol car. "You're a detective, right?"

"Yes.

He held the door open and followed Maharos inside. The shop was much more spacious than appeared from the outside and was crammed with furniture, mostly ultramodern living room sets, and lamps. Maharos sat in a white leather couch, spread the photos from the envelope on a low coffee table. He asked Woodridge if he recognized anyone in the pictures.

Maharos watched Woodridge's face as he went through the stack. He thought he hesitated when he came to Horner's picture. When he had examined them all, he pointed to one.

"Sure, I knew Burnstein. Poor guy."

"Did he ever come into your steam room?"

"No. I met him through his friend, Harwood. Lance is a decorator too. One of our competitors, you might say. I guess you people took him out of competition." He laughed, then suddenly grew serious. "I'm sorry, I didn't mean to make light of it. It's hard for me to believe that Lance would kill Frank. They were so happy together—most of the time."

Maharos got up as though to leave. Suddenly he turned to face Woodridge. "What do you know about the times when they *weren't* so happy together?"

Woodridge tugged at his earring. "Well, they—I guess you know they had a few spats. Who doesn't?"

Through Maharos' mind ran the question: Was there someone jealous of the relationship between the good-natured nurse and the handsome decorator—jealous enough to murder Burnstein?

"Did Frank or Lance have anyone else on the side?"

The young man shifted his gaze from Maharos. He said nothing for a few moments. Finally, "You've got to understand, Lance is a very intense person. Frank was an easygoing guy. Everyone was his friend. Whether or not either one had affairs with anyone else, I honestly don't know."

Maharos extended his hand. "Well, thanks for your help."

"Not at all. By the way, I'm curious. Who were those other people you showed me?"

"Oh, just some people we're trying to get information about."

"Are they gay?"

"Why? Do you know most of the gays around here?"

The thin man shrugged. "I'm quite active in the gay rights organization in northeastern Ohio. I know a number of men and women who are involved."

"How about Youngstown and Akron?"

"Yes, they're in our chapter."

"What if the people in these photos were not open about their homosexuality? Would you be likely to have any contact with them?"

"Maybe, maybe not. I've been to parties where there are what you people like to call 'closet gays'— doctors and lawyers, for example, who feel it would damage them professionally to be known as homosexual."

"Without asking you to identify any individual, are any of the people in the pictures I showed you known to you as closet gays?"

There was no hesitation in his answer. "No."

Maharos sank back in the car seat. "Well, so much for the gay connection. He glanced at his watch. "Let's call it a day. I'll head on home, fix myself a TV dinner and see if I can get any bright ideas watching reruns of *Hill Street Blues*."

Vandergrift looked straight ahead as she drove. "I was wondering, since you don't have plans for dinner, how would you like to come over to my place? I'll fix us a couple of steaks I've got in the freezer. I'm not a great cook but you won't starve."

Maharos' weariness suddenly left him and he breathed a little faster. "Sounds good to me. I'm sure I can get brighter ideas watching you than from watching Frank Furillo."

She glanced at him from the corners of her eyes and a smile tugged at her mouth.

SEVENTEEN

RANKINS STEPPED BACK, cocked his head first to one side then to the other, then moved forward and brushed back a wisp of hair from the face of the corpse. Needed more color. He touched the bristles of a small camel's hair paintbrush to the surface of a jar of pink rouge and lightly stroked it onto the cheeks of the dead woman. With the tip of his little finger, he spread the rouge so the edges faded into the pallor of the facial skin.

"Good job, Jackson."

He hadn't heard Peterson come in, but nodded without looking up. Even after three years, Ephraim Rankins had to think for a moment when he was called "Jackson." Jackson Wiliams. One l in Wiliams. Seven letters in each name. He'd picked the combination because it sounded like "William Jackson", his old asshole buddy at Lima State. It was the name he'd given Peterson when he was hired. Didn't want anyone to be looking up his record. Even got a new social security number to go with the name. Duane Jackson in Pittsburgh had done that for him.

Jason Peterson placed his hand on Rankins' shoulder, patted it gently. "Let's take her in to the chapel. The family will be here any minute."

They wheeled the gleaming steel gurney on which the casket rested through the door of the embalming room, down a corridor and through the double doors of a dimly lit chapel. A dozen rows of seats flanked the maroon-carpeted center aisle. Two large baskets of gladiolas were already in place at the front of the chapel; their sweet scent permeated the air. They positioned the casket between the flower baskets.

Peterson glanced at his watch. "It's quarter past six. Why don't you get your dinner, Jackson, then come back and relieve me before you take off for the rest of the evening."

Rankins left the mortuary and walked down Wales Road. Three blocks north, he turned into Fern. Near the building where he rented an apartment, he turned into a narrow alley. A row of attached wooden garages lined the alley. He stopped in front of the unit that bore a tarnished number 8, unlocked the door and pushed it up. A moment later, he backed out his green van.

It was early on a mild evening in late June and there was little traffic on the streets of Massillon, which lies south of Akron, west of Canton. He drove to the takeout window of a Kentucky Fried Chicken restaurant on Lincoln and waited while his order was processed. When the smiling young woman passed the sack through the window, he placed it on the seat alongside him and drove east. Soon he had swung onto State Route 21 until he reached Massillon's southern outskirts. A dirt road led to a wooded area where he parked and ate while seated in the van. He followed his unvarying routine: a bite, seven chews, swallow.

You are still one short of your quota. The lady doesn't count, you know.

He half turned toward to the back of the van and nodded. "I know," he said.

The other tribal leaders have presented their gifts. You are the only one—

"Look, I know. It has to follow the schedule, right?"

Just so you remember. You know the consequences—and the reward. Don't forget the reward.

The voice taunted him. "Yeah, yeah. Damned right, I haven't forgotten. Just so *you* don't forget. You promised."

There was no response and he turned to peer into the rear of the van, feeling the sharp pain in his back as he twisted. He rubbed the part of his back, where the scar was, and relieved the spasm. He had thought there would be no more pain after the operation, what was it—three, four years now. That Italian doctor had said that removing the disk would take care of the problem. Well, at least the leg pain was gone. But whenever he twisted a certain way he still had sharp pain in the lower back. That would last forever, he guessed.

It had all started when he lifted that bag of feed. The fat son of a bitch, Hamberger, didn't care how hard he worked him. The bag was supposed to weigh fifty pounds. Shit, it probably was half again that heavy. When he tried to heave the bag into the back of the pickup, he had felt a searing pain in his lower back and down his left leg. He'd fallen to the ground writhing, while Hamberger stood over him, prodding him with a foot, telling him to stop faking and get back to work. Somehow he'd managed to finish out the day, but when he'd tried to get up the next morning, he couldn't move. Finally, he'd crawled out of bed and crept on hands and knees along the floor to the stairway and boosted himself up on the handrail. He inched his way downstairs to the phone, called Hamberger to tell him he couldn't come in to work but would try to make it the next day.

"Don't bother. You're through. You can pick up your check." Hamberger had slammed the phone down so hard, Rankins' ear rang.

Dr. Theodore Long at the Jefferson Medical Group clinic prescribed some codeine but it helped only for a short time. Two weeks later Rankins was no better. His left leg became so weak it would collapse under him. Several times he almost fell while walking. Just as bad was the pins-and-needles sensation in the sole of his left foot every time he put it on the ground.

"You've got a ruptured disk and you'll probably need an operation," Long told him, and referred him to an orthopaedic surgeon in New Philadelphia.

He asked, "How much is this going to cost?"

Long said, "You got hurt at work, didn't you?"

"Yeah."

"Well, Workers' Compensation should pay for it. Haven't you filed a claim?"

Rankins said he didn't know how to go about filing a claim, and Dr. Long told him he would have to do it through his former employer. He went from the doctor's office to the feed store, limping badly, his trunk listing to the right. Behind the counter, Hamberger scowled when he saw Rankins walk in. "I said you're fired."

"I need some papers filled out so I can file for compensation."

Hamberger walked around the counter and stood in front of Rankins. He lowered his face so that their noses almost touched. "You're a fake, a crazy goldbricking dwarf. Get the hell outta here before I throw you out."

Elsie Harrelson, the woman who owned the house in New Philly at which Rankins roomed, watched him limping around. Finally she asked why he wasn't going to work. He told her what had happened.

She wiped her hands on her apron and gave a short laugh. "Noah Hamberger won't give you nothin'. You better see a lawyer."

She had a nephew who knew someone with a similar problem. From the nephew she learned that George Horner in Canton was the best compensation lawyer around. She told Rankins, "Canton ain't that far. Why don't you call this Horner and see if he'll take your case?"

The twenty-five-mile ride to Canton, on his black Yamaha motorcycle, was pure torture. While Rankins waited in the lawyer's anteroom, he had to get up every five minutes and pace the floor to try to relieve the ache in his leg. He filled out the blue forms the secretary gave him and, finally, was beckoned into Horner's private office.

The lawyer looked up from reading the form Rankins had filled out and saw the pain in his face.

He asked, "Have you seen anyone but this Dr. Long?"

"No."

"Would you like to see an orthopaedic surgeon here in Canton, or would you prefer to be treated in New Philly?"

"Makes no difference to me. I just want to get rid of this pain."

Horner gave him Dr. Russell Marino's name and address. "Maybe he can see you today. I'll have my secretary call."

Luckily, Marino had a cancellation and would fit Rankins in.

Dr. Marino's examination confirmed what Dr. Long had told him. He had a herniated disk. "There's a test we'll have to do, but I'm pretty sure it will show what I expect."

The nurse gave Rankins a requisition and directions to the Stark Medical Imaging Laboratory. "After you finish the scan, go home. We'll get in touch with you and tell you what you have to do next."

It was six-thirty in the evening by the time the technician placed him on the examining table enclosed by a huge sewer pipe-like tunnel for a magnetic resonance imaging study. It was all he could do to keep from screaming with fear, confined in the apparatus. In spite of the air conditioning, he was drenched with sweat by the time he emerged.

The red-labeled warning on the bottle said, "Do not drive after taking," but Rankins gulped down two of his remaining codeine tablets before getting back on his motorcycle to return to New Philadelphia in the dark. He stopped four times along the way, got off the cycle and paced to try to shake out the ache that drilled into his left leg.

For the next two days, he remained in his room, lying on his back on the floor next to his bed. The only way he could get relief from the pain was by putting his legs up on the bed to flex his knees and hips.

Mrs. Harrelson was shocked to find him lying in that odd position when she came in to tell him that Dr. Marino's office was on the downstairs phone.

Rankins hobbled down to take the call. Dr. Marino's nurse told him, "Your scan showed that you have a large disk rupture. Dr. Marino has made arrangements for you to go into St. Agnes Hospital here in Canton. You need to be there by three this afternoon."

"Is he gonna operate on it?"

"He'll let you know when he sees you tomorrow morning."

When Rankins told Mrs. Harrelson he was going into the hospital, she could see he was in no condition to drive up on his motorcycle. "I'll call my nephew and have him run you up to Canton," she said.

He put a few belongings into his beat-up suitcase and waited until the nephew arrived in his pickup to drive him to the hospital.

Rankins crushed the empty Kentucky Fried Chicken bag and tossed it out of the window of his van. He drove back along State Route 21, past the mass of gray buildings that housed Massillon State Hospital, until he reached the city. He was thinking about Jason Peterson. That slimy, smooth-talking son of a bitch, he thought. He says all these nice things to Rankins' face, but in his mind he's probably thinking how he could screw him.

Watch out for Peterson. He's a slimy, smooth-talking son of a bitch. Says all these nice things to your face, but in his mind he's thinking how he can screw you.

Rankins turned his head slightly and spoke to the back of the van while he drove. "That's just what I was thinking."

He drove to his garage, locked up the van, then walked back to the mortuary.

Peterson was waiting for him upstairs in the office. He got up from his desk when Rankins came in. "I'll grab a bite and be back in about an hour. Some of the Prattle family are in the chapel. See if they need anything, please."

Rankins followed the funeral director with his eyes as he walked out of the office. When he heard the downstairs door close, he took the small Bible out of his pocket. It fell open at Psalm 18. Rankins started to read:

"The waves of death were all around me,
The waves of destruction rolled over me
The danger of death was around me . . ."

EIGHTEEN

ANNIE MAHAROS was unusually quiet as she sat across from her father in Darrow's restaurant. Al Maharos' attempts to make conversation were met with brief nods, shrugs or one-word responses. He had just finished telling her about Karen Vandergrift. Annie had looked at him with those big brown eyes, long eyelashes fanning while he spoke. Her mouth was set the way Marcie's was when she was peeved.

"Look, baby, I don't like living alone. You know that."

"Then why did you leave Mom?" Her voice was tight. Close to tears.

"Hey, wait a minute, baby. You know better. It wasn't me that wanted out of the marriage. We've been through that before, we don't have to rehash it now, do we?"

Annie's head dropped. Her hair fell over her eyes. "It's only that—"

He waited but she didn't finish. He reached across the table and put his hand on hers. "I want you to meet her, okay? Don't make any judgments until you have a chance to see what she's like."

Annie raised her head. Her eyes were teary. "Sure, Dad. I want you to be happy even if it means I'll be losing you."

He smiled and shook his head slowly, "Annie, Annie, how can you say that? You're *never* going to lose me. No one is ever going to come between us. Ever."

Her lips quivered. "Promise you won't marry her right away."

"I'm not going to run off and get married to anybody—yet. Listen, I don't even know if Karen'll marry me if I ask her, which I haven't done anyway."

He took his handkerchief out of his pocket and handed it to her. She wiped her eyes, looked up at him and smiled weakly. "When am I going to get to meet her?"

"That's better. How about next Sunday?"

She bobbed her head up and down.

"How about some dessert?" He waved at the waitress.

Annie ordered a piece of dark Dutch chocolate cake and was working to get the few remaining crumbs on her fork, while Maharos drained his coffee cup. He said, "Come on, I've got to get you back to your mother."

They walked out of the restaurant, his arm around her shoulders, her arm around his waist.

* * *

The detective squad room was its usual bedlam the morning of June 30. In one corner of the large room, divided by low partitions into a dozen small cubicles, Detective Third Grade Schaeffer was booking a twenty-five-year-old black man who had been caught in a closed liquor store, filling a pillow case with bottles of Johnnie Walker Black Label. The perp sat opposite Schaeffer in a straight-backed wooden chair, his hands cuffed behind him. He shouted, "I want my lawyer. You motherfuckers ain't givin' me my fuckin' rights."

Schaeffer was batting away at his computer, looked up. "I read you your fuckin' rights. You already called your lawyer. I don't see him running his ass down here at eight in the morning."

"I ain't answerin' no more questions 'till my lawyer gets here."

"No one's asking you any questions. Anyway, what's to question? Why you were doing your Fourth of July liquor shopping at four AM, in a store that closes at eight PM?"

In another cubicle, Detective Second Grade Andrews sat with a two-hundred pound woman in her late fifties. One shoulder strap of the woman's housedress was completely ripped exposing a bulging brassiere. She wore no shoes or stockings, her feet were black with dirt. "Can you imagine, the son of a bitch was tryin' to rape me!" She shrieked. Andrews leaned away from the woman, trying to cover his nose with a handkerchief. No, he couldn't imagine anyone trying to rape her.

Two of the other three detectives on the day watch were out responding to calls. Maharos sat at his desk, his feet up on one of its corners. He was reviewing his notes on a stabbing homicide he had investigated three months ago. He was due to testify on the case in Mahoning County Common Pleas Court at ten. Although he had to be present at ten, he knew he'd be lucky if he took the stand by eleven. The lawyers' motions and their conferences with the judge at the start of the day's proceedings could devour as much as an hour. More likely it would be close to noon and, since the direct questioning by the district attorney and the cross by the defense attorney would undoubtedly take more than an hour, his appearance would run up against the noon recess. He would have to be back when court reconvened at two. Another day shot.

Maharos had trouble concentrating on his reading. Last night, when he had phoned Marcie to be sure he could take Annie to meet Karen Vandergrift on Sunday, he had run into resistance. It was Fourth of July weekend; Marcie and Sam had made plans for a Sunday picnic with the family. Finally, after a rare shouting match, his ex-wife agreed that Al could take Annie on Saturday instead. As things turned out, it was just as well. Saturday was the Fourth of July and Karen had the day off. Otherwise she would have had to make complicated shift switches.

At nine-thirty, Maharos put on his jacket and started out the door on his way to court. Halfway down the corridor, he heard his name called. He turned to face Shelly Ehrlich, the *Herald* reporter.

Ehrlich said, "What have you got for me on the Horner investigation?"

"Still working on it. Nothing new to report."

"What's the connection with Harwood in Canton?"

"I haven't established that there's any connection."

"How about the Graves case in Canton and the Hamberger case in New Philadelphia?"

"Same answer."

Ehrlich smirked. "How are you getting along with Deputy Vandergrift."

Maharos had been walking while Ehrlich, at his side, fired questions. He stopped and faced the reporter, bristling. "Are you getting personal?"

"Not unless you are."

Maharos smoothed Ehrlich's tie, snugged the knot close to the reporter's chin. "My personal life is no concern of yours. Do I make myself clear?" He did not wait for an answer and walked off, leaving Ehrlich staring at his back. Just as he reached the door to the parking lot, Maharos turned. He was grinning. He called back down the hall, "You're a good reporter, Shelly. I respect you for that."

It was three-fifteen when the judge leaned over and excused Maharos. He had been on the witness stand from eleven-thirty until twelve-fifteen. After the lunch recess, he returned but found that the lawyers were in the judge's chambers arguing a plea-bargaining arrangement. No agreement had been reached, so the legal maneuvering resumed.

Maharos smiled pleasantly as he passed the jurors on his way out of the courtroom. Several avoided his glance, others sat stone-faced with their arms crossed. The defendant glared at him.

The sign on the door of the corner top floor office in the two-story professional building on Boardman Canfield Road read:
    Marc Sussman, PhD
    Clinical Psychologist

In the lower corner of the glass panel was a small sign that said, "Walk in. Please be seated."

Maharos had made his appointment for five and was five minutes early. No one else was in the small waiting room, furnished with a love seat and two upholstered chairs. He leafed through a four-month-old copy of *People* magazine while he waited. From an overhead speaker, an FM station played music by Mantovani. In three minutes, Maharos' lids drooped.

At precisely five o'clock, he heard the sound of a corridor door closing. Moments later, the waiting room door to the inner office opened. The face that peered out belonged to a fifty-year-old rotund body wearing a rumpled shirt, the top button undone, the knot of the orange and black tie pulled down. Marc Sussman's smile showed teeth that were encircled by a full dark beard and mustache. His dark eyes were overhung by thick eyebrows. With all that facial hair, none was left over for the top of his head. His shiny pate was wreathed by a fringe of graying hair.

"How do you do, Alexander the Not-So-Great."

"Same to you, shrinker-of-heads."

Maharos followed Sussman into his office. He glanced around at the cluttered cubbyhole. The single window was covered by a thick, brown drape, a bookcase along one wall was crammed with books and bound journals, the desk top was covered with papers, folders and stacks of unbound journals. As Maharos sank into one of the two upholstered chairs, motes of dust rose and danced in the light from a desk lamp, the only light in the room.

Maharos said, "I see your cleaning lady hasn't made it in again this year."

Sussman shrugged, "You want a sharp office or a keen mind? So, how're things, Al?"

"Not too bad, Marc."

"What do you hear from Marcie—and Annie?"

Sussman had counseled the Maharoses during their marital problems. He was the psychology consultant to the Youngstown Police Department, a relationship of twelve years. Old-timers thought it was bullshit. They claimed they weren't about to lose any sleep if they shot the ass off some rapist or a knife-wielding junkie wired on PCP. On the other hand, even the most hard-nosed admitted that the black-bordered plaque hanging in the headquarters lobby included several of their late comrades who had used their hard palates for targets.

"Marcie's happy. Annie's whatever a teenager is supposed to be."

"And you?"

"I'm doing okay."

DEAD END

"Still eating and sleeping alone?"

Maharos grinned. "I didn't come here to use your couch for myself. Your sizable bill goes to the city. I want your thoughts about someone who's going around juking some citizens."

"'Juking'? Who are we reading now, Leonard? McBain? Or is this Youngstown PD new-speak?"

Sussman listened while Maharos told him about the series of homicides. The psychologist scribbled notes in a long yellow pad on his lap, occasionally grunting as Maharos talked. When he finished, Sussman scanned his two pages of notes. Nodding, he said, "Heptamania."

"What?"

"I shouldn't have to define it for *you*."

"*Hepta*. That's seven in Greek."

"Smart lad. Heptamania is a fixation on the number seven."

"Why seven?"

"Seven is a very important number: seven days in the week, you crap out—or win—with seven in dice, Rome was built on seven hills, the guy in the Grimms' fairy tales wore seven-league boots—"

Maharos broke in. "You sail the seven seas, drink Seven-Up, Snow White and the Seven Dwarfs—"

"There you go. The guy you're looking for is a heptamaniac."

"Guy?"

"Sure. You've heard me lecture on the subject. Serial killers are almost all white males in their early thirties with histories of bad childhoods—broken homes, abandoned in infancy. This one has an obsession-compulsion with the number seven. He commits his murders on the seventh of the month, he delivers the death blow by shooting his victims through the seventh vertebra in the neck and the seventh vertebra in the thoracic spine. I suppose if the lumbar spine had seven vertebrae instead of five, he'd shoot them there too. He even kills them along Interstate 77."

Maharos said, "Is heptamania common?"

"Well, there are a lot of people running around who have an obsession-compulsion related to seven—they wash their hands seven times, count to seven repeatedly throughout the day, chew each mouthful seven times, and so on. But they're otherwise normal—they don't go around killing people. In fact, they're not even considered psychotic. Neurotic, maybe."

Sussman stared at the ceiling in deep thought, tapping his lips with his pencil. "I'm trying to think where I've seen a patient who was a heptamaniac who was also psychotic, a schizophrenic as I recall. It might have been at Massillon State Hospital or Lima State, I'm not sure. I'll give it some thought. If I can remember, I'll let you know."

Maharos started to get up. "Well, your profile is a big help. I'll have everyone in the department checking out the restaurants. See who chews everything seven times."

Sussman rocked back in his chair. "You know, there are two things that puzzle me."

Maharos sat back down.

"Most serial killers commit their murders at random. They may have *some* pattern in selecting their victims, like erasing all the prostitutes in the world, or homosexuals, or taking out the population of priests. But for the most part they have no *specific* individuals in mind. They'll take anyone who fits their particular specialty. You've found a connection between at least two of the victims, right?"

"Uh-huh, a hardware salesmanager type in Canton, plus a guy from Tallmadge who sold men's clothing and was a gambler."

"It wouldn't surprise me if you found that your killer knew *all* his victims. What I'm saying is, that these may not be random killings."

"What's the other thing that puzzles you?"

"You can account for murders on the seventh of each month except February, right."

"Uh-huh."

"It's not likely that your heptamaniac would miss one month. Someone with a compulsion like this killer is on some kind of mission: holy, satanic, sexual, who knows. He's got to account for the seventh of every month until he fulfills whatever his end is."

"You think we've missed one?"

Sussman nodded. "I think you've overlooked February's member of your murder-of-the-month club."

Again Maharos started to get up. Sussman went on. "One other thing. I'm going to stick my neck out and make a prediction. The next one is going to be the culmination of whatever this character's mission happens to be. It seems to me that he may have been building up to the next one—which, incidentally, may be the last."

"Why's that?"

"July seventh. Seven-slash-seven. Seventh day, seventh month."

NINETEEN

"CALL STARK COUNTY Sheriff's Office," the message on Maharos' desk read. He found it when he returned, following his conference with Dr. Sussman.

He phoned Vandergrift. "What's up?"

She sounded excited. "I think we've got our February connection."

For a moment the meaning escaped him. Suddenly, it registered. "You've filled in the February homicide?"

"Can you meet me here. We'll have to go down to Parkersburg and check it out."

"Parkersburg, West Virginia?"

"Uh-huh."

"Tell me about it."

"Well, it occurred to me that we had been looking only at the *Ohio* homicides that fit the MO. On a hunch, I got a computer run of the homicides under investigation by county sheriff's offices in the other states through which Interstate 77 passes. I found that a guy named—" He heard the rustle of papers "—Abelson was killed in what appeared to be a traffic accident just off State Route 68, a few miles from I-77 near Parkersburg. At first, it looked like a routine one-car accident. The car was found burning in a ravine. The investigating sheriff thought it had gone out of control and crashed. There were two badly burned bodies in the wreckage."

"Two?"

"Uh-huh. Abelson and a married woman—not his wife. When the coroner autopsied the bodies, he found that they'd both been shot before they burned. The man had been shot twice in the back. The woman was shot in the head."

"When did this happen?"

"February seventh."

On the way to Parkersburg early the next morning, Maharos filled Vandergrift in on his meeting with Dr. Sussman. When he had finished, she said, "So the psychologist thinks July seventh will be the Big One. Wonder what that means."

"Who knows. *Every* homicide is a big one to the victim. You don't get much deader whether you die in May or in July."

"What about his idea that the killer is on some kind of mission?"

"That's *his* theory. We won't know until—or unless—we figure out if all these victims have some connection," said Maharos.

Maharos and Vandergrift had not been together since the night she had prepared dinner for them in her condo. The wine and candlelight had been prelude to what they both knew would happen. By dessert time, they were two consenting adults tearing off their clothes and falling onto the bed.

They had spoken on the phone several times since, but it had been all business. Now, driving down to West Virginia in Maharos' unmarked car, they both carefully avoided any mention of that evening until they had gotten the discussion of their investigation out of the way.

For several minutes, while Maharos drove along the freeway, they both fell silent. Then, as though on signal, they started speaking together.

They laughed. Vandergrift said, "You first."

Maharos said, "I haven't enjoyed myself so much for years, as I did last Monday. I'm looking forward to Saturday. I want you to meet Annie."

"I feel the same way about Monday evening." She smiled.

"What's funny?"

"Anyone listening to us, would think we're a couple of adolescents talking about our date last Saturday night."

He nodded. "It isn't easy being workmates and playmates at the same time. First time for me."

"Me too. That's one reason I never dated any of the deputies I work with. Somehow with you it seemed, well, different.

After all, it's not as though we're in the same department. I mean, this is really a temporary arrangement—you and me as partners."

Maharos grinned. "And here I thought my lovemaking had impressed you. Oh well, I guess I'm just a one-night stand."

She punched his shoulder. "You know what I mean."

They crossed the bridge over the Ohio River at Marietta, and a few miles below the West Virginia border reached Parkersburg.

The deputy of the Wood County Sheriff's Office who was on duty at the reception desk told them that the sheriff was out. However, he had left word that they were to speak to Deputy Sheriff Aaron Lincoln, who was in charge of investigating the Abelson case.

Lincoln was a tall black man with a build like a wide receiver. The copper-colored, football-shaped trophy engraved "MVP" on the bookcase behind his desk, was a reliable clue to his having been a pretty good one. He followed Maharos' gaze to the trophy. "That's from last year's Copper Bowl game. We won."

"Copper Bowl?"

"The cops against the sheriffs. We play every year."

Vandergrift said, "Cutesy name, Copper Bowl."

Lincoln smiled. "Nothin' cutesy about the way we play it."

Maharos looked at the man's biceps bulging at the edges of his short-sleeved uniform shirt and could believe it.

"What can you tell us about the Abelson case?"

Lincoln read from a thick manila folder lying on his desk.

"Theodore Abelson, forty-three, Caucasian, resided in Lubeck—that's a couple of miles south of here. Divorced. Abelson worked as a salesman for Halliday Ford. He had been in this area about three years. Moved here from Canton where his ex-wife still lives. She's remarried."

At his mention of Canton, Maharos and Vandergrift looked at each other.

"Frances Salter, née McGuire, forty, Caucasian. Resided at 833 North Chelsea, Parkersburg. Married. Worked as secretary-bookkeeper at Halliday Ford for nine years.

Husband Michael Salter, unemployed. Worked as driver for PTS—that's Parkersburg's local bus line—until terminated for DWI on 20 December. Present whereabouts unknown. Last seen in Parkersburg on 1 February. Is currently subject of APB, wanted for questioning in homicides of Abelson and Mrs. Salter."

Maharos interrupted. "Was he reported missing before his wife was killed?"

"No." He went on. "At 11:10 PM, 7 February, a motorist on State Route 68, two miles west of I-77, near Vienna, observed flames in a ravine fifty yards from the highway. He stopped and, looking down, saw a car on fire. Neither the driver or any other person was in the vicinity. He assumed that there were people in the car but because of the fire, he was unable to get close enough to render aid. He drove to a farmhouse one mile from the scene, roused the occupant and phoned us. A deputy in Vienna responded at 12:08 AM, extinguished the remaining fire and, removed the bodies of a man and woman, later identified as Abelson and Salter."

Lincoln took from the folder a small packet of papers stapled together. "Here's the medical examiner's report. It's got a lot of words I won't try to pronounce so you'd better read it for yourself, if you're interested."

Maharos placed the report on the edge of Lincoln's desk and he and Vandergrift pulled their chairs up close so they could read it together. Polaroid photographs mounted on pages in the report depicted the bodies, most of the skin burned black. Fragments of charred clothing hung off the corpses. In another group of pictures, taken after the burned clothing had been removed, segments of skin that had been protected by clothing stood out stark white in contrast to the blackened portions.

They shuffled rapidly through the pictures until they came to the pages on which were mounted close-ups of the gunshot wounds. The woman had been shot once, at the base of the skull. Her head had not been burned in the car fire, and a dark circlet surrounding the bullet entry site represented powder burns, indicating that she had been shot at very close range. The bullet had exited through a ragged hole in the right cheek.

When they came to the close-up of Abelson's gunshot wounds, Maharos and Vandergrift huddled closely, their heads touching.

The photos showed the characteristic two entry sites: one over the base of the neck, the other between the shoulder blades. *The signature wounds.*

One additional photo showed an exit wound in Abelson's neck.

Maharos said, "Did you recover the bullets?"

Lincoln said, "Yeah. The pathologist got one from Abelson's body that had not exited. I think it was in his breastbone. We recovered another in the car wreckage. We're not sure which of the bodies it passed through."

Vandergrift said, "There were two exit wounds, so one bullet is missing."

"Right. We went through what was left of the car but couldn't locate it."

Maharos said, "What about the ballistics?"

Lincoln shuffled through the papers in the folder and pulled out a report from West Virginia State Crime Laboratory. It described the markings on the deformed bullets. They had been shot from a twenty-five caliber gun, probably a Beretta.

Vandergrift said, "First time he's used a Beretta, isn't it?"

Maharos said, "Yeah." He turned to Lincoln. "No match on the ballistics?"

Lincoln shook his head. He looked from Maharos to Vandergrift. Puzzled. "How come you're interested in this case, and what did you mean, 'first time he's used a Beretta.'?"

Maharos said, "Didn't your chief tell you? I explained it to him when I phoned down last night. We've got a couple of homicides in Ohio with MOs that fit these—at least Abelson's."

Lincoln said, "Nobody told me nothin'. Sheriff Smith was already gone when I came on watch. He just left word that you'd be here and that you wanted to go over the file. Nothin' about why. What's this *couple* of homicides'? You think Salter's runnin' around the countryside shootin' up others besides his wife and her friend?"

"We don't think it was Salter," said Vandergrift.

"Excuse me, ma'am?"

"We don't know *who* it is, but I doubt if it's the husband. Abelson was probably the target. She just got in the way."

Lincoln looked at Maharos for confirmation and got a nod.

Maharos and Vandergrift went over the file, but there was little else of interest to them. Abelson had no family or close friends in Parkersburg. He was living in a house he had rented shortly after arriving from Canton three years before. He had no police record, his credit rating was unblemished.

They asked Lincoln for photocopies of the file and waited while they were made.

On their way back to Canton they made plans to look up Abelson's ex-wife, find out what she might know about a connection between Abelson and the other victims.

"Sussman was right. He said there might have been a February victim," said Maharos.

"Actually, we've got a bonus," said Vandergrift.

"Bonus?"

"Uh-huh. The woman. If Sussman is right about the killer aiming for seven victims, he's already met his quota."

"Well, only Abelson had the signature. I think you put your finger on it when you told Lincoln that Abelson was the target. Mrs. Salter happened to be in the wrong place at the right time."

Vandergrift said, "You know, there's one thing that's puzzled me. We haven't really discussed it."

"What's that"

"All of these bodies have been found on country roads. We've assumed in every case except Hamberger, that the killer somehow gets into the victim's car and has him drive to where he kills them. He leaves the body in the car. How do you figure this guy gets back?"

Maharos said, "That's bothered me, too. One way would be to have an accomplice who follows the car with the victim and the killer. After the job is done, they ride back to town."

She shook her head. "I don't buy that. Serial killers are loners. I can't imagine this one being different."

"I don't think much of that idea either. Of course, he could always get on the road and hitchhike, but, again except for Hamberger, these killings have all taken place at night and I can't imagine anyone stopping on the interstate in the dark to pick up a stranger, can you?"

"No. How about this: the killer parks his car at a predetermined place, off the side of the country road where he had decided he's going to take his victim. He does it in daylight, then hitches a ride back to where he's going to pick up the victim that night."

Maharos nodded idly. Now he could kick himself for not insisting that casts be made of the single tire track he'd seen at the Hamberger murder scene. "That's a possibility, but it's still taking a chance he would get picked up by a sheriff or highway patrol officer for hitchhiking on the freeway."

Vandergrift laughed. "Reminds me of the riddle where this farmer has a fox, a chicken and a bag of grain. He wants to take them across a river in his canoe."

Maharos said, "Yeah, I remember. He has room for only one item at a time, besides himself, in the canoe. He can't leave the fox alone with the chicken or the chicken alone with the grain, . The puzzle is: how to get all the items over to the other bank. Did you ever figure it out?"

"Sure. The farmer bought a bigger boat."

Maharos said, "No, no, no. You missed the whole point. The farmer eats the chicken, plants the grain and brings home a fox stole for his wife."

"Of course. How could I be so stupid!"

They rode in silence for several miles, gazing at the green fields on either side. It was approaching late afternoon and dark clouds appeared in the western horizon over some low hills. A few flashes of lightning reflected against the darkening sky, and gusts of wind bowed the tops of trees that bordered the interstate.

Maharos said, "We're going to catch it in about an hour. Maybe we should think about stopping for dinner. Let it blow over."

What he was *really* thinking was that they could hole up for the night in a motel along the way.

Vandergrift smiled as though she had similar thoughts. She placed her hand on his arm. "Wish we could, Al. But I caught late watch tonight. I'm afraid I have to be back early."

Disappointed, he drove on. By the time they reached the outskirts of Canton, large drops spattered the windshield. He dropped her off at the entrance to the sheriff's headquarters with sheets of rain slanting down around them. He declined her invitation to come in and wait until the worst of it was over, preferring to head back to Youngstown immediately.

TWENTY

LIEUTENANT ED BRAGG stopped chewing on his hamburger long enough to register a frown. "Whatta ya' mean 'It was *her* idea.' Who's runnin' the show?"

"Look, Ed. This is a joint venture between us and the Stark County Sheriff's Office. No one has a monopoly on coming up with ideas. I suppose if it came to making a policy decision, my seniority would outweigh Vandergrift's. As it turned out, she came up with the thought of checking the other states for homicides with the same MO, and it paid off."

Bragg grunted. "Listen. I don't know how much longer I'm gonna be able to hold off the media. Gayle What's-Her-Name from Channel 8's been pushin' me for a public statement. They know somethin's goin' on. Can't we throw 'em a bone to chomp on?"

Maharos shook his head slowly. "Christ, Ed. Anything we say now will just open the tap and maybe wash this whole investigation down the sewer. We're *really* close. I can feel it. What's today, Thursday? July second? Just stall for another week. Maybe we can wrap things up by then." Maharos glanced at his watch. "Did you want me for anything else?"

Bragg glowered at him for a moment. "Runnin' off to Canton, right?"

"Uh-huh. We've got an appointment to question the ex-wife of Abelson, the guy who was killed in Parkersburg."

Bragg was getting ready to explode. "You're goin' back to Parkersburg?"

"No. She lives in Canton."

Bragg waved him out and swiveled to gaze out the window.

* * *

DEAD END   135

Maharos and Vandergrift walked up the steps of the small red brick two-story house on Orchard Street in Canton. The name over the doorbell read "G. Swenson."

The woman who came to the door was a hefty blonde who looked about forty. She wore white shorts and a loose-fitting sweatshirt with hand-painted, sequined doodles covering most of the front. Maharos flipped his shield case open. Vandergrift was in her tan uniform, gun belt on her hips.

"Mrs. Swenson? We're the ones who called about—"

The blonde said, "Yeah. Come on in."

She followed behind the pair and gestured to the small living room. The officers sat on a sofa facing Mrs. Swenson.

Maharos said, "As I told you on the phone, we'd like to ask you a few questions about your former husband, Theodore Abelson."

"Uh-huh. And like I told you, I haven't seen him for over three years—ever since he moved down to West Virginia. That was just after our divorce."

"Did you have children?"

"Yeah. Gloria is ten and Sandy, that's Sandra, is eight." She peered out the window over Vandergrift's head. "Wonder where they disappeared to? Oh, there they are, playing in the yard across the street."

"What about child support and alimony?"

"Well the alimony stopped after I remarried. Ted paid child support for the girls until he—died. He had insurance that we got after his death. That takes care of the child support." Her tone became adamant. "I don't get it. I told the West Virginia police all about it when they came up here and questioned me right afterward. What's all this got to do with your investigation?"

Vandergrift said, "Some new evidence has come up that may help us get the person or persons responsible. I can't go into detail for obvious reasons but we're trying to find out as much as we can about Mr. Abelson."

"What kind of 'obvious reasons'? His girlfriend's husband did it, didn't he?"

"Well, we're not sure of that now. What I meant by 'obvious reasons' was, we want to keep this investigation as confidential as possible. If the killer doesn't find out where we are in our search, our chances of making an arrest are much better. That's why I'll ask you not to tell anyone about this inquiry."

She shrugged. "Okay by me. I didn't have a hell of a lot of use for Ted after he walked out on me and the girls to go chasing some twenty-year-old. But nobody deserves to be killed the way he was." She smiled. "Although to tell you the truth, there was a time when I could have strangled him with my two hands." She quickly covered her mouth with her hands. "Oops. Maybe I said the wrong thing to you cops."

Maharos said, "Don't worry; you're not a suspect."

He brought out his list of seventh-of-the-month homicides.

"Mrs. Swenson, do any of these names seem familiar to you?"

She glanced through the list shaking her head. When she came to Burnstein. She stopped. "This name seems familiar." She continued down the list. She pointed to that of Henry Gibson. "I heard of him, too."

Vandergrift said, "Did you know them? Or did your ex-husband know them?"

She looked thoughtfully at the ceiling. "I don't know *how* I know them. But the names are familiar."

"Could it be you read about them?"

She smiled as though she saw the light. "Of course. They were killed. I read it in the papers. That's how I knew the names." Her face grew serious. "Did the same guy that killed Ted kill—" She stopped in midsentence and fixed a stare on Maharos. "Wait, Ted *did* know this guy." She pointed to Burnstein's name. "Wasn't he a homosexual who was killed by his boyfriend?"

Maharos nodded.

She said, "Yeah, just a couple of months before Ted died."

Maharos said, "Actually, it was a month. But how do you know Ted knew him?"

She dropped her head in thought for a moment. "Well, he was late with the child support check right after the first of the year. This wasn't like him, so I thought maybe the check was lost in the Christmas mail. I phoned him to find out about it.

It turned out that he had been away for a week—went to Florida over the holidays. He said he would mail it right away." She stopped and reflected, "Gee, that was his last check. The next month he was dead. Anyway, when I was on the phone with him, he told me he had read about this Burnstein being shot. He said it like he knew him."

Maharos said, "Did he say how he knew him?"

She stared at the carpet, thinking, then slowly shook her head. "I don't remember if he told me or not."

Vandergrift leaned forward. She was barely on the edge of the sofa. "Mrs. Swenson, this is terribly important. Please, try to recall if your ex-husband said anything that might give a clue as to how he knew Burnstein."

Her brows were drawn down. "I'm trying, I'm trying." Finally she looked up. "I'm sorry. At the time I was only interested in the check.. If Ted said anything about how he knew Burnstein, I didn't pay any attention to it."

"Do you remember his words, when he mentioned that he'd read about Burnstein's death?"

"Let me see if I can remember. It was something like, 'Hey, I read that Burnstein was killed. He was a fairy but a real nice guy.'"

Vandergrift pressed her. "Wouldn't you have asked him how he knew Burnstein?"

Swenson shrugged. "Maybe I did, or maybe I didn't much care."

Maharos said, "Mrs. Swenson, this may be a little embarrassing for you to answer. But you do know that some men have both heterosexual and homosexual tendencies. Is there any chance that your ex-husband was one of those?"

"Ted? You gotta be kidding. He was a woman-chaser all the way. That's why we finally split. No. He was definitely not a homo."

"Maybe he knew Burnstein from his work. Where did he work?"

"Ted was a car salesman. He worked for Quality Chevrolet for a few years, for Stanley Plymouth, for Chick Hadley Toyota Agency. That's one thing about car salesmen. They move around a lot. For all I know he sold the guy a car or two."

Vandergrift said, "Burnstein was a nurse at Mercy Hospital. Was your ex-husband ever there as a patient?"

"No. He was healthy, Ted was. He was never sick. He was a macho athlete. Used to play softball in a league. Every Sunday morning. Soon as the weather got warm enough."

"Was he ever injured playing?"

"No—Wait, I take that back. He broke his ankle sliding into base once. I almost forgot. It's got to be at least three, four years."

"He must have been treated in a hospital, wasn't he?"

"Yeah, but it wasn't Mercy. It was that place over on Fifth. I forget the name."

"St. Agnes?"

"That's the one."

The officers looked at each other. Vandergrift's hands were in her lap, her fingers crossed.

TWENTY-ONE

ST. AGNES WAS the oldest hospital in Canton. The central section, built in 1915, was a dull grey granite from the outside. Wings of a lighter hue had been added, giving the entire complex the appearance of a bird in flight. Inside, the wood and vinyl floors gleamed and smelled of lemon cleanser rather than the usual medicinal hospital odor.

The volunteer at the reception desk directed Maharos and Vandergrift to the office of the executive director.

Mother Superior Agatha Cavanaugh sat erect at her desk in her white robe, a large cross suspended from a chain around her neck. She peered through wire-rimmed glasses as Maharos made the introductions and began to explain the purpose of their visit.

"First, could you check your records and tell us if you had a nurse here named Frank Burnstein? It would have been about three or four years ago."

She nodded slightly. "I don't have to check. I remember Mr. Burnstein. We don't have many male nurses. He worked here for about two years. I can get the exact years for you, if you wish."

Maharos said, "Yes, that would be helpful."

She started to pick up the phone on her desk, then waited with her hand poised over the telephone. "Was there some other information you wanted?"

Maharos took from his jacket pocket the list containing the names of the six men and one woman they had connected with the serial killer. "Yes, we'd like to know whether any of these people were patients here. If they were, we'd also like to know when they were hospitalized."

Mother Agatha took her hand off the phone and a faint smile touched her lips. "You know, of course, that all patient information is privileged. I couldn't give you any information from the records without a release from a responsible family member and the attending doctor in each case."

Maharos nodded. He had expected a roadblock. He also knew that today was July second. In less than a week someone would be taking an unscheduled trip down I-77 for an appointment with a pair of bullet holes in the back. "Yes, I know that, Mother Agatha. However, this is a homicide investigation. Actually, all of the people whose names I've given you are dead, they're homicide victims. I'm sure we could get permission from the families. We could also get a court order, if necessary. But we're working under some time constraints here. I was hoping that we could get a simple answer to whether these people were patients in St. Agnes, and, if so, when. We can take it from there. We're not interested in their medical problem."

She tapped her chin with an index finger then toyed with the cross at her chest for ten seconds. Finally, she picked up the phone.

Maharos and Vandergrift sat in the small anteroom outside Mother Agatha's office for twenty minutes. They sipped coffee out of Styrofoam cups until a stocky woman in her mid-forties came in carrying a sheet of paper. She knocked on the door to Mother Agatha's office and entered. A minute later, she came to the door and asked the officers to step inside.

Mother Agatha said, "This is Mary O'Brien, our record room librarian. Here's the information I believe you asked for."

Maharos and Vandergrift read the neat handwritten notations opposite each of the names on the list they had given the director. Three had been patients in St. Agnes: Marlon Graves, Henry Gibson and Theodore Abelson. All the dates of hospitalization overlapped. Opposite the other four names, Ms O'Brien had written, "No." Underneath the list of names she had recorded the dates of employment for Frank Burnstein. He had been a nurse at St. Agnes during the time the three murdered men had been patients there.

DEAD END 141

A wave of exaltation went through Maharos. They had found the key. They were almost home free. Almost.

Mother Agatha moved some papers around on her desk and cleared her throat. Their time was up. She said, "Is that all?"

Maharos said, "It's a big help, and thank you, Ms. O'Brien. I wonder if you could tell us just one other thing—well, *three* things. First, the three men that you've marked as being patients here—were they all in the same room? Second, was Frank. Burnstein one of their nurses? Third, who was the doctor in charge of each of the three?"

Mother Agatha looked down at her desk and shook her head, "Now, *really*. You're taking advantage of my good nature. I give an inch—" She turned to the record room librarian. "Mary, would you take these people back to the Record Room and find the answers to the questions we've just heard? The officers are *not* to see the patient's records. Is that clear?."

"Yes, Mother."

Vandergrift said, "Thank you, Mother. You've been a tremendous help."

Mother Agatha nodded as Vandergrift and Maharos filed out after the librarian.

The moderate-sized, windowless record room, was in an adjacent corridor. All the walls were fitted with shelves on which were manila folders containing patient records. Mary O'Brien's desktop was covered with stacks of charts. A microfiche reader stood on a long writing table in the center of the room. There was a green six-drawer file cabinet next to the librarian's desk.

O'Brien took three, oblong sheets of microfilm from her desk and placed them next to the reader. She asked the officers to take seats opposite her, across the table. It was obvious that she was positioning them so that they could not see the image projected on the reader screen. Vandergrift glanced sideways at Maharos and smiled faintly. Maharos thought the precautions were ridiculous. Even if they could have read what was in the record, they would probably not understand the terminology.

Moving the microfiche platform from side to side and up and down, O'Brien examined each sheet carefully in the viewer. She made notes on a blank piece of paper which she handed Maharos when she had finished. "As you see, these three men were all in 320-West, but the physician in charge of each patient was different. I've written the names of the three doctors down here." She pointed to the sheet. "I checked the nurses' daily progress notes to see if I could tell whether Mr. Burnstein had signed any, but I couldn't be sure of the nurses' signatures. I'll take you over to the head nurse's office. Maybe she can check her records to see what ward he served on."

Maharos and Vandergrift followed the librarian to an office across the hall where a gray-haired nurse in a crisply starched white uniform sat at a desk. A plastic name tag on her collar identified her as Helen McNamara, RN.. She listened while O'Brien explained her errand, then shook her head. "Our employment records indicate only the days on and off duty for each nurse. They wouldn't tell us which ward a given nurse was working on. A record like that would be hard to keep because, except for the head nurse on each ward, we move the nurses from one ward to another from day to day depending on the workload. Frank Burnstein was never a ward head nurse. The only way we could tell which nurse was on duty for any particular patient would be to look in the patient's record and see who signed the nurse's progress notes."

O'Brien explained that she had tried but was unable to get that information.

The nurse said, "What room were these patients in, Mary?"

"Three-twenty West."

McNamara nodded, "Frank was on 3-West at least part of the time he was here. I'm not certain if the dates were the same as those of the patients you're interested in, but that's the best I can do."

As they walked through the lobby on their way out, Vandergrift glanced at Maharos. He walked slowly, thinking.

She said, "I'll bet you're thinking the same thing I am. We know there's a connection between four of the men that are dead: the three patients and the nurse. But where does that lead us? Obviously, none of them is the killer. The three that were patients didn't even have the same doctor."

Maharos suddenly stopped. "Wait a minute. I'd like to take a look at the room they were in. Maybe we'll get some ideas there."

The woman at the reception desk was talking on the phone as they passed on their way to the elevator. Each of the other visitors in the elevator held a blue card that read "Visitor's Pass." A white-coated doctor stood alongside in the elevator car, his hands clasped behind him, staring at the roof.

Vandergrift whispered to Maharos, "Got a spare stethoscope in your pocket?"

He whispered back, "Don't need one. I can hear your heart beat from here."

She stepped on his foot.

They got off on the third floor and followed a sign indicating the direction of Rooms 300-320. As they passed the rooms, they peered in. Most were occupied by two patients. A few contained a single bed.

Room 320 was at the end of the corridor away from the nurses' station. It was larger than the others. From the doorway they saw that it contained four beds, a patient occupying each. If this was a four-bed room and if Gibson, Graves and Abelson had been patients assigned to it, who had occupied the fourth bed?

Maharos said, "You see what I see?"

"Uh-huh. Sure would like to talk to the man who had been in that fourth bed three years ago. I'm afraid it's going to take an edict from the pope to find out who it was."

"Probably, but let's give it a try. We'll start up here and work down."

They stopped at the nurses' station. Vandergrift, who was in uniform, did the talking. None of the nurses on duty had been working at St. Agnes longer than two years. Maharos knew that questioning them would be a waste of time.

Back on the first floor, they walked into the record room surprising O'Brien. "I thought you'd left," she said.

Maharos said, "We have something else to ask you: How can we find out the name of the fourth patient in 320-West at the time Graves, Gibson and Abelson were there?"

As he spoke, she stood shaking her head. She was almost in tears. "I can't give you any information without Mother Agatha's permission."

Vandergrift said, "Ms. O'Brien, we certainly don't want to get you into trouble. But this is a murder investigation, and I'm sure you can appreciate the importance and the urgency of collecting all the information we need."

O'Brien's face was crimson. "Please, officer. I *can't*. Believe me, I can't." She buried her face in her hands.

Maharos sighed. "Okay. Let's talk to Mother God."

Mother Agatha's office door was open. When the pair walked in, her thin lips compressed into a thinner line. Vandergrift fingered the handcuffs on her belt as they walked to her desk. If Mother Agatha was intimidated, she did a great job of bluffing. She pointed a bony finger at them. "If you don't leave this minute, I'm calling the police."

Maharos said, "What do you think *we* are? Keystone Kops?"

"Why don't you two go away and leave us alone?"

"Mother Agatha, there's someone running around killing people. Not only is that a violation of the law, if you'll look in that black book on your desk you'll find it's also a violation of one of the commandments. I think it's number six."

"Detective Whatever-Your-Name-Is, I don't need any of your sarcastic remarks."

"How can I get through to you that you hold the key to our finding out who killed several people connected with this hospital? Now please, it's not asking too much for you to try to find out—and it does not in any way, shape or form violate your patients' right to privacy."

Mother Agatha breathed in and out rapidly. Some of the fire went out of her eyes. "What is it you want to know now?"

"Three men who were patients in Room 320-West three and one-half years ago, have been murdered in the past year. In addition, Frank Burnstein, who probably was on duty on that ward at the same time, was murdered. As you know, that room holds four beds. We would like to find out who

DEAD END

occupied the fourth bed at the time these other people were here."

"You think he was the one who killed them?"

"We won't know until we find him and question him."

Mother Agatha adjusted her glasses. "Well, why didn't you say so in the first place?" She was getting to play detective and looked as though she planned to enjoy it.

Mother Agatha took off her glasses and polished them with a tissue. "Let me see, Mary, what would be the best way of finding out who occupied 320-West during the dates we're interested in? You don't keep any such record, do you?"

"No, Mother. I do have a list of all the admissions and discharges. The list shows what room patients occupied at the time they were discharged from the hospital."

"All right. Let's start with the admission and discharge dates of the three patients we know occupied that room. Let's see, they were Gibson, Abelson and Graves? You have that on the microfiche of each of these patients, right?"

"Yes, Mother."

"Now, start with the admission date of the first of these patients and go through the list of discharges from that date on. . ." She spent five minutes giving Mary O'Brien detailed instructions on the data to be retrieved.

When she was finished, she turned to Maharos. The look on her thin face said: Am I an investigator, or what?

Maharos gave her his most admiring look. It said: Anytime you're ready to leave the cloth behind, we're ready to pin a shield on you.

Vandergrift glanced sidelong at Maharos and hiked up her slacks. With all that bullshit floating around. . .

TWENTY-TWO

IT WAS AFTER five when Maharos and Vandergrift left the hospital to grab a quick supper before they returned to Vandergrift's office. Mary O'Brien's search would take an hour, perhaps two. Although it was well past her normal quitting time, she had agreed to stay on and get the required information. She had said she would call Vandergrift to report her findings.

At quarter past seven, O'Brien was telling them, "I've got three names for you: Cornelius M. Jarnow, Daniel X. Maloney and Robert T. Banks. Each of them was in 320-West during part of the time that Gibson, Abelson and Graves were hospitalized."

Vandergrift had taken the call. She said, "Then the fourth bed in that room would have been occupied by one of those three?"

"Well, not necessarily."

"What do you mean?"

"You see, my records show the room these patients occupied *at the time they were discharged.* If someone who was *admitted* to 320-West had his room changed while he was in the hospital, his name wouldn't show up on my list."

"Because he would have been discharged from a different room?"

"Exactly."

"Does that happen very often?"

"Not really. Most patients remain in the same room throughout their stay."

Vandergrift said, "Well, I guess we'll have to play the odds on this one. Do you have the addresses of the three names you gave me?"

DEAD END

"Yes. Now remember, the addresses are almost four years old, so I don't know where these people are now."

Jarnow and Banks had Canton addresses. Maloney had been living in North Canton.

The phone book listed Banks at the same address he had four years ago when he was a patient at St. Agnes.. Maloney was not listed in the North Canton book and Jarnow was not in either the Canton book or city directory.

Although it was now eight o'clock, Maharos felt they should visit Banks at his home. Early the following day they would try to track down the other two men through the Ohio Bureau of Motor Vehicles.

While Maharos waited in the lounge, Vandergrift changed out of her uniform in the locker room. She came out wearing a brightly patterned summer dress and carrying a large beige handbag that obviously held her thirty-eight caliber snub-nosed revolver. The purse had no clasp; its Velcro fastener could be opened as fast as Maharos could reach his shoulder holster. They took Maharos' unmarked car.

Banks' listed address was a one-floor bungalow in a street of tract homes. Except for differences in exterior paint color and window covering, one house looked the same as the others.

At close to nine o'clock on one of the first days of July, it was still light enough for two teenaged boys to be playing one-on-one at a basketball hoop suspended over a garage door. They were good. The kids stopped playing to stare at the two white officers when they started up the walk, then they resumed play.

Maharos pressed the doorbell and a woman's voice from inside shouted, "Who is it?"

"Police officers."

From inside the house, a blaring TV was tuned to a baseball game. The door cracked open, held by a chain. A woman's face peered out. Her eyes, white against her dark skin, were open wide.

Maharos showed her his gold shield. "I'm Detective Maharos. This is Deputy Vandergrift. Is this Robert Banks' residence?"

The door remained open only as far as the chain would allow. "What you want? Robert ain't done nothin'."

"Is he there, ma'am? We'd like to talk to him."

Vandergrift had her hand inside the handbag, on the butt of the revolver.

"Wait a minute." The woman turned toward the back of the house and shouted, ""Robert, it's the *po*-lice. They wants to talk to you."

She left the door open a crack and disappeared inside the house. A moment later, a lean, six-foot man appeared in the opening in the doorway. He wore a T-shirt and basketball shorts. He had a small mustache, and a few hairs hung from his chin as a scraggly beard. He could have been any age from thirty to forty. "Who you be lookin' for now?"

"Mr. Banks?"

"You sure you got the right Banks?"

"Robert T. Banks?"

"Yeah, I'm Robert Thomas Banks. What you come to see me 'bout?"

"Mr. Banks, were you a patient in St. Agnes Hospital about four years ago?"

Hesitation. "What about it. Workman's Comp'sation paid my bill."

"Mr. Banks, would you mind if we came in and discussed why we're here? It's not about your bill."

Banks did not answer, but the door closed, the chain was removed and the door reopened. He gestured the officers inside.

The front door opened directly into a small living room. It was darkened except for the blue light reflected from a TV screen on the faces of two small boys who sat on the floor in front of the set.

Banks led Maharos and Vandergrift into a small kitchen. They sat, the two officers on one side of the kitchen table, Banks opposite them, a half-scowl on his face. The woman who had answered the door stood alongside Banks. Her hand rested on his shoulder.

Vandergrift smiled at her. "Are you Mrs. Banks?"

She nodded without speaking, did not smile back.

Maharos said, "Mr. Banks, when you were a patient at St. Agnes, do you remember the other men who were in the room with you?"

He cocked his head. "Man, you know how far back that was? 'Bout four years."

Maharos said, "Let me give you some names. See if they are familiar. Marlon Graves?"

Banks shook his head,

"George Gibson?"

"Nope."

"Ted Abelson?"

"Lemme hear that one again."

"Abelson, Ted or Theodore Abelson."

"Maybe that one sound familiar. I'm not sure. What you want to know for?"

"We're investigating some—cases. They involve these men."

Banks looked more at ease now. Maharos, watching the man carefully, saw his wariness dissipate. A black man faced by two white police officers, at first not sure what crime he was suspected of. But now he knew he had done nothing wrong, he wasn't in trouble. "Wha'd they do? Park in a loadin' zone?"

Mrs. Banks laughed, she also felt the tension ease.

"This is a homicide investigation."

Banks' eyes rolled up. "Uh-oh. One of these guys off someone?"

Maharos ignored the question. He wasn't going to tip his hand yet, although he was already sure Banks was not the fourth man they were looking for. "Do you remember how many men were in the room with you?"

Banks pursed his lips in deep thought for a few seconds. "Two or three. No, three. Yeah, three and me."

"Do you remember their names?"

"Uh-uh. Only the one you said. Abel-somethin'. Wait a minute. There was one guy had an Irish name."

"Maloney?"

"That's it."

"How about the fourth?"

"Don't remember who it was."

"Does the name Jarnow ring a bell?"

He shook his head.

Mrs. Banks had been standing silently, her arm around Banks' shoulder. She said, "Robert, you know that foreign man, was in the room with you?"

Banks looked up. "Oh yeah. Don't remember his name though."

Maharos said, "Cornelius?"

Banks shrugged. "Might be."

Vandergrift said, "Incidentally, Mr. Banks, why were you in the hospital?"

"I had a operation. I was ruptured. From lifting. At Timkin."

"How long were you there?"

He looked up at his wife. "You 'member, Sarah?"

"'Bout four, five days, maybe a week."

Vandergrift said, "Do you remember a male nurse named Frank Burnstein."

A wide smile lit up Banks' face. "Swishy guy? Yeah, I remember him. He was goo-o-o-d. You call for a bedpan, he come right away. Better than a lot of the lady nurses. Know what I mean?" He suddenly became serious. "Hey, he didn't kill nobody, did he?"

Maharos said, "No. As a matter of fact he was killed. That's why we're carrying out this investigation—one of the reasons."

"He killed?" Banks appeared shocked. He glanced up at his wife. "Hear that, Sarah? Nice little faggy nurse be dead."

Maharos said, "What do you remember about Maloney?"

"What you mean?"

"Well, was he young, old? Anything peculiar about him? How did you get along with him?"

Banks thought for a moment. "'Bout my age, close to forty. Talked a lot. Yeah, joked around with the nurses—lady nurses. Wasn't very sick. Don't know why he in the hospital. Maybe like me, you know. Ruptured."

"Do you remember if he had a wife? Anybody that might have come to visit him?"

He laughed. "Man, how you spec' me 'member all those things?"

"What about Cornelius Jarnow? What was he like?"

"The foreign guy?"

"Yeah."

"He an a old man—maybe fifty. White haired. Talk funny. Wife used to be with him most the time. He *real* sick. Kinda green, know what I mean? Him an' me didn't talk much. He didn't talk to nobody—even his wife."

Vandergrift said, "Did you leave the hospital before any of the others?"

"Lemme see. That Abel guy, he leave a day or two after I come in. I don't 'member about Maloney. The other guy, he there when I come in an' he there when I got to go home."

"Do you remember who took the bed Abelson was in after he left?"

"Nope. I don't even 'member if *anyone* took his bed. Seem to me, for a day, maybe two, there only three of us after Abels went home."

"You, Maloney and Cornelius?"

"Right."

Maharos said, "Well, you've been a help. I'm sorry we came barging in on you like this.

Banks walked them to the door. "I sure hope you find who kill that fag nurse. He he'p me. He he'p me a lot."

Back in the car, Maharos said, "What do you think?"

"Well, I'm sure Banks is not the one we're looking for. It's either Maloney or Jarnow."

"Or neither."

She said, "Or someone else we don't even know about."

TWENTY-THREE

IT WAS CLOSE to midnight by the time Maharos walked into his apartment. He had dropped Karen Vandergrift off at her condo a little more than an hour ago. At the door they embraced in what could have been prelude to much more. Vandergrift was first to make the break. "Get out of here, Maharos, before I change my mind. We've got a big day ahead and I have to report at six-thirty for muster." She felt Maharos' hardness against her thigh. She pushed him away. "Take your friend home. See you tomorrow."

Reluctantly, Maharos got back in the car. He knew it was more than sexual attraction with Karen. It certainly was that. But it was also the desire to have her near him all the time. To tell her his thoughts, to listen to hers. He could almost forget that his partner was a woman. Almost. But the camaraderie that he had with some of his male partners was also there with her. He had confidence in her ability to think, to act, and if necessary, to protect him, such as he had with only a few of the men with whom he worked.

He had to report to headquarters in the morning for a briefing with Bragg. Tomorrow (it was almost that now) was the third day of July. Only four days left. Would the seventh be like that other seventh, "a date...of infamy"?

* * *

Maharos awakened to the sound of shots, sat up quickly, then realized it was only kids getting an early start on Fourth of July firecrackers, smuggled across from Canada.

This morning, the face that looked back at him in the mirror while he shaved, was more haggard than usual. He was getting too old for late dates, he told himself. The thought of settling down was more appealing than ever.

At headquarters Ed Bragg was his audience of one as he reviewed the latest developments in the Horner investigation. It now involved so many other people, victims as well as suspects, that he had almost forgotten it had started, for him, with the investigation of George Horner's murder.

In Bragg's office he had set up an easel on which he placed a large pad of paper. With a Magic Marker, he listed the names of the victims and the dates of their deaths.

Alongside each of the names he listed the suspects, matching them with the victims:

1/7 Burnstein—?Harwood
2/7 Abelson/Salter—?Michael Salter
3/7 Graves— ?
4/7 Gibson— ?
5/7 Horner— ?Nancy Taylor, Sally Horner
6/7 Hamberger—?Young
7/7 ? ? ? — ?

Those who were linked to St. Agnes Hospital in Canton formed a second list:

Burnstein
Graves
Gibson
Horner

Finally, he listed separately the other three men known to have occupied Room 320-West at the hospital:

~~Robert Banks~~
Daniel Maloney
Cornelius Jarnow

The line through Banks' name, Maharos explained, indicated that he was not a viable suspect. But from the description Banks had given him of the other two, he didn't believe either of them was the killer he was looking for.

The lieutenant rocked back and forth in his chair. "Where do you go from here?"

"St. Agnes seems to be the focal point right now. First, I've got to talk to the widows of Gibson and Graves. See if they remember who else was in the hospital room with those two men. The next thing is to locate Maloney and Jarnow. See what they know. Maybe one of them *is* the person we're looking for. Where Hamberger and Horner fit into the picture, I don't know."

"You only got a few more days. I suppose you could use some help, but right now I don't have a warm body to give you. Speakin' of warm bodies, how you makin' out with the lady sheriff?"

Maharos ignored the comment. "She's smart and a hard worker."

"Could you get some extra hands from her end?"

Vandergrift had already asked Sheriff McAllister for assistance and had been turned down. Maharos simply told Bragg that Stark County could not provide more help.

His first stop, after leaving Bragg was the records office. He gave Karen Hennessy the names of Jarnow and Maloney and their last known addresses.

"I'd like you to run a check of these through LEADS." The Law Enforcement Automated Data Systems connected the police department with the Bureau of Motor Vehicles.

Hennessy held up the sheet of paper Maharos had handed her. "You want a driver's license check or a vehicle license check?"

"Both."

"Both?"

"And I also want you to run the names through your mentioned file." He was referring to a computerized file containing the names, aliases and addresses of anyone mentioned in any case investigation or field interview.

Hennessy said, "You want all that?"

"Still asking questions?"

She glared at him for a moment before viciously attacking her computer keyboard.

He said, "I'll phone in for the report in about an hour."

* * *

Bonnie Graves answered Maharos' phone call with a husky voice that had not fully awakened. It took her a moment to remember him. "Oh, sure. That cute detective. Boy, you get up early." It was eight-thirty.

Maharos said, "Bonnie, your husband was a patient at St. Agnes Hospital in Canton, wasn't he?"

There was silence for ten seconds. "St. Agnes in Canton? Oh yeah. Must have been about five years ago. He had a hemorrhoid operation. What makes you bring *that* up?"

"Remember, I had asked you where he might have met Henry Gibson, the man who wrote you the condolence note? Well, in checking, we found that Gibson and your husband had been in the same room at St. Agnes. It was about three and one-half years ago."

"Gee! How'd you find out about that?"

"Plodding, dull leg work, that's how."

"Huh?"

"The reason I'm calling you is to see if you recall the other patients who were in the room with Marlon."

There was silence at her end.

"Hello. Are you still there?"

"Yeah, yeah. I'm thinking. Gee, my head's a blank right now. Maybe after I've had a cup of coffee I can remember something."

"All right, let me give you a number where I can be reached. If I'm not there, leave a message where I can call you back." He gave her the number of the Stark County Sheriff's Office.

When Maharos arrived in Canton, Vandergrift had already contacted Harriet Gibson.

"She said her husband had been admitted as an emergency for a bleeding peptic ulcer. She was peed off that they put him in a ward instead of a private room, as they had requested. She doesn't remember anybody else who was in the room. In fact, she thought there had been only *two* others besides Gibson, not three."

"Did she recognize the names of either Graves or Abelson?"

"No. I even tried Banks, Maloney and Jarnow. Negative on all three."

Maharos shook his head. "We're making great progress."

A deputy stuck his head in the door. "Call for Detective Maharos."

It was Karen Hennessy. She was abrupt, no greeting, simply: "Daniel Maloney has not renewed his driver's or vehicle license in Ohio for the past three years. Cornelius Jarnow is deceased. That all?"

He thanked her. She hung up without responding.

Vandergrift said, "Probably means Maloney has left the state. Scratch two more prospects."

"What about Hamberger? Think there may be a St. Agnes connection there?"

"I called his widow in New Philly before you got here. There's no answer at the house. The Tuscarawas County Sheriff's Office there is making inquiries to find out where Mrs. Hamberger went. They think she's staying with her sister in Minnesota."

The deputy came in to tell Maharos he had another call. "We'll start charging you our phone answering service fee."

It was Bonnie Graves. "I'm sorry I sounded so foggy when you called before. You know, I thought and I thought, but I can't remember who was in Marlon's room. I can't even remember that guy Gibson who sent the letter. I'm real sorry. I wish I could help you."

Maharos said, "Do you remember how many other men were in the room with your husband?"

"No."

"Bonnie, maybe it will help if you try to picture the room. Think where he was in relation to the windows and the door."

"Well, I'm trying to picture the room. Let's see, Marlon was over near a window. Then there was another man near the door on the same side of the room. Then there was another man in the bed directly across the room from Marlon."

She stopped. Maharos could hear her muttering to herself. "You know, I can picture the fourth bed. It was across the room, like on a diagonal from Marlon. I don't think there was anybody in that bed. No, I'm pretty sure there were only three people in that room, although there were definitely four beds. Does that help any?"

"Maybe it does. Thanks Bonnie."

"Call me if you need anything else, hear?"

Vandergrift said, "Well?"

Maharos stared at the wall over her shoulder, scratching his chin. "That's two of them that say there were only three people in the room."

Vandergrift said, "Banks also said there were only three beds occupied after Abelson was discharged."

"Right. The point is: they didn't always fill the fourth bed."

"Want me to check with Saint Agatha?"

"You mean Saint Agnes."

"They just *named* it after Agnes. Agatha runs it."

He shook his head, "What a heretic. Call me if you find out anything interesting. I'm going back to Youngstown. Don't forget about tomorrow. We're going to picnic with Annie."

"I haven't forgotten. Anything I can bring."

"No. I've ordered a deli basket."

A television sound truck and crew was standing out on the street in front of police headquarters when Maharos pulled into the parking lot. Although that was not unusual, when he had left for Canton earlier there were no police stories on the burner big enough to warrant coverage by the mobile unit. He recognized Gayle Olson, from Channel 8, who spotted him as he walked toward the steps leading to the building. Pulling on the sleeve of the cameraman, the reporter hurried toward Maharos, speaking a lead-in to the microphone she held as she walked. "Detective Alex Maharos, what can you tell us about the developments in the Horner murder case?"

Maharos did not break stride. He had known it was just a matter of time before word of his investigation became public. He didn't know how much information had leaked. Perhaps there had been new development while he was on the road from Canton. He had to get upstairs and talk to Bragg, find out what the hell was going on. "I have nothing to report at this time. Our investigation is still under way. I'm sure you can understand the sensitivity of—"

Olson broke in, "Do you have any suspects in custody?"

"No." He was halfway up the steps.

"Is an arrest imminent?"

He had reached the door and hurried inside without answering.

Fuming, Maharos passed the door to Records on his way to the squad room. Hennessy was typing away at her computer. He opened the door. She glanced up and immediately returned her eyes to the keyboard.

He spoke quietly and deliberately. "I know where the news leak came from. When I get proof, I guarantee you the person responsible will be looking for work—and the Civil Service Board won't be able to do a goddam thing about it." He slammed the door and took the stairs two at a time.

Bragg held his hands out, palms up when Maharos asked him about the leak. "I don't know any more about it than you. Shelly Ehrlich called me half an hour ago. Told me he was going with a story that we suspected Horner was the victim of a serial killer. That we had a good lead and it was a matter of time before we made an arrest. Said he knew the trail of killings led to several other towns and cities in the eastern half of the state. Shit, the son of a bitch knows as much as we do. I didn't confirm nothin', of course."

"He's going with it anyway?"

Bragg pointed to the window and the street below. The mobile TV crew were packing up and getting ready to leave.

At his desk, Maharos called Vandergrift and told her that news of their investigation was about the become public.

She said, "Tell me about it. I've got newspeople around here like flies on a pile of manure. I've been noncommittal, of course. But it's going to be tough to move around from here on in. By the way, I spoke to Mother Agatha. She confirmed that they often have one or two beds open in that four-bed room on 3-West. The hospital generally runs pretty close to full occupancy, and that room is used for industrial patients. But when no semiprivate or private rooms are open and a patient has to be admitted for a life-threatening condition, they'll put the emergency case in the four-bed ward."

Maharos said, "Have you been able to contact Hamberger's widow?"

"Not yet. I did check with Mercy Hospital. Remember, that's where Burnstein was working when he was killed. Thought maybe there might be a connection between him and

Hamberger or Horner there. Neither one has ever been a patient at Mercy."

Maharos was pleased that Vandergrift was using her initiative, looking into angles that hadn't occurred to him. He reminded himself that it was her idea that had led to the discovery of Abelson as one of the victims. Not only did it complete the chain of murders, but by linking the February victim with Burnstein and St. Agnes Hospital, it provided a major breakthrough in their investigation.

Vandergrift said, "One more thing. We got a positive on the fiber analysis."

"Fibers?"

So much had taken place in the investigation that, for the moment, he had forgotten about the navy blue fibers that had been found at the scenes of the Hamberger and Horner murders. Vandergrift was telling him that the crime lab had found the fibers to be identical, probably from the same source: a sweater worn by the killer.

When he hung up the telephone, he leaned back in his chair, folded his hands behind his head and closed his eyes to think. The St. Agnes lead had seemed so promising a few hours ago. Now all the lanes had ended in brick walls.

The phone on his desk buzzed. "Call for you on five."

"Pohs ee-stek, Alexander," the pleasant voice said. Only one person he knew greeted him in Greek.

"Kah-lah ehf-khah, Markos Sussman. What's new in the head-shrinking business?"

Dr. Marc Sussman said, "I have something for you. Not sure what you can do with it but, remember, I told you I'd check about some patients I had seen who had a compulsive obsession with the number seven?"

"Heptamania?"

"Yeah. Well, I went back over my old records and came up with three names: Ronald Baker, he'd be twenty-five now. Saw him in consultation at Massillon State Hospital six years ago.

"Monica Dudek, thirty-three years old. I saw her as an office patient five years ago.

"Ephraim Rankins, now he'd be thirty-two years old. Saw him in consultation at Lima State Hospital six years ago."

Maharos said, "Do you have addresses for them?"

"Only for Monica Dudek. Want it?"

"Hold onto it, but I don't think it's worth while wasting time following it up. Our killer is not a woman."

"I agree. Baker is still at Massillon State Hospital. He had a number of psychogenic problems, heptamania was the least of them. The most debilitating was mental retardation. He was what we used to call an *idiot savant*. He'd been institutionalized since he was fifteen. Could do all sorts of arithmetic tricks—multiply two columns of seven figures in his head, tell you what day of the week any date in history fell on, things like that. But he couldn't dress himself without help."

"Does he get out of the hospital?"

"Only with supervision. His mother or another relative takes him out for dinner once in awhile."

"Tell me about the other one. What's his name, Rankins?."

"Okay. I was only teasing you with the first two. This one may be promising. He was in Oakwood Forensic Center for eight years. Diagnosed as a schizophrenic."

Maharos said, "Only it wasn't called Oakwood then. It was Lima State Hospital for the Criminally Insane. You want me to ask you why he was in Lima State, right?"

Sussman chuckled. "Okay, game's over. He was in for suspected homicide. Supposedly killed his landlady. He passed M'Naughton, incompetent to stand trial. By the time he got out eight years later the DA figured he had no case."

"Sussman, you're a prick."

TWENTY-FOUR

HE HEARD SUSSMAN chuckle. "Wait, Al. Don't hang up on me, there's more. This guy has a history going back to childhood. Ever hear of Bellefountain?"

"No."

"It's in Cleveland—a residential therapy center for disturbed children. Anyway, Rankins—or Rankin, as he was known then—was placed there by the Akron Child Care Agency for a year or so. Seems the kid's foster father had been killed in a farm accident while the two of them were working together. The foster mother suspected that Rankins was somehow responsible although charges were never brought. After a battery of tests, Bellefountain diagnosed him as having superior intelligence but a borderline schizophrenic."

Maharos digested the information. So we're dealing with a kook. "How old was he then?"

"Seventeen. He was eighteen when he got out. Bellefountain treated him with medication that seemed to bring him back to the real world. Trouble is, unless he continued to take it, he'd be back in La-La land."

"How long did they follow him?"

Sussman said, "He was lost to follow-up after they sent him back to Akron. The next time he surfaced was when he was admitted to Lima State, a full-blown schizophrenic That's when I first saw him. It was only a one-shot consultation. I recommended that he be given one of the antipsychotic drugs. What happened after that I don't know. You can probably get more information from the people at Lima State."

"Any more you can give me about the form his schizophrenia took?"

He heard Sussman rustling some papers. "According to my notes, he got messages right out of the Book of Numbers."

"You mean the Old Testament?"

"Uh-huh. He was Ephraim, leader of the seventh tribe of Israelites."

Maharos shook his head slowly. "And I'm Moses, King of the Jews."

Sussman laughed. "I'm disappointed. I always thought you could walk on water."

Maharos said, "Thanks for the information Marc—even if I had to pass one of your psycho-stupid tests to get it."

He was about to hang up, had a thought. "Oh, one other thing. You said this guy was known as Rankin when he was in that place in Cleveland."

"Yeah. At Bellefountain his name was Edwin Rankin. By the time he got to Lima State, he was Ephraim Rankins."

"So what's the big deal. Most of the guys in lockups have a string of AKAs that stretch a city block."

Sussman's clucking in the mouthpiece stung his ear. "Al, you're not paying attention. Heptamania. Each name has *seven letters.*"

TWENTY-FIVE

MAHAROS WAS ON the line to Vandergrift as soon as he finished talking to Sussman. In his gut he felt that the psychologist's information was going to lead him to the killer, but his experience told him that he was a long way from the solution. He had trouble trying to sound calm when he passed along what he had learned, but his partner made no effort to hide her excitement.

Vandergrift said, "What's the next step?"

"Let's start with Horner's office, see what we can find out. How long will it take you to get here?"

"I'm on my way."

Nancy Taylor, George Horner's former secretary, was putting the cover on her word processor as Maharos and Vandergrift walked into her small cubicle at quarter past five.

A faint smile on her lips. "Well, Detective, more questions for me?" A glance at Vandergrift, in uniform. "I see you brought reinforcements."

Maharos remained deadpan. "We're checking to see if a certain party had been one of Mr. Horner's clients."

Nancy Taylor hesitated. "I'd better check with Mr. Bost before I give you any information." She got up and walked out without offering the officers a seat.

A minute later she returned. "Mr. Bost would like to see you." She led the way down the corridor to Harrison Bost's office. Bost got up and, smiling, greeted the pair. Maharos introduced Vandergrift. Nancy Taylor remained standing at the office door.

Bost said, "I understand you want to know about one of George's clients. Some new developments in the case?"

Maharos said, "Possibly. Mr. Bost, did Mr. Horner have a client named Ephraim Rankins?" He dropped on the desk a faxed sheet he had received from Oakwood Forensic Center. It contained front and profile mug shots of Rankins.

Bost glanced at the photo. "Nancy, could you check the files?" He turned to Maharos. "Is this the man?"

"Yes."

Taylor went back to her office and Bost gestured the officers to a pair of chairs. "I had rather expected I might be hearing from you. I heard something on the news about a serial killer. Do you think it could have been George's murderer?"

Maharos said, "We've made some progress, but I'd rather not say anything more specific as yet. I'm sorry the news was leaked. It's going to make our job more difficult."

Bost nodded gravely. "I understand."

Taylor returned with a manila file folder and placed it on Bost's desk. The attorney flipped it open. "Ephraim Rankins?"

Maharos' pulse raced. The pieces were coming together. He nodded. Bost pushed the file across his desk. "Read it for yourself."

Maharos and Vandergrift sat side by side, heads together as they opened the file. Vandergrift touched an index finger to a line on the first page and turned to face Maharos. He read, "Employer, Noah Hamberger." Another piece fell into place.

But why?

That would wait. Now, at last, he knew who he had to find.

Maharos said, "Could you have this file copied for us? And would you have a current address for Rankins?"

Bost looked up at Taylor, questioning. She shook her head. "Only the one in the file."

Vandergrift said, "That's New Philadelphia. It's three years old. Any way of knowing if he's still there?"

The secretary flipped to the back of the file. "Afraid not. The last contact we had was three years ago." She removed a paper from the folder, read it silently for a moment, shook her head slowly and handed it to Maharos. It was a letter, written on lined paper, a page torn from a notebook. The writing was uneven, some words small, some large, some in script, others printed in block letters.

GEORGE HORNER
Why don't YOU answer my calls?? WHAT happened to the money YOU were supposed to get for ME.
EPHRAIM RANKINS

Maharos said, "Did Mr. Horner answer him?"

Taylor took the last letter out of the file. Stapled to it was an envelope bearing the printed return address of the law firm. The envelope was addressed to Rankins at the New Philadelphia address. Stamped across the front of the envelope was "Return to sender. No forwarding address." Horner's reply to Rankins' note was a three-paragraph explanation and apology. Horner had tried to return all of his clients' calls and a check of his phone log showed that every call had been returned, although not always on the day it was received. The log also showed that on two occasions there had been no answer when Horner had tried to return Rankins' calls.

Vandergrift said, "So our man must have left New Philadelphia about the time Mr. Horner wrote this letter."

Taylor said, "Rankins was getting checks from the ICO. They may have a more recent address."

"ICO?"

"Industrial Commission of Ohio. I can call their Columbus office for you and find out, if you'd like."

"Please."

Taylor went back to her office with the file. Maharos noticed how her attitude had changed now that she was no longer a suspect. He said, "I think we're getting pretty close, Mr. Bost. I'm sure I don't have to tell you how sensitive this information is, and how important it is..."

Bost held up a hand. "Of course. I won't say a word about it. And I'll caution Nancy to keep quiet as well." He smiled broadly. "I must congratulate both of you. When I hadn't heard anything, I had assumed you had come to a dead end. I don't know how you did it, but I'm impressed. I wouldn't want to be a criminal and have you two dogging me."

Maharos said, "Thanks for your confidence, but we don't have the killer yet."

Nancy Taylor came back shaking her head. "Closed. Half-past five on a Friday—and a holiday weekend at that. You know government offices..."

Bost said, "They won't be open until Monday. Guess you'll have to wait, or try to find his present whereabouts from some other source."

Maharos said, "We'll work it out. Thanks for your help." He took the photocopy of the Rankins file that Taylor had brought in, wrote out a receipt and placed it on Bost's desk.

Lieutenant Ed Bragg was getting ready to leave for the day. His eyebrows shot up as he glanced through the glass wall panel separating his office from the squad room. Maharos and Vandergrift had just walked in. Bragg beckoned them to his office and leaned back in his swivel chair, a corner of his mouth turned up in an attempt at a smile.

Maharos introduced Vandergrift. She grasped his big hand firmly.

"So you're Al's partner in this case," Bragg said.

Maharos was thankful the lieutenant avoided making a sexist remark, although he had warned Vandergrift of Bragg's bias.

"Yes sir." Vandergrift stood rigidly at attention. Unsmiling. Maharos had trouble suppressing a grin. She was showing the son of a bitch she was just as much a grunt as any of his male underlings.

"Sit down, take it easy. I don't know what Al told you about me, but I haven't bitten a deputy sheriff yet." He chuckled. Vandergrift smiled weakly, said nothing.

Maharos said, "We've got a pretty good line on our suspect, Ed." He told Bragg about the visit to Harrison Bost's office.

"Sounds good. I think it's time we get you some help. I'll check around, see who's available."

Maharos tapped the cover of Rankins' file. "We picked up a copy of his record from the lawyer's office. We'll go over it now. See if we can get a lead as to where he might be. We're going to have to work fast. The news hawks are already on our backs. The last thing we need right now is more sweaty bodies to add to the scenery."

Bragg shrugged. "Okay. I'll try to have someone for you by tomorrow. Just don't get yourselves in a jurisdictional bind in case the guy turns out to be out of bounds for us." He pushed himself up from his chair and brushed lint from his trousers. "Look, I gotta run. Glad to have met you, Sheriff. You got one of my best men here." He winked at Vandergrift. "Don't let him get hurt."

They followed Bragg out of his office. Maharos looked at Vandergrift and shrugged a shoulder at the lieutenant's last remark. She raised an eyebrow in response and silently mouthed, " 'Don't let him get hurt.'"

Detective Sean Norris and the elderly couple he was interviewing were the only other occupants of the squad room as Vandergrift sat head to head with Maharos at his desk. They were reading copies of letters and Workers' Compensation forms in Rankins' file. Vandergrift made notes in a spiral notebook.

Maharos said, "Looks like Noah Hamberger was fighting to deny Rankins' claim of back injury. Says there were no witnesses."

"Yeah, but this sheet shows that the Industrial Commission Appeals Court ruled in favor of Rankins."

"Uh-huh. Here's the initial report of the doctor who operated on him. Russell Marino. He's in Canton. Know him?"

"Not personally, but he's well known in the city. Orthopaedic surgeon, I believe."

"Here's the St. Agnes Hospital admission note," Maharos said. "'Patient was admitted with a history of industrial back injury. MRI scan confirmed clinical impression of herniated disk between L4 and L5 on the right. Patient admitted for laminectomy.' I guess that means taking out the ruptured disk."

Vandergrift leafed through a sheaf of papers. "Here are the bills: Dr. Theodore Long, New Philadelphia; Dr. Russell Marino, Canton; Stark Medical Imaging Laboratory, Canton; St. Agnes Radiology Group; St. Agnes Anesthesia Group; Dr. Harold Schneider, Canton; St. Agnes Hospital. Boy! He accumulated a mess of bills."

"It don't come cheap."

They glanced at copies of checks from the state Industrial Commission that had been sent to Rankins. The last was dated three years before.

It was seven-thirty when Maharos closed the file folder, blew out a deep breath. "Not much help there. I'll get Records to see what Bureau of Motor Vehicles has. Meantime, why don't you try to get in touch with Dr. Marino. Maybe he's been seeing the guy for checkups and has a recent address. Use my phone, I'll use the one at the next desk.

Vandergrift placed a call to the number listed on the physician's letterhead. The exchange operator told her that the office was closed until Monday. "Dr. Marino is not on call, but Dr. Lathrop, his associate, is taking calls. I'll connect you with him."

Before Vandergrift could protest, the exchange operator was patching her through to another number. A child's voice answered. "My daddy and mommy are eating dinner. Is this a 'mergency?"

"Yes, it is, sweetheart. Let me speak to your daddy, please."

The child called loudly and a few moments later a man's voice answered. "This is Dr. Lathrop."

Vandergrift introduced herself and said she was trying to reach Dr. Russell Marino.

"Dr. Marino is out of town for the holiday weekend. Is there something I can help you with?"

"Maybe you can. I'm trying to get the current address of a patient Dr. Marino operated on at St. Agnes' about three years ago."

"*Three years* ago! *This* is the emergency?"

"Look, Doctor, I can't explain but it *is* urgent. Do you remember one of his patients named Ephraim Rankins?"

Curtly, "No."

"Is there someone who can look up Rankins' record and see what his address is?"

"You mean *now*? This evening?" More annoyed.

"Yes."

"Who did you say you are?"

"Deputy Sheriff Vandergrift, Stark Count—"

"I'll call you back. What's your number?"

"I'm calling from the Youngstown Police Headquarters. The number here is—"

"Youngstown! That's *Mahoning* County. I thought you said you were a Stark County sheriff."

"Listen, Doctor, I'm investigating a homicide, a murder case."

"I *know* what a homicide is, Sheriff." A loud sigh. "All right, give me your number in Youngstown."

After she hung up, she sat staring at the phone, her jaw set. Maharos was watching, amused. "He give you a hard time?"

She nodded. "I caught him at dinner. Maybe his steak was tough. Is your BMV trace going through?"

"Yeah. They've got a skeleton staff on. Probably won't get back to me for at least a few hours."

Five minutes later, Maharos' phone buzzed. He listened and passed the phone to Vandergrift. The caller was a woman who identified herself as a secretary in the office of Drs. Marino and Lathrop. She said that Dr. Lathrop had been called to the hospital for an emergency, but had instructed her to meet Vandergrift at the doctors' office in Canton. She would try to get the information on Rankins.

Daylight was rapidly fading at 8:45 PM when Vandergrift pulled up to the parking lot of a one-story office building, one block from St. Agnes Hospital in Canton. A directory on the wall outside the building listed Dr. Russell Marino and Dr. Edward Lathrop, Orthopaedic Surgery, Suite 112. The lobby door was locked so she pushed the bell button and peered, shielding her eyes, through the glass door. She heard the click of high heels on the vinyl floor, and a moment later a young red-haired woman was at the door. She appraised Vandergrift, looked up and down at her tan uniform before unlocking the door.

As the two walked along the corridor toward the doctors' office, Vandergrift said, "I appreciate your coming down so late. As I explained to Dr. Lathrop, we're investigating a homicide, so this is urgent."

"Oh my God. Who was killed?"

"Well, I can't go into that right now, but we're trying to locate Ephraim Rankins. Dr. Marino operated on him about three years ago. We thought the doctor might have been following him, you know, for checkups and there might be a current address in his file."

The secretary thumbed through the folders on one of the shelves. "No Rankins here. Let me try the inactive file." She moved to another stack of shelves, picked out a manila folder. "Yes, here it is. Dr. Lathrop asked me to remind you that the medical information on the chart is confidential, but I can give you the last address we have."

"That will be fine."

She leafed through the chart. "The last address we have is the Akron YMCA."

"When was that?"

"About three years ago."

"Nothing since?"

"No, I'm sorry."

Vandergrift's lips compressed. A YMCA address was not likely to be for long. Still, there might be a forwarding address. She thanked the secretary and headed for home.

Vandergrift unbuckled her holster, kicked off her shoes and took a beer out of the refrigerator. She sprawled on an easy chair in her living room, reviewed notes she had scribbled in her spiral notebook during the day. She would type up her report when she returned to the office day after tomorrow.

With the cold beer in one hand and the phone in the other, she got the number of the Akron Y and placed the call. The desk clerk said that no Rankins was registered.

"Could you look up your records and see if you had an Ephraim Rankins three years ago? If so, I'd like to know when he checked out and whether he left a forwarding address."

"Three years ago? Wow!"

"This is a homicide investigation."

"I'll try. See what I can find."

Vandergrift had just finished eating a hamburger she had broiled when the YMCA desk clerk called back.

"You're lucky. We put our records on computer just a little more than three years ago. I found Rankins' registration."

Her pulse leaped.

"He was here for a month. Left no forwarding address."

TWENTY-SIX

A SHOWER OF red and white and blue sparks filled the sky. It was followed by another and another.

"Wow, that's *beau-u-u*-tiful!" Annie's mouth gaped open as she stared up at the fireworks display. Gradually, the flashing sparks faded as they fell in slow motion toward the ground. A few echoing booms remained as the bright flashes of exploding rockets in the shy were replaced by blackness.

"I guess that's the finale," Maharos said.

They got up from the Boardman High School stadium bleacher seats and shuffled slowly, following the crowd out of the stands toward the parking lot. Vandergrift, dressed for the warm night in blue batik shorts and a white halter, led the way. Annie held a tight grip on her father's hand. She spoke softly. "She's nice, Daddy. I like her." Maharos squeezed her hand in reply.

They had picked up Annie at ten that morning. Marcie hadn't come to the door and Annie was ready. Maharos was relieved. He would rather not have the two women appraising each other face to face.

They'd picnicked on fried chicken and sliced ham, potato salad and cole slaw, served on a blanket spread on the grass at Firestone Park. Around them, hundreds of other families celebrated the Fourth in much the same way. They swam and sunned. And they talked. Vandergrift found Annie easy to talk with. Maharos listened, watched and smiled a lot. Vandergrift looked good in a one-piece bathing suit, lavender with a large white floral pattern. Cut low over her chest, high over the hips and buttocks. Very slight bulge at the belly. Small breasts with nipples pointing through the material.

Even with her short cut, wet hair hugging her head like a helmet, she looked good.

Late in the afternoon, they folded the blankets and dressed in the locker rooms. They stopped at the Hungry Bear, a franchised fast-food restaurant for a light supper of salads. It was dusk when they got back to Youngstown for the fireworks display at the Boardman High School stadium.

Although he avoided talking to Vandergrift about the hunt for Rankins in Annie's presence, half a dozen times during the day Maharos' mind wandered to it. Early that morning, he had spoken to Frank Fiala, who was on duty, briefing him on the state of the investigation, and instructing him to follow up with the Motor Vehicles trace. In addition, Fiala was to run Rankins' name through the files of the Ohio Bureau of Criminal Investigation, headquartered in London, Ohio, and the FBI's National Crime Information Center. Several times he was tempted to call headquarters and find out what Fiala had learned. He resisted the temptation. If Fiala had something urgent to report, he could rouse him on the beeper. Meantime, he would enjoy his day with Annie and Karen.

As he walked out of the stadium, the acrid odor of cordite, from the exploding fireworks, hung in the air. He stopped, sniffed. Stared at the ground, thinking. The association of odors plucked a key in his memory bank.

Vandergrift looked back. Maharos and Annie had stopped. She walked back to them. Her expression questioned him. He looked up smiling and shook his head. "Nothing."

They drove Annie home three abreast in the front seat. At the house, Maharos walked Annie up the path leading to the front door. At the porch stairs she reached up, hugged her dad tightly around the neck. Then she sprinted back to the car, leaned in and kissed Vandergrift. Self-conscious, she quickly turned and ran up the front steps to the house. Over her shoulder, she called, "Thanks. 'Night." Maharos stood watching while his daughter disappeared inside the house. His chest was bursting with pride and with joy.

They rode in silence for two minutes before Vandergrift said, "That was me, twenty years ago."

"Annie?"

"Uh-huh."

"Like her?"

She faced the windshield and nodded. Maharos noticed the glistening in her eyes. "She likes you, too."

That could be the daughter I will never have, thought Vandergrift. It had been years since she had given the subject much consideration. Before the divorce, like any wife, she had expected that one day she'd be a mother. One day, that is, after Tom's law practice had become established. But the marriage had ended first and afterward she was gun-shy, avoiding permanent attachments. Before she knew it, she was thirty, thirty-five, now thirty-six, pushing forty. She didn't think she'd want to be tied to an infant—squalling, bawling, at this stage in her life. Yet it *would* be nice to have a daughter. An Annie. *This* Annie?

At Maharos' apartment, where she had left her car earlier that day, they went upstairs silently. No preliminary small talk as they pressed their lips and bodies together, barely inside the door. His hand slipped to the small of her back. She pressed herself against him while they moved, like ballroom dancers, toward the bedroom. He unfastened her halter while she unbuttoned his shirt, lightly ran her tongue over his nipples. Her hands stroked him below. He unfastened his trousers and burst out.

Afterward, her head on his chest, she murmured, "Talk about fireworks!"

Maharos said, "Can you stay?"

She shook her head. "Got to grab a shower and get back for early report."

A few minutes later, he watched, lying on his side on the bed, head propped on an elbow, while she dressed.

She stood before the mirror, plumped her hair. Took a small vial of perfume from her purse and placed a dab behind each ear. Smiling, she bent to kiss him. He started to get up. Gently, she pushed him down. "Don't get up. I'll find my way out."

The fresh perfume aroma lingered after Maharos heard the front door close. Again, as when he had walked from the stadium, his memory was jogged by association of odors. He stared at the cracks in the ceiling without finding the answer.

Maharos awoke to the sound of church bells. Remembered it was Sunday. He reached over to the phone and placed it on his chest while he punched in the numbers. Fiala answered with a voice that was still hoarse with sleep. Maharos said, "Sorry to call so early. Wanted to get you before you left for church."

"You could have waited. I'm sleeping in. Henny and the kids have already went to mass by themselves. You want a report, right?"

"Got anything?"

He waited while Fiala got his notes.

"Okay, here it is. BMV has a registration of a motorcycle owned by Ephraim Rankins. A Yamaha."

"Address?"

"New Philly. Last registration was three years ago. No reregistration since then."

"Did he sell the cycle?"

"No record of a sale. Maybe it was scrapped."

"Shit."

"Yeah. He hasn't renewed his driver's license for three years either. Ohio Bureau of Criminal Investigation has him listed for incarceration at Lima State. Served eight years. He was released to a halfway house in Akron. Saw a counselor for two years. Last contact was when he moved to New Philly. Everything seems to stop at New Philly."

Maharos said, "Well, not *everything*. He hurt his back there and went to St. Agnes Hospital in Canton for a back operation. After he left the hospital he apparently moved to the Akron YMCA. That's where we lose him."

Fiala went on, reading from his notes. "NCIC has nothing on him after Lima State. I called Lima State. Incidentally, they don't call it Lima State any more. It's Oakwood Forensic Center."

Maharos said, "You've *really* been on the stick. What did you find out?"

"They dragged out his file. Was arrested on suspicion of aggravated assault, homicide. His landlady. Never came to trial, a M'Naughton ruling. While he was in the joint, he was a good boy. Took some medicine that straightened out his head so they had no reason to keep him. The DA didn't think he could get a conviction, so the homicide charge was never pressed after he got out. Don't forget, this was eight years later. Go try to find witnesses."

Maharos was curious about the murder pattern. "Was the landlady murdered with the two-shot technique we're seeing now?"

Fiala said, "We'll never know. They never found the whole body."

"Whole body?"

"Hair, teeth, finger that might have been hers."

"Jesus."

"She was a sixty-year-old widow who'd lived in the same house for thirty years. Steady as a rock. Rankins was her only roomer. And, oh yeah, in his closet they found a meat cleaver with traces of human blood and hair that matched strands from her comb."

Maharos said, "What was he doing with a meat cleaver?"

"He had a job trimming and dressing carcasses in a wholesale butcher factory. For all anybody knows the landlady might have ended up on the shelf in the pet foods section of a supermarket."

"Nice thought."

"Anyway, he had a friend in Lima State, guy named Willie Jackson. They were a husband-wife team. Jackson's still there."

Maharos said, "Does he know where Rankins is?"

"I'm coming to that. The assistant warden I talked to was real helpful. After I told him what we were after, he called Jackson in and called me back on a conference line."

"You had a chance to question Jackson?"

"Yeah. I gave him some shit about me being a lawyer who was trying to find Rankins because someone had left him some dough."

"Think he bought it?"

"Who knows. Anyway, he says he hasn't heard from him since he left the joint. Says if I send him the money, he'll try to find him and give it to him. I guess he ain't so crazy even if he is in a nuthouse."

"Did you ask him how he was going to find him? Maybe he's got a contact on the outside."

"Yeah, I asked. He says once in a while he has spiritual contact with him."

"Uh-huh."

Fiala said, "Jackson's keeper says they checked the log book for visitors and the mails. There was no record of Rankins having any contact with Jackson after he left. I don't think they got around to checking for spiritual visitations."

Maharos had flinched while he listened to Fiala's recital. He was a sworn officer of the court and had misrepresented himself to a mental patient, posing as an attorney. With an assistant warden, no less, as a witness.

. "Hate to lay this on you, Frank, but we may have a problem with this information."

"Conning the con?"

"Uh-huh. This guy Jackson's a nut case. If we ever catch Rankins and get to prosecute, we've given his lawyer an early Christmas present."

Fiala's voice was tight. "I thought of that, Al. Tell you the truth, I got carried away. I figured, if this is what it takes to nail the bastard, I'm gonna go for it. The clock's runnin' down, Al., otherwise I'd a taken a trip out to Lima. I may have greased a loophole for some slick lawyer, but fuck it. Maybe I ought to turn in my shield, but until I do, Job One, as I see it, is to catch the son of a bitch."

Maharos could feel the man's anguish. Fiala was his partner. Right or wrong, he had reasoned that the end justified the means. He had to offer words of consolation. "Frank, don't let it get you down. I probably would have done the same."

Fiala blew a big sigh into his ear. "Thanks, Al. Lemme see, if there's anything more in my notes. Oh yeah, when Rankins was there, he worked in the prison lab, his job was listed as 'Pathology Assistant.' I think that's a fancy title for a guy who sweeps the place out. I guess that's all I have for you."

"Okay. Go back to sleep. You had a hard day, Frank."

Maharos swung his legs out of bed. It was seven o'clock, July fifth. Two more days until the seventh. So much to do in two days. He could feel the tension building in his gut.

He finished shaving and splashed Canoe on his cheeks. He inhaled the fragrance. The odor was not sweet. Musty? Lemony? His nostrils tingled. He would later recall that there seemed to be an audible click as his brain synapses made contact.

"Holy Mother of God!"

The sound of his own voice startled him for a second. He threw his clothes on, slammed the door shut and leaped down the stairs, three at a time. His garage was one of a row behind the apartment building. He cursed as he fumbled with the lock on the garage door, threw the door opened and backed out. The tires screeched as he sped out of the driveway and headed downtown.

TWENTY-SEVEN

DETECTIVE SAM EMERSON was the duty officer at Youngstown PD. He looked up and said, "Shit, Maharos. It's Sunday morning. You want me to check all the labs from Marietta to Cleveland?"
"Right."
"It'll take a dozen extra men."
"I don't care what you need. Do it!"
Maharos was at his desk fifteen minutes later when he got Lieutenant Bragg's call. "What's this all about, Al?"
Maharos had expected the call, and the question. "You heard from Emerson?"
"Yeah."
Maharos summarized Fiala's report, but said nothing about the possible damage to the case in the way the information had been obtained. He told Bragg that Rankins had been working as a pathologist's assistant when he was institutionalized at Lima State. "I don't know if you remember, Ed, but one of the lab reports, the one on Marlon Graves,—"
"Which one was he?"
"Graves was the cloak and suit salesman from Tallmadge who was killed on the way to see his bookie. They found him in his car near Barberton."
"When was that?"
"March."
"Okay. I remember."
"The lab reported that they found traces of glutaraldehyde in the dirt in his car. It didn't come from Graves' shoes."
"What is that shit?"
"Glutaraldehyde?"
"Yeah."

"After I got the lab report, I spoke to the chief technician at the Stark County lab. It's a preservative, in the same family as formaldehyde."

Bragg said, "You mean that stuff in the medical examiner's lab that stinks to high heaven?"

"Uh-huh. In fact, I smelled something and that's what got me thinking about the glutaraldehyde. It's used in labs to prevent tissue from rotting. They call it 'a tissue fixative.' I think he said it's the same thing as embalming fluid."

"You mean like tanning leather?"

"Well—yeah, I guess so."

"And you think this Rankins may be working somewhere in a lab and tracked some of that stuff into Graves' car?"

Maharos said, "Well, at the time, I thought maybe one of the lab techs might have tracked it in, so I never followed up on it. After hearing that Rankins had some experience as a lab assistant, I thought maybe that's what he's been doing lately."

Bragg was silent for a few seconds before he spoke. "Yeah. Tell you what you do. Get in touch with McCormack in Vice. Tell him what we're onto. Ask him for three of his people. We're gonna have to get moving on this thing and we don't have the manpower in the Detective Squad. Another thing, this is getting out of our jurisdiction. We can't be sending our people all over the state. We don't know where this guy is. I want you to be sure you have someone working with you from each of the local police agencies where you take the hunt. But I want you to stay with it, Al. And remember, you're in charge."

"Okay, Ed."

Maharos' jurisdiction stopped at the city limits. Bragg was making sure that they had arrest powers in each of the localities that the investigation took them.

Chester McCormack, the head of the Vice and Criminal Intelligence Unit, was with his Sunday foursome on the golf course. He called back at noon. Maharos explained the problem and what was needed. McCormack asked him why they had waited so long before calling for help.

Maharos said, "Up till now, we thought we could handle it with the personnel we've got. Besides, we haven't had a viable suspect until now."

"You think this Rankins is your man?"

"Yes."

"Okay. I don't have three people to spare but I'll let you have one."

"When."

"This is Sunday, you can have him Tuesday at the latest."

"No good. Tuesday's too late. This guy's getting ready to hit. We expect him to do it on the seventh, that's Tuesday. We've got to locate him before that."

McCormack's voice exploded in Maharos' ear. "Jesus Christ, Maharos. What kind of fuckin' deadlines you handing out? You sit on a case for a month, then expect me to send help yesterday. I'll do the best I can, but I'm not making any promises." He hung up muttering.

Maharos phoned Vandergrift and told her of his conversations with Bragg and McCormack. "I'd like you to stay on the case with me, Karen. Do you see any problem?"

"I'm sure I'll be able to stay on, and I'm glad that we'll be getting help. We can sure use it. We've got a lot of ground to cover."

"Except I'm not sure when we'll get it. Unless we get to this guy before the seventh, we may have another homicide on our hands."

Vandergrift was silent for a few seconds, then, "You've got a good analytical mind, Al. Based on the people he's already killed, who do you think he's got targeted for Tuesday?"

"I was about to ask you the same question."

Vandergrift laughed. "I asked first."

"I've been thinking about it, of course. This guy's anger seems to be aimed at people connected with his back injury: his employer, the lawyer who handled his comp claim, the nurse who took care of him at the hospital and three guys who were in the hospital when he was. If I had to make a bet on who has been left out, I'd say it was the doctor who operated on him. What do you think."

Vandergrift said, "I agree. That would be Dr. Marino."

"Yeah. We'd better warn him."

"He's here in Canton. Want me to do it?"

"Uh-huh. Be sure to emphasize that he's not to spread it around. We'll arrange for close surveillance and protection for him, at least through the seventh. The best thing, of course would be for him to quietly leave town for the next couple of days. He'll probably be a lot safer."

Vandergrift said, "I'll see what he says and let you know."

After Maharos hung up, he sat staring at the phone. His conversation with Vandergrift reminded him of a question that had puzzled him since he had learned that Rankins, Graves, Abelson and Gibson had all been hospitalized at St. Agnes. While there must have been some contact between Rankins and the other three, where had it occurred? Nothing he had learned pointed to Rankins being the fourth patient in the room. He made a note to find out where in St. Agnes Rankins had been. At the moment, his job was to find Rankins.

* * *

Vandergrift parked in the circular driveway in front of the Marinos' large, white, Georgian home. Three boys between the ages of three and ten were wrestling on the spacious lawn in front of the house. When they saw the car with the large sheriff's shield decal on the door, they stopped and warily walked over to it. Their eyes and mouths gaped open. Vandergrift smiled. They did not smile back.

"Hi. I'm here to see Dr. Marino."

Silence.

"Is your dad inside the house?"

Three heads wagged.

The door opened a moment after she rang. A dark-haired, broad-shouldered man about six feet tall, dressed in blue jeans and a T-shirt, stood at the door. He appeared to be in his mid-forties. His eyebrows were slightly raised and he appraised her through piercing dark eyes.

"Hi, I'm Karen Vandergrift from the Sheriff's Office. I'm the one who just called. You are Dr. Marino?"

"Yes. Come on in." He ushered her into a spacious hallway. Black and white floor tiles in a checkered pattern led to a staircase that spiraled gracefully to the center of the hallway. "Let's go into the study." He pointed to a doorway.

A woman's voice called from upstairs. "Who is it, Russ?"

"It's the sheriff who phoned a little while ago."

A moment later, a slender woman, late thirties, straight light brown hair, wearing khaki shorts and a brown halter, bounded down the stairs. Her Reeboks squeaked on the tile floor. She extended her hand to Vandergrift, "Hi, I'm Kim Marino. Excuse my appearance. We'd just got home when you called. We took the kids to Cedar Point for the weekend."

Vandergrift smiled. "I'm Karen Vandergrift, Stark County Sheriff's Office. God, Cedar Point! I remember my folks taking me there when I was a kid. Do they still have the roller coaster and the rides?"

"Yep. Still there. Did you grow up around here?"

Vandergrift shook her head. "No. We were living near Columbus." Her face turned serious. "I'm sorry to disturb you on a holiday weekend. Maybe we should get down to business."

The walnut-paneled study was lined with bookshelves. Beside a window was a semicircular desk. Marino gestured to a leather-covered armchair, and after Vandergrift was seated, he and his wife sat on a matching love seat facing her.

Vandergrift said, "Dr. Marino, do you remember a patient you operated on about three years ago, named Ephraim Rankins?"

Kim Marino looked relieved and started to get up. "I guess this is about one of Russ' patients. You don't need me."

Vandergrift put out her hand. "If you don't mind, I'd like you to hear what I have to say, too."

Marino looked at the ceiling, reflecting. "Rankins? Offhand I don't recall anyone by that name. Can you refresh my memory? What was his problem?"

"I believe you operated on him at St. Agnes for a ruptured disk."

A smile came to Marino's face and he nodded. "Okay. I know who you mean. Very short guy. Looked like a jockey. A little peculiar, too."

"What do you mean, 'peculiar'?"

"Well, maybe I shouldn't say it, but Rankins was kind of a religious freak. He came to the hospital with one of those boom boxes and tapes of hymns and sermons. We tried to get him to cut down the noise level, but he paid no attention to the nurses or me or anybody. We had him in a four-bed ward until the other guys in the room got so annoyed by the religious stuff, we had to move him to a room with an old guy who was deaf and shut the door. What about him?"

He had been moved to another room. *That's* why the fourth bed in the ward was empty. Like Maharos, she had wondered where Rankins had come into contact with the other three patients: Gibson, Graves and Abelson.

Vandergrift said, "We've been trying to find him and question him about a series of homicides."

Marino laughed. "Oh, come on. You mean, that little squirt is a murderer?"

"I don't want to make any accusations, but there is a strong possibility that he may be involved in several murders."

Marino's smile disappeared. His brow furrowed. "Who do you think he killed?"

Vandergrift briefly told the Marinos about the homicides she and Maharos had been investigating and the time pattern of the killings. "All the victims have been involved in Rankins back injury. Since you performed the surgery, we theorize that if he is the one who killed the others, you may be a target."

Marino did not appear worried, although his wife did. She said, "Do you have any idea where this man is?"

"No. We're not even sure he's responsible for the killings. We *won't* know until we find him."

Kim Marino said, "What do you think we should do?"

"All the murders have taken place on the seventh of the month. The police psychologist thinks Rankins has an obsession-fixation on the number seven. If that theory holds up, he'll strike on July seventh."

She put her hands to her face. "My God! That's this Tuesday."

Marino put his arm over her shoulder. "Come on, honey. Let's not get carried away. This thing is one big hypothesis. I wouldn't even dignify it with the label 'theory.' They're not sure Rankins killed all those people—they don't know if he's in this area. Even if he *is* the guy they're looking for, who knows *who* his next target may be? Could be anyone. He probably doesn't even remember me. As I recall, he got a good result from his surgery. Why the hell would he want to kill me?"

Vandergrift did not want an argument with this bullhead. But he didn't seem to be getting the point. She spoke patiently, "Dr. Marino, we're not dealing with someone who thinks normally. This man is a former mental patient who is apparently acting out some sort of strange role. He is unpredictable."

Marino shook his head. "How can you be inside the head of someone you don't even know? Someone who may not even be the person who has committed these murders?. I'm sorry, I can't buy it."

Vandergrift nodded gravely. "You may be right. I hope you are. But we have the duty to inform you that you *may* be in danger."

Kim Marino, who had been listening thoughtfully, said, "Russell, you're not being fair with Sheriff Vandergrift. She's trying to warn us. I think we ought to take her advice. What do you think we should do, Sheriff?"

"Both my partner Detective Maharos and I feel it would be advisable for you and your family to quietly leave town until after the seventh."

Marino exploded. "Get out of town? That's impossible. I've got elective surgical cases scheduled through the end of July. There are office appointments—you know how long a patient has to wait for an appointment in my office? Two months! I can't just wave goodbye to these patients."

Kim Marino said, "What about Ed Lathrop? Can't he take care of your patients? That's what you've got a partner for, isn't it?"

Marino brushed the question off with the back of his hand. "Ed's as booked up as I am. Look, leaving town is out of the question. Let's not even discuss it. Sheriff, if we assume for the moment that Rankins is the killer, is my family in any danger?"

Vandergrift said, "Honestly, I can't answer. All I can tell you is that so far the murderer has only gone after men, the ones I told you about, with one exception, a woman who was with Abelson. From the evidence we have, we think she was killed because she was in the way."

"What makes you think that?"

Vandergrift was not about to tell him about the victims' signature wounds, nor the fact that Frances Salter, Abelson's paramour, was shot through the head rather than through the spine. She simply said, "I can't go into any more detail at the moment."

Marino persisted. "You mean there are some things you haven't told us?"

She nodded. "We've spent a lot of time on this investigation. We've gathered a lot of information. Some of it can't be revealed because if—when we catch the person responsible, we want an airtight case. We don't want the murderer slipping through on a technicality."

The turn in the conversation seemed to have an effect on Marino. He chewed his lower lip for a few seconds. He turned to his wife. "Kim, why don't you take the kids to Evansville and spend a week with Bud and Helen?"

Kim Marino shook her head vigorously. "I'm not going to run off to my sister's and leave you here. If you come along, fine. Either we all go or none of us."

"Kim, it's just not possible for me to leave now. But that's no reason for you and the kids to be sitting ducks for some nut."

Vandergrift could see that the Marinos were not going to leave town. "Well, if you insist on staying, I want you to know that we plan to give you protection and keep you and your family under close surveillance."

Kim said, "For how long?"

Vandergrift shrugged, "As long as it takes."

She was not unhappy with their decision. Marino was going to be bait for their trap by his own choice.

TWENTY-EIGHT

MAHAROS SPOONED CEREAL from his plate, his eyes glued to the twelve-inch screen of the TV set on the corner of his breakfast table. A school bus was pictured, lying on its side. Bodies were strewn on the ground, some covered by shirts or other articles of clothing. The camera shifted to a smashed car, wheels in the air like the legs of a dead horse.

"Eight deaths have been confirmed. Twelve people critically injured, have been taken to three hospitals in the Akron-Canton-Youngstown area. The accident had occurred shortly after ten last night at the intersection of U.S. 224 and State Route 44, between Rootstown and New Baltimore."

The announcer told how the bus, filled with parishioners of the First Baptist Church of Barberton had been returning from a holiday outing, when it collided with a car containing six teenaged boys and girls, all from the Youngstown area. The cause of the accident had not been established. The death toll was expected to rise.

Maharos shook his head slowly. This was close to home. He wondered how many of the dead and injured he knew. He wiped his mouth and carried the dishes to the sink.

"Meanwhile, the world is anxiously watching the events as they unfold in the Mediterranean, where Pan Am Flight 304 has been taken over by terrorists."

He glanced to the screen while he rinsed the dishes.

"After briefly circling airports in Cyprus and Messina, where requests for refueling were denied, the 747, with 328 passengers and crew aboard, has landed in Libya"

What a world, he thought. He shrugged into his holster and suit jacket. At the mirror in the front hall he adjusted his tie and hat. What a world. Not ten miles away, they were stuffing bodies into bags. Halfway around the world, no one knew what was about to happen. One thing was fairly certain: some people were going to be hurt or killed. In that perspective, *his* problem was little more than the brief twinkle of a star in the galaxy. In ten years, only those directly connected to any of today's events, would remember. In twenty years, no one would remember.

The first thing Maharos saw as he walked into the squad room Monday morning, was a guy sitting at his desk. Cleaning his nails with a straightened paper clip. Medium height, stocky, balding, wearing a blue suit. Looked about thirty-five. A plastic ID clipped to his coat pocket.

"You Maharos?" He raised his eyes without moving his head.

"Yeah."

Kept picking at his nails with the paper clip. "Ike Show." He pronounced it to rhyme with "cow.". "McCormack said you need help."

Show. A recent transfer from the Cincinnati PD who had been assigned to Vice, Maharos recalled the name but hadn't met him before. He vaguely remembered Fiala mentioning complaints from guys in Vice about the new guy, but Maharos had listened with half an ear. Departmental politics didn't interest him.

Maharos gave him a cold fish look. "Mind if I use my chair?"

Show took his time getting up, tossed the paper clip at the waste basket and missed. Maharos kept looking at the paper clip lying on the floor until Show slowly walked over, picked it up and flipped it into the basket.

Maharos said, "McCormack fill you in?"

Show shrugged. "Some nut case wanted for a bunch of homicides."

Maharos took the investigation file from his desk drawer. It was three inches thick. He slid it to the corner of his desk. Show riffled through it like a deck of cards. "You expect me to read all this shit?"

Maharos began to breathe heavily. One more word and he was ready to jam his fist down the guy's throat. He looked out of the window. The sun was bright, the sky a deep blue—a glorious July day. Finally, he said quietly, "I think you'd better read it." He got up and walked to the Mr. Coffee machine in the corner of the squad room. He needed to get away from this prick more than he needed the coffee. He watched as Show rapidly skimmed the file, hardly pausing to read.

Carrying his coffee in a Styrofoam cup, Maharos went down the corridor to Records. The girl at the computer was someone he hadn't seen before. She smiled pleasantly and announced Karen Hennessy was on vacation. Best news he'd had so far that day. He asked her if her database had the medical labs in eastern Ohio. She punched a few keys, nodded looking at the screen. "I can get that for you. Want it by category?"

"What categories have you got?"

"Blood analysis labs, pathology labs, spectrographic analysis—whatever that is—"

"Get me a list of the pathology labs."

"Okay, but first let me bring up a zip code map, and you tell me what area you want to limit the search to."

Maharos decided to search the northeastern Ohio sector, since almost all the homicides had occurred in that zone. He felt that's where they would probably find Rankins. Five minutes later, he walked back to his desk with a printout sheet containing a list of thirty-five pathology laboratories, most of which were in hospitals.

Show was no longer looking at the file. He sat, hands in trouser pockets, the chair tilted, teetering on its back legs. Maharos resisted an urge to sweep the chair out from under him. From the file, he took a copy of Rankins' mug shot. He handed it to Show along with the list of pathology labs. "This is the guy we're looking for. This is where I want you to look."

Show said, "Why don't I just call the places on the list."

"Because he may be using an alias. I want you to show the picture."

"Want me to handle *all* these places?"

"Did McCormack send anyone else.?"

"I'm the only one got stuck with this shit."

Maharos said, "I'm trying to get someone else assigned. Maybe from Patrol. You can share the list with the other person when we get him. Meanwhile, start on the places around here. I'll fax Rankins' mug shot and description to police agencies in all the cities on the list. Ask them to send their people around to the labs in their area. We haven't got much time."

Show's eyebrows shot up. "Got a deadline?"

"If you'd read the sheet, you'd know that this guy operates on a schedule."

"What'd I miss?"

"Each of the homicides has occurred on the seventh of the month. Today is July sixth."

"No shit!"

"No shit."

Lieutenant Ed Bragg walked in as Show was leaving. He gestured for Maharos to follow him into his office. "Who was that?"

"One of McCormack's men. A real wiseass."

"Did he send just one?"

"Said that's all he could spare. Jim Spencer said he'd assign me someone from his unit."

"Patrol?"

Maharos nodded. He outlined to Bragg his plan for the investigation. Bragg nodded his approval. "I'm giving you Emerson and Fiala. Could you use a couple of uniforms?"

Maharos said, "I can use as many bodies as I can get. They can help with the check of the labs, see if we can locate this Rankins."

The phone on Bragg's desk rang. He answered it and looked at Maharos while he listened for a full minute. Finally, he said, "He'll be right there."

Hanging up Bragg turned to Maharos. "That was the chief. He wants to talk to you."

Sometime in the long distant past, Chief of Police Bennett Atwell had taken a course in administration. The one thing he learned was: delegate authority to people you can trust, and stay the hell out of their way. His division captains and lieutenants were given *carte blanche* in the day-to-day work of the department. Atwell's job was to keep the peace with the mayor's office and the city council, keep the press happy and see that the budget wasn't cut. He managed all three.

Lucinda Brown, Atwell's secretary smiled at Maharos when he walked into the only carpeted office in headquarters. "Go right in, Al"

Atwell was seated at a desk that was so uncluttered, it looked as though it had just been uncrated. In spite of his apparent detachment from the rest of the force, he knew everything that went on. Copies of daily reports reached him every morning, and he read each one. By ten AM Lucinda Brown had filed away each report—the written copy, that is. The gist was filed in Atwell's head. He ran one of the most efficient departments in the state without ever raising his voice above normal level.

He riveted his dark eyes on Maharos. "I hear you're getting close."

Maharos nodded, "I think so, Chief."

"You haven't much time. You expect him to act on the seventh, right?"

"That's his pattern."

"Any idea who's next?"

Maharos reviewed what he and Vandergrift had discussed, that Dr. Marino in Canton was the likely target.

"Canton is out of our jurisdiction. I know you're working with Stark County Sheriff's Office. You want to stick with this case, am I right?"

"I've got a lot of time on this one, Chief."

"Okay. Just make sure they get warrants and whatever papers are needed. Double-check their surveillance methods. Assume nothing. Do I make myself clear? I know I'm not talking to a rookie, but I want you to know for the record where I stand."

Maharos' smile was thin. Atwell did not hand out compliments often. "I appreciate your confidence."

Atwell said. "I wouldn't have anyone but you handling this investigation, Al."

The chief glanced at his watch, Maharos got up from his chair. Atwell gestured for him to remain seated. "Stick around. I've called a press conference for ten. That's twenty minutes from now."

Maharos studied the chief's face, his smooth skin, the color of rich mahogany, his kinky gray-black hair. "Nobody told me."

"I'm telling you. I want you to brief them on the status of your investigation."

"How far do you think I should go?"

"I'll leave it to your judgment. It might be a good way to get the word out on the man you're looking for. Save some shoe leather if the publicity turns him up."

Maharos said, "They're gonna want to know if Rankins is a suspect."

Atwell shrugged. "You can say he's being sought for questioning in connection with a series of homicides in this area. Period."

Maharos thought that explanation would not satisfy the reporters like Shelly Ehrlich. His skepticism was read by the chief. *"Of course* they'll press you. Just repeat that he's wanted for questioning."

The phone buzzed. Atwell held the receiver to his ear. "Tell them to wait another five minutes. . .How many are there?"

He replaced the receiver, looked at Maharos. "There are only three, two print and one TV."

Maharos was not surprised that there were not more. "Did you see the news today?"

Atwell nodded. "The crash near Akron?"

"Yeah. That and the plane hijacking."

"Guess there are more important things than a serial murderer running loose."

Maharos said, "Not to me right now."

TWENTY-NINE

THE TV SET in the corner of the small lounge of Stark County Sheriff's Office was tuned to the five o'clock news. Maharos and Vandergrift watched as images flashed by showing the hijacked plane, still on the ground in Libya. An update of the bus-auto collision between Akron, Canton and Youngstown took up most of the remainder of the half-hour telecast. They listened to interviews with injured victims in their hospital beds, relatives of several of those who had been killed and with police officials trying to piece together the cause of the tragic accident.

Vandergrift said, "They'll probably go through the sports and weather before they get to Rankins."

Maharos said, "*If* they get to Rankins. A week ago I was trying to keep these news monkeys off my back. Where are they when you need them?"

Vandergrift held up a hand. "I think this is it."

The blond anchorman with sensuous lips appeared on the screen. "Law enforcement agencies in northeastern Ohio are attempting to locate and question a thirty-two-year-old man in connection with a series of unsolved murders that go back to January of this year." The mug shot of Rankins filled the screen. "Ephraim Rankins, formerly a patient-inmate at Oakwood Forensic Center for the Criminally Insane, and now believed to be in this area, is wanted for questioning in the killings of George Horner, a Youngstown attorney; Henry Gibson, a Canton executive; and Frank Burnstein, a nurse who had been employed at Mercy Hospital in Canton. At a press conference today, Youngstown Chief of Police Bennett Atwell, intimated that there may be a connection with at least three additional homicides."

The picture on the screen shifted to the interview with Maharos in Atwell's office. The reporter's overvoice said, "Detective Alex Maharos, of the Youngstown Police Department, would not say whether Rankins was a suspect in the killings."

MAHAROS: Mr. Rankins is known to have some connection with several of the victims, but at this time we are not accusing him of any crimes.

Rankins' picture was shown again.

MAHAROS (overvoice): If anyone knows of Mr. Rankins' present whereabouts, we would like them to contact any of the law enforcement agencies...

In the office of Hartman's Ambulance Service in Massillon, John Henderson was alone, sprawled out on a lounge chair in front of the TV set. He was dressed in white from his jacket to his shoes. Henderson drove ambulance for Hartman's. The other member of his crew was across the street having supper.

Henderson was waiting for the sportscaster to come on with the daytime baseball scores. Today, he had his sawbuck riding on the Red Sox against the Yankees. He listened without interest while the announcer went on about some Arab nuts grabbing a plane. Shit, *that* was news? Happened every other day it seemed. He paid a little more attention when the car-bus accident was shown. He recognized the intersection. They should have a four-way stop sign instead of just the stop sign on 44. He wondered who got the ambulance calls on that one. Probably the larger outfits out of Akron or Canton.

When Rankins' image appeared on the screen, Anderson's eyes opened wide. The face was familiar. He sat on the edge of the chair now, listening to the words of the announcer and the interview with Maharos. I know that guy, he thought. The second time Rankins' face appeared he said aloud, "Jesus Christ!" He snapped his fingers and spoke again to the empty room. "Peterson's." He reached for the phone book.

* * *

The paging speaker in Stark County Sheriff's Headquarters intoned Vandergrift's name. She answered using the phone in the lounge.

The operator said, "Are you taking the calls on Rankins?" She acknowledged.

On the line was Rich Laufer, sergeant in the Massillon Police Department who had just received the call from Henderson identifying Rankins. "He says the guy is called Wiliams. One 'l,'" said Laufer. "Works for Peterson's Mortuary here in Massillon. You can call Henderson for more information." He gave her a phone number.

Vandergrift thanked him and hung up. "We may have something, Al. Take the other extension."

Henderson was waiting for the call. Vandergrift identified herself. "I understand you think you know the man we're looking for."

"Yeah. I'm pretty sure it's the guy who works for Peterson's Funeral Home. I've seen him several times when I've delivered bodies there. I drive ambulance for Hartman's. Only the guy's name is Wiliams, or something like that."

"Could you describe him for me?"

"Well, he's a little squirt—almost like a midget, know what I mean? Doesn't say much. Kind of funny that way."

Maharos, his ear to the extension phone, wagged his head.

Vandergrift said, "Okay, we'll check on the information. We appreciate your help."

She started to hang up when she heard Henderson's voice, still on the line. "Hey!"

"What?"

"Is there any reward?"

Vandergrift glanced over at Maharos. He shook his head.

"No, I'm sorry. But your action as a responsible citizen is greatly appreciated."

"Sure. Thanks a lot."

* * *

At 5:15 PM, Rankins knocked on the door of Jason Peterson's office and stuck his head in the door. "I'm finished downstairs. Okay if I take off?"

The funeral director, seated at his desk, glanced up. "Okay, Jackson. Goodnight. See you tomorrow."

Rankins hesitated at the door. "I'm off tomorrow, remember? I switched from last Sunday."

Peterson's brows knit. "Oh?"

"I worked last Sunday. You said I could have Tuesday off."

Peterson nodded, remembering. "You're right. See you Wednesday."

Rankins walked the short distance to the garage that housed his van and drove it out.

The sun, starting to dip toward the western horizon, still shone brightly. The ten-mile drive to Interstate 77 took him less than fifteen minutes. He was now in Canton. As he approached the on-ramp to the freeway, he slowed, then turned off on a side street. He debated whether or not to pass the doctor's office once again. Decided he had no need. He had done his surveillance well the preceding week. He drove on to Whipple Road, reaching its intersection with the I-77 on-ramp. This time he drove on to the interstate. Continued unhurriedly past the Akron-Canton Airport. At State Route 619 he left the interstate and drove east for another three miles. He was now in open country, fields with scattered patches of woods, weathered barns, farmhouses. A narrow dirt road appeared, leading into a densely wooded area. There were no signs or other markings to identify the dirt road. He steered the van on to the road, stopped and set the dashboard odometer to zero. For the last four minutes he had passed no vehicles.

The dirt road, barely wide enough for the van, was deeply rutted and clumps of weeds poked out of the earth. Fifty yards farther on, the road made a gentle bend and the paved county road behind him was no longer visible.

Rankins crept along at less than five miles an hour, following tire tracks the van had made when he had explored the road two days before. At one point he got out and examined the tracks, was satisfied that there were no fresh marks over the ones he had made before. In scouting the area, he had driven along the dirt road to its terminus, two miles further on a pile of charred wood and an open pit lined with a few cement blocks, the foundation of a small, burned-out farmhouse.

Now he checked his odometer, decided he did not have to go any farther. He was surrounded by trees and thick bushes. A few yards ahead, he came to a clearing with enough room on either side of the road to turn the van around facing the way he had come in.

He climbed into the back of the van and slid the side door open. The rays of fading sunlight that filtered through the forest reflected on the bright chrome handlebars of the motorcycle that leaned against a wall inside the van. He lifted a wide plank from the floor and made it into a ramp from the doorway to the ground. He carefully guided the Yamaha onto the ramp and, standing alongside, balanced it the short distance to the ground.

Rankins walked alongside the cycle, steering it through narrow gaps in the underbrush, moving away from the van, until he was twenty yards from the road. He placed the cycle on its side under a bush and went back to the van for a black plastic tarp, which he used to cover the motorcycle. He scattered loose branches and leaves on the tarp and stood back examining it, satisfied that his cache was well hidden. He'd be back for the cycle tomorrow—but not in the van. Maybe he'd return as a passenger, guiding the driver along the dirt road. Prodding the back of his head with the barrel of a gun. Or he'd be driving, with his passenger bound and gagged in the back of the car. But one way or the other, he'd be back tomorrow.

Dusk was rapidly settling as he started the van and slowly drove out of the woods. When he reached the paved road, he drove toward the interstate, but stopped after he had gone a hundred yards. He got out and walked back to the dirt road carrying a whisk broom which he used to obliterate his tire tracks for ten yards into the dirt road. He retraced his steps to the paved road, walking alongside the dirt road to avoid leaving footprints.

Ephraim Rankins hummed and he talked to his invisible friends in the back of the van as he drove back to Massillon. He was already feeling the flush that he experienced before each of the earlier sacrifices. *This* was the one they had all led to. *This* was the one that really counted.

THIRTY

"IN CASE OF emergency please call 836-9976." Vandergrift, squinting in the rapidly fading light of day, read the sign on the door of Peterson's Mortuary to Maharos who stood alongside.

They turned to the sound of car tires on the gravel driveway. A gray and blue patrol car with a yellow "Massillon Police Department" decal on the door pulled up and parked. A tall, lean police officer stepped out and approached. "Hi. I'm Matt Clemens. You the guys Sergeant Laufer talked to?"

Maharos said, "Yeah. Know where we can find Peterson?"

"He lives next door." Clemens pointed to a two-story red brick house just visible through the hedge that separated the funeral home parking lot from the owner's driveway. He led them around to the front door.

A woman in a flower print house dress answered the doorbell. Through the screen door, she glanced from Maharos to Vandergrift. Spotting Clemens, she smiled in recognition. "Hi, Matt. What's up?"

Clemens had mentioned that he'd moonlighted for the mortuary on a number of occasions, driving an escort car in funeral processions. He introduced Vandergrift and Maharos to the woman, Maureen Peterson.

Maharos said, "We're trying to locate one of your husband's employees. I believe you know him as Jackson Wiliams."

Mrs. Peterson opened the screen door. "Would you like to come in?"

She led them into a spacious center hallway. Jason Peterson, dressed in slacks and a sport shirt, a newspaper in his hand, appeared at the entrance to the living room that led off the center hall. He saw Clemens and greeted him. "Anything wrong, Matt?"

"These officers are looking for that little guy who works for you."

"Jackson Wiliams?"

Maharos said, "Yes sir."

"Anything wrong?"

"We'd like to ask him a few questions. Part of an investigation we're conducting. Know where we can find him?"

"I imagine he's home. Maureen, do you know his address?"

Maureen Peterson said, "It's that two-story red brick apartment building corner of Bridges and Fern. It faces on Bridges but I don't know the exact address. It's just about three blocks from here."

Vandergrift said, "Could we look up the address in your phone book?"

Peterson said, "I don't think he ever put in a phone. Matt, you know the building, don't you?"

Maharos' brows went up. No phone? Who didn't have a phone in this day and age? Peterson noticed Maharos' expression. "You're thinking about the phone? I know it seems odd, but Jackson—well, he's a very private person. Wouldn't you say, dear?" He looked at his wife for confirmation.

"Yes, I'd call him a *very* private person."

Vandergrift said, "Mr. Peterson, when did you see Wiliams last?"

"A little after five this evening when he left work."

"So you wouldn't expect him back until tomorrow morning?"

"Well, yes—except he won't be in tomorrow. He's got the day off."

Maharos said, "Tuesday is his day off?"

Peterson smiled. "In this business we don't stick to regular days off. If we have a funeral on Saturday, he would work that day and take off another day during the week instead."

"Is that why he's off tomorrow?"

"Yes—well, partly."

Maharos kept looking at him for an explanation.

Peterson went on. "We *did* have a funeral Saturday and he worked. But, actually, he had requested tomorrow off several weeks ago. Wasn't it a few weeks ago, Mo?"

His wife nodded.

"Has he ever requested a day off in advance before?"

Peterson thought for a moment. Looked at his wife for the answer.

Maureen Peterson touched her husband's arm. "Yes he did, dear. Last month, remember? He wanted to be sure he could be off—I don't remember the date but I could look it up."

Peterson smiled, "That's right. Now that you mention it, I do remember that there've been several times in the past few months he'd tell me a few weeks in advance that he wouldn't be coming in on such-and-such a day."

Maharos said, "Was it always the same day or date each month?"

Peterson thought a moment. "I'd have to look it up."

"If it's not too much trouble."

Mrs. Peterson said, "I was just working on the books. I've got the information right here on my desk."

Maharos said, "I'd appreciate that." He watched as she went into the small study off the center hall, and turned back to Peterson. "How long has Wiliams been working for you?"

Peterson puffed out his cheeks and let the air out slowly, thinking. "Let's see. It's almost three years now I think. I could have my wife look that up too, if you want."

"Maybe later. Is he a licensed mortician?"

"Mortician assistant, we call him. He isn't licensed. I am, of course."

"How did you come to hire him?"

"He answered an ad."

"Do you know what he had done before he came to work for you?"

"I think he had been working on a farm. To be honest, I never checked the references he gave me. I hired him as a janitor. At the time, I had another man who helped me preparing remains, but he took sick. Wiliams filled in for him and did such a good job that I trained him myself rather than someone I'd have to pay industry scale."

Maharos said, "By the way, what kind of car does he drive?"

"As far as I know he doesn't have a car. He lives only a few blocks away and he always walks to and from work."

Maureen Peterson was approaching them, carrying a ledger book. Peterson asked, "Have you ever seen Jackson drive a car, Mo?"

Maureen Peterson shook her head. "Only the hearse. I guess he takes buses if he has to go any distance. Funny, I'd never thought too much about how he gets around before." She opened the ledger. "Here are the days he's had off this year."

She pointed to the dates. He was off usually one day each week. Since January, Wiliams' days off had included the seventh of each month. Maharos took it in, without comment. He said, "Do you have last year's record of days off?"

She flipped the page. In the preceding year the dates Wiliams had off, were randomly distributed.

Vandergrift said, "Mrs. Peterson, you just said that Mr. Wiliams drives your hearse. Then he must have a valid license, right?"

Mrs. Peterson looked at her husband. Both appeared flustered. Finally, Peterson said, "I—I'm sure he has one. He certainly knows how to drive."

Vandergrift said, "Have you asked to see it?"

"I must have at one time."

Maharos said, "Do you actually remember seeing it?"

Peterson's face turned red. He looked from Maharos to Vandergrift, then back to Maharos. "I don't understand what this is all about."

Maharos didn't care whether or not the guy was driving with a valid license. Probably it had never been renewed. That explained why his current address had not been filed with the BMV. He tried to sound casual. "We just want to ask him some routine questions. It's in reference to an investigation we're conducting."

"You already said that. What kind of investigation?"

Maharos hesitated. Although the evidence against the man was piling up, until he was certain Rankins was the person they were hunting he was reluctant to make a definite statement. "A homicide investigation. I can't go into any more detail at the moment, but I'll be glad to answer all your questions after we've talked to your employee." He turned to Clemens. "Could you take us to the apartment building where he lives? We'll follow you in our car."

Maharos followed Clemens and Vandergrift out of the door and walked rapidly toward the car. The sooner he got away, the fewer questions he'd have to answer. Peterson stood at the open door, the newspaper hanging from his hand, a perplexed look on his face.

Rankins lived in a square, red brick, corner apartment building. Sturdy oak trees lined the curbs on either side of Fern Street, their branches forming an arbor over the roadway.

The building contained four apartments, two on each floor. Clemens pulled the patrol car to the curb on Bridges Street, in front of the building. Vandergrift, driving an unmarked Olds, parked on Fern, along the side of the building. It was half-past eight but still light. Clemens remained in his patrol car.

Maharos waited at the car while Vandergrift walked around to the back of the building. In a few moments she came back. "There's no fire escape," she said. "There's a back door but it's locked. It looks as though it leads to the basement."

Maharos and Vandergrift walked to the front of the building. The outer door led to a small vestibule with an inner door that was locked. Inside the vestibule, they read the names next to the row of four bell buttons on a brass plate mounted on a wall. Wiliams' name was opposite the top button. Maharos pressed the bell button and they waited, but there was no response. Twice more he rang without an answer.

Vandergrift said, "Let's try one of the others. Maybe one of them is the caretaker."

The name card opposite the lowermost button read "Warner." A few moments after Maharos had pressed the button, a metallic man's voice came through the flutes of a small amplifier set in the bell button plate. "Yes?"

"Mr. Warner?"

"Who is this?"

"Police. Can we talk to you?"

A few beats of silence, then, "Wait a minute."

They heard a door open and a moment later a form appeared at the thick glass panel set into the door separating the vestibule from the inner hallway. A man, was shielding his eyes as he pressed his face against the glass.

Maharos held up his shield and Vandergrift pointed to the star badge pinned to her shirt. The door remained closed. "What is it you want?" His voice was muffled behind the thick glass.

Maharos called, "We're trying to find Jackson Wiliams."

"His apartment is upstairs. Ring his bell."

"There's no answer."

"Then he's not home."

"Who's the caretaker of this building?"

"I am. I own the building."

"Can we come in? We'd like to talk to you."

"What about? I thought you wanted Wiliams."

Maharos was becoming irritated. "Mr. Warner, why don't you open the door so we can talk without shouting."

"How do I know you're who you say you are. There's been a lot of robberies around here."

Vandergrift stepped outside the vestibule and beckoned to Clemens seated in his patrol car, elbow resting on the window frame. He came up the walk. "What's the problem?"

She explained that Rankins did not answer and the owner-caretaker would not let them in. "Maybe you could talk to him."

Clemens stepped to the glass vestibule door. Warner appeared to recognize the Massillon PD uniform. A moment later he opened the door and scowled, while the three filed into the small inner lobby.

Maharos said, "Mr. Warner, please take us to. Wiliams' apartment. Maybe he's there but isn't answering the doorbell."

Warner said, "What's he done?"

Maharos said, "We're investigating a case and we need to talk to him."

Warner hesitated, then shook his head slowly and led the way up the stairs. He pointed to the door on the left at the head of the stairs. "That's Wiliams' apartment."

Maharos stood to the side and knocked. When there was no response, he called, "Mr. Wiliams?"

Silence.

He turned to Warner. "Do you have a key to this apartment?"

"Why?"

"We'd like to take a peek inside. See if he's asleep or sick. Maybe he didn't hear us."

"Now, wait a minute. I can't let you in. You should know that's against the law."

Clemens said, "We could get a warrant. . ."

"So get a warrant."

"If I have to go to all that trouble I won't be happy."

"I don't give a shit if you're happy or not."

Clemens glanced around the hallway. "When were you last inspected for termites, Warner?"

"*Termites!* Where do you think you are, California? We don't have no termites here."

Clemens brushed his hand over the wood molding halfway up the wall. He held up his fingers. "Looks like termites to me. I'll have a building inspector out in the morning. You can bet your ass he'll check for termites. Probably make you have a full fumigation. Everybody'd have to leave the building 'till it's over."

Warner took a deep sighing breath. "Wait here. I'll get the master key."

* * *

Ephraim Rankins was still humming as he turned the van into Bridges Street. He passed Beech, Cedar and Daphne. As he approached Fern, the next cross street, he saw against the darkening sky the profile of the overhead light rack on the car parked in front of his apartment building. The danger flag in his head shot out like a banner in a high wind. His foot gentled down on the brake and he turned right on Fern, away from the apartment building.

He drove for a little more than a block, then stopped at the curb. He was breathing rapidly. *So* close to his goal now. Couldn't take a chance on being stopped. Just one more day, that's all he needed.

For ten minutes he drove around aimlessly, then turned back and passed the apartment building. The patrol car was still there. He kept going.

In Rankins' apartment, Matt Clemens said, "Do we toss the place?"

Maharos shook his head. "Not without a warrant."

Warner said, "Damn right. You shouldn't even be in here."

Clemens said, "Hey, we're just checking out a report of a possible break-in. We're just protecting our citizens, for crissake."

"*Some* protection."

Warner stood by in Rankins' apartment while Maharos and Vandergrift looked into each of the rooms, being careful not to touch anything. Clemens remained in the living room, his legs apart, thumbs hooked into his gun belt.

Warner said, "What the hell are you looking for? You can see he's not here."

No one answered him.

The apartment was uncluttered and spotlessly clean. The living room was furnished with a maple couch upholstered in a plaid tweed material. Early Sears. In addition, there were two matching chairs and a small drop-leaf table. Maharos was struck by the barrenness of the room. He looked for newspapers, magazines or books. There were none. There were no pictures on the walls, no carpeting on the floor.

From a cramped vestibule off the living room, doors led to a small bathroom and the bedroom. In the vestibule there was a linen closet, the lower half of which was taken up by a small washer-drier combination. Maharos pointed to the unit. "Does this come with the apartment or do the tenants buy it?"

Warner said, "The previous tenant put it in and left it when he moved out. I think he sold that, and all the other furniture in the apartment to Wiliams."

Vandergrift said, "Did Wiliams add any furnishings?"

Warner slowly scanned the rooms, shook his head. "I think it was all here when he moved in."

The linen closet shelves held two neatly folded sheets, a pillow case and two towels. Nothing else. An ironing board was folded into a wall of the closet, but there was no iron in sight. Apparently, Rankins simply folded his laundry without pressing anything.

From the small bedroom, a single window covered by white lace curtains looked out to an alley separating the building they were in from the unit next to it. The furnishings were as stark as those of the rest of the apartment—a maple bed, a dresser and a straight-backed chair next to the bed. On the seat of the chair was a ghetto blaster, a large radio-tape player with amplifiers at either end. A cardboard carton under the chair was filled with tapes in plastic containers. Maharos used his foot to move the chair so they could get a better view of the tapes. Most were unlabeled, but on a few of the plastic containers, labels had been pasted.

Vandergrift bent down and turned her head sideways to decipher the crude hand-lettering of the labels. She read off several: "'Kings,' 'Psalms', 'Proverbs'..."

Maharos said, "I haven't been to Sunday School in over a week, but aren't those the books of the Bible?"

Vandergrift said, "Uh-huh. Looks like our boy's into religion."

"Or religion is into him."

A closet in the bedroom held a dark blue suit and three pairs of jeans. Two black ties hung on a tie rack fastened to the closet door. On the floor of the closet were a pair of black shoes shined to a high gloss. Vandergrift pointed to the clothing. "Looks like he goes either to work or to funerals."

Maharos said, "Funerals *are* his work."

A high shelf in the closet held a small pile of what appeared to be dirty laundry. Maharos stood on his toes and peered into the back of the shelf. Although there was no light in the closet, he made out a pile of dark blue wool that could have been a sweater. He resisted the temptation to pluck a few strands of the wool and run a test of them against the fibers found at the scenes of several of the murders. He was almost certain they would match, but he was too good a cop to risk blowing his case by obtaining evidence in this manner. He'd have to come back with a warrant.

As he started to follow Warner out of the bedroom, from the corner of his eye he saw Vandergrift bend, reaching toward the shoes on the closet floor. He half-turned and shook his head vigorously. She got the message, straightened up and followed him back into the living room. She said, "Mind if I use the bathroom for a minute?"

Warner said, "Go ahead."

She closed the bathroom door and scrutinized the room. Two towels hung on a wall bar. She pushed aside the shower curtain over the bathtub. A cake of soap sat in a soap dish. Nothing unusual. The medicine cabinet held a razor, shaving cream, toothbrush and toothpaste and a small bottle of aspirin. On the back of the top shelf, a brown bottle was filled to the top with tablets labeled "Young's Pharmacy," with an Akron address, and typed instructions which read, "Take one tablet twice a day." The lower left hand portion of the label identified the medication as Lithium Carbonate, 300 mg. Typed in the opposite corner was the expiration date, four years ago. Vandergrift vaguely recalled that lithium was used to treat certain forms of psychosis. She didn't need the pharmacopoeia to know that the medicine had no physiologic effect on the brain while it sat on the medicine cabinet shelf. She flushed the toilet and walked back to the living room.

Warner was nervously glancing from one of the officers to the other. "Come on. You've seen all you need to see. Let's get out of here."

Maharos was in the kitchen. He called to Vandergrift and wordlessly indicated the calendar hanging on the wall. July 7 was enclosed in a large red crayon circle.

THIRTY-ONE

THEY ASSEMBLED AT seven AM the next day, the seventh of July, in a room in Stark County Sheriff's Headquarters. Two rows of folding chairs faced a chart on an easel.

Sheriff Sherman McAllister's chair was next to the easel. A small wooden desk in front of him was clear except for a chipped coffee cup that said in large letters, "I'm The Chief—That's Why." He nodded to Maharos seated in the front row facing him.

"Maharos, you've been on top of this case longer than the rest of us. This is a cooperative operation. Why don't you make the assignments."

Maharos stood alongside the chart, opposite McAllister. Seated facing him were Vandergrift; Ike Show; Les Cassidy, a Youngstown patrol officer on temporary assignment to Maharos' investigation; Detective Lon Kinkaid from the Canton PD; and two other uniformed sheriff deputies of the Stark County unit, Don Grimes and Walt O'Malley.

Maharos spent fifteen minutes reviewing the homicides and the evidence implicating Rankins. Although most of those present were familiar with the case, he felt it would do no harm to refresh their memories. Kinkaid and the Stark County deputies were hearing some of the details for the first time. They sat with pads on their knees, making notes as Maharos spoke. "We've got a lot of manpower for this operation. In addition to those of us here, Officer Matt Clemens and another uniform of the Massillon PD have been staked out at Rankins' place since last night."

Detectives Frank Fiala and Sam Emerson of the Youngstown squad had spent the preceding day canvassing labs in a search for Rankins. When Maharos reported that the suspect had been located in Massillon, the two detectives were recalled by Bragg to their regular duties.

To the unit assembled in Canton, Maharos said, "We're using a lot of people, but we expect this will be a short operation."

Kinkaid said, "How short?"

"Based on his pattern, one day. Today."

Les Cassidy said, "He never showed at his place last night, did he?"

"No."

"Do we know what he's driving?"

"No. His employer says he doesn't have a car. There's no current BMV registration under Wiliams or Rankins. We've tried some variations of the names. No luck."

Maharos looked around the room. There were no more questions. He pointed to the chart. "Show, you'll be on the stakeout at Rankins' apartment in Massillon, along with Clemens and the other local officer—I believe his name is Conrad. The three of you can work out how you want to do it, but I want at least two of you there all the time."

Show said, "In the apartment?"

"We got a court order to get inside, so two of you will be in Rankins' apartment. The other member of the surveillance unit will be downstairs in Mr. Warner's apartment. He's the building owner. He's moved out for the next forty-eight hours to let us use the place. We've also arranged for the other tenants to stay somewhere else until this operation is over. You'll be in radio communication with each other, of course. Work out a schedule so one at a time can get relief. Here are the directions to the apartment building. You'll find Clemens and his partner there. One of them is in Rankins' apartment the other is in Warner's place now." Maharos handed Show a piece of paper.

Show leaned back in his chair, the corner of his mouth turned up. "Think the three of us are enough to handle him?"

Maharos glared at Show's face. For ten seconds he did not speak. Then, quietly, "We don't need that. If you want out, say so now." He looked steadily at Show in silence for another ten seconds. Show said nothing. His eyes dropped to the floor. The smirk stayed on his lips.

Maharos returned to the chart. "Detective Kinkaid will be in Dr. Marino's home. Mrs. Marino has agreed to remain in the house all day with the children. Lon, your watch will last until about six when Dr. Marino gets home. Deputy Vandergrift and I will be with him all day, while he's making rounds at St. Agnes Hospital and seeing patients in his office. We'll stick with him after he gets home, so you'll be relieved."

McAllister said, "So, Dr. Marino is business as usual?"

Maharos nodded. "He insisted on it. In a way, it may turn out best for us."

"You mean he's bait?"

Maharos half-smiled. "I wouldn't have put it quite like that. Vandergrift and I will be staying close by the doctor, but in the background. We don't want to spook Rankins, but we do want him to make his move. That's the only way we're going to force him out in the open where we can get him."

"Assuming Dr. Marino is the target."

"Yes sir, that's our assumption."

Maharos went back to the planning board. "Grimes and O'Malley will be in a surveillance van parked in the driveway of the house next door to the. Marino home. We found a place there where they'll have a good view of both the front and back of the house.

McAllister said, "What about the people next door. Is the surveillance going to bother them?"

"No. They're out of town. In fact, they asked the Marinos to keep an eye on their place."

Maharos pointed to Les Cassidy's name on the chart. "Cassidy, you're going to be our communications coordinator. You'll be here in Canton. We've got two lines cleared so you'll be in contact with the unit in Massillon, and with Detective Kinkaid and the deputies in the van. Vandergrift and I will be in touch with you at regular intervals until this is over. You can beep us at any time." He paused and walked to the center of the room. "You're all experienced in this sort of thing. I know it's him against all of us, but he's smart and he's dangerous. The fact that he didn't show at his place last night probably means he knows we're looking for him. Maybe he's running now and won't try for another victim. But don't count on it. Be careful."

He stood waiting for questions, then signaled that the meeting was over.

* * *

The doctor's lounge in the surgery suite at St. Agnes Hospital was a room about fifteen by twenty feet, walls painted a light beige. The furnishings were a couch covered in brown vinyl and four matching chairs; a coffee urn and a stack of Styrofoam cups occupied a small table in the corner. A door at the back of the lounge led to the locker-filled dressing room where the surgeons changed into scrub suits before entering the operating rooms.

Vandergrift sat on the couch next to Maharos waiting for Dr. Marino to come out of the OR. She was out of uniform, dressed in light tan slacks and a plain white blouse, a gold chain at her neck. She carried a large shoulder purse that held her service revolver. Maharos wore what he called his FBI outfit, a striped gray seersucker suit, blue tie with regimental maroon stripes.

The staff doctors who wandered in and out of the lounge nodded pleasantly to them, and they nodded back. Marino had told them, "If anybody asks, just say you're waiting for me. I have docs visiting me from other hospitals all the time."

An hour after he had left them, Marino came bustling into the lounge. His green scrub suit was blood-stained, his cloth shoe covers caked with plaster of Paris. The surgeon ripped off his paper mask and cap, tossed them into a wastebasket. He flopped wearily into a chair and blew out a deep breath. "Tough case. Let me grab a cup of coffee and I'll get dressed."

Fifteen minutes later, Marino, in street clothes covered by a long white coat, walked briskly toward the wards to make rounds. Maharos and Vandergrift tagged a few steps behind him. On each of the wards they waited at the nurses' station while he went from room to room accompanied by a nurse pulling a rack of charts. At the X-ray Department they watched Marino view some x-ray films and scans with one of the radiologists. By eleven-thirty, the doctor had retrieved his suit jacket from the doctor's coat room and the three were making their way to the hospital parking lot.

Maharos and Vandergrift in an unmarked blue Oldsmobile followed Marino who was weaving his tan BMW in and out of traffic as though trying to lose them. They pulled into the parking lot next to his office building as he was getting out of his car. Marino entered through a door in the back of the building and Vandergrift started to follow him, but Maharos grabbed her sleeve. "Hold it. We'll take the patients' entrance in front. I don't know if Rankins is watching, but in case he is, we're patients."

Vandergrift said, "Shouldn't I limp a little?"

"Careful, or I'll have him put you in a body cast."

The two officers were shown into a small room used by the office staff for coffee and food breaks. They helped themselves to lunch from a well-stocked refrigerator while Dr. Marino, who said he never ate lunch, was busy with a stream of patients that had filled the waiting room. At one point he stuck his head in the door. "See why I just couldn't run off and hide? Most of these people have had appointments for over a month."

In Massillon, Show pulled his Chevrolet behind the dark blue Ford with the antenna jutting from the top, parked at the curb across the street from the entrance to Rankins' building. In the lobby, he pushed the call button to Warner's apartment. A sandy-haired man in a sport shirt came to the vestibule door and peered through the glass. Show noticed that the man had his right hand at his hip under the sport shirt. He flashed his shield. "I'm Ike Show, Youngstown PD.. You expecting me?"

The man relaxed, smiled and brought his right hand up from his hip as he opened the door. He said, "Hi. I'm Joe Conrad." He reached to his back pocket and brought out a wallet. He flipped it open to show his Massillon PD shield. "Yeah. They told us you were coming. My partner, Matt Clemens, is upstairs."

Show said, "The guy—what's-his-name, Rankins—never showed?"

"Not yet."

"He won't."

Conrad stared at Show.

Show went on, "Guy's probably long gone out of here. This stakeout's a waste of everybody's time."

Conrad shrugged. "I sure hope so."

"I'm going up."

"Okay. I'll tell Matt to let you in. Apartment 4, upstairs." He unclipped a walkie-talkie from his belt and spoke into it while Show went upstairs.

Five minutes later, Matt Clemens, in a Hawaiian sport shirt long enough to cover the small automatic in a clip-on belt holster, came downstairs and knocked on the door of Warner's apartment. When Conrad let him in, he flopped into a chair. "Show's gonna stay in the apartment while you grab something to eat. I'll hold down this end until you get back."

"Okay. He don't think much of this operation."

"I know. He told me. Maybe he's right."

Conrad said, "Did you tell him to keep an eye on the back of the building from the kitchen window?"

"Uh-huh."

"Think he will?"

Clemens shrugged.

Conrad passed Clemens the walkie-talkie. "I'll be at Wendy's."

Clemens watched through the window that looked out on the front of the building as his partner walked up Fern Street. Wendy's restaurant was two blocks away on Castle. Show's indifferent attitude had annoyed him. Maybe the boredom was natural after you had waited through a number of stakeouts. Clemens was relatively new to the routine.

Detective Lon Kinkaid sat in Kim Marino's kitchen. He was reading the Canton paper, occasionally glancing up to look out the window that faced a spacious backyard. He wore a short-sleeved shirt. His tie was dragged down and the top shirt button open. His shoulder holster held a Colt .38, something which had the Marino children fascinated from the moment he'd taken off his sport coat. On the table in front of him, a walkie-talkie cackled from time to time as the crew in the surveillance van reported. Earlier, he had stood on the back porch watching the three Marino boys playing on a swing and slide set and crawling in and out of a log cabin playhouse. Now they were in the basement recreation room watching TV cartoons. Kim Marino was at the stove in a pair of shorts, a halter and an apron. She said, "I suppose there's something good in everything. Since I've been confined to this house arrest, I've gotten a lot of junk cleaned out of drawers. Things I hadn't looked at in years."

Kinkaid said, "Whatever you're cooking smells awfully good."

"It's chicken cacciatore. I got the recipe from Russ' mother."

"You a *paison* too?"

"You kidding? With this face? No, I was little Kimberly Murphy before. . ."

The static and hiss of the walkie-talkie broke in. "Check the side door, Lon. It's open."

Kinkaid was out of his chair and ran to the door that opened to the driveway from the basement. He turned the knob and the door opened. "Shit!"

Kim Marino was alongside, her eyes wide open. "What's wrong?"

"The crew in the van reported that the side door was open. I put the dead bolt on. Someone unlocked it." He ran down the basement steps. Seated in front of the screen were the two younger boys.

He shouted. "Where's your brother?"

The two boys looked up, frightened by Kinkaid's loud voice. The three-year-old began to cry. The five-year-old sat on his haunches, his mouth open.

Kinkaid shouted again. "Where's—" He had forgotten the name of the other boy.

The five-year-old shrugged without speaking and stuck his thumb in his mouth.

Kim Marino had followed Kinkaid. She grabbed the older of the two by the shoulders. "Where's Victor?"

The boy wailed. "I don't know!"

Kinkaid said, "Mrs. Marino, if you'll look through the rest of the basement and check upstairs, I'll look outside."

He grabbed the walkie-talkie from the kitchen table and ran out the side door, talking into the two-way radio. "Dog one, did you see the kid leave?"

"Negative, dog two. The door opened a crack and closed. There's a hedge that covers our view of the lower half of that door."

Kinkaid glanced up and down the driveway. Victor was not in sight. He ran to the front of the house. The boy was not there. He ran around to the back. The backyard was separated by a picket fence from the house behind it which faced the next street. The sides of the backyard were enclosed by low boxwood hedges. He ran to both sides and checked the yards of the adjacent houses but did not spot the boy. As he passed by the log cabin playhouse, he looked through one of the small windows. Seated on the floor, reading a comic book, was Victor.

The boy looked up and smiled. "Hi, Detective. Did you come out to play with me?"

Kinkaid blew out a deep breath. "Not right now, kid. Come on back in the house., okay?"

THIRTY-TWO

EPHRAIM RANKINS thought he had gone blind. Around him was blackness. It took him a moment to remember that he had been asleep on the floor in the back of the van. He was parked five miles south of Massillon, in woods off Richville Drive, on what was little more than a dirt path . He had driven there last night, cautious about returning to his apartment after spotting Clemens' patrol car in front. The police car was gone when he drove by again, but instinct told him to be wary now that he was so close to his goal.

His supper, a fried fish sandwich, lay half-eaten on the dash, even more tasteless now than when he had bought it last night at the drive-in window of a fast-food joint. Now he was hungry and thirsty.

A rooster's crow from a farm half a mile away told him that dawn was about to break. He got up, stretched and relieved himself outside the van.

He knew he would have to move soon. Even though he was in a remote rural woods, he wasn't sure who might come by at daybreak. After the sun crept over the horizon, he drove toward a country general store he had passed on the road near Richville, three miles back. He waited twenty minutes until the storekeeper, a wizened man in his seventies unlocked the door and grunted a good morning. The old man looked quizzically over the wire-rimmed glasses that hung low on his nose. "You ain't from around here, are you, sonny?"

"No."

"Didn't think so. Seen them Pennsylvania plates. Where you from?"

"Pittsburgh."

Rankins helped himself to a quart of milk and a package of sliced ham from the refrigerator case and brought the items to the counter along with a loaf of bread. After he had paid, the storekeeper waved him off. "Drive careful."

Rankins headed east, and soon he was entering the northbound ramp to I-77. He drove to a highway rest stop and parked between a motor home and a truck. His breakfast consisted of a ham sandwich washed down with the milk. He remained parked in the rest area throughout the morning and early afternoon. Periodically, he got out of the van and strolled through the nearby fields and woods. Every hour or so a state highway patrol car pulled in and parked for a few minutes. Through the back window of the van, Rankins observed the officers get out of the cars and stretch or go to the men's room. The green van with the Pennsylvania plates caused the highway patrolmen no more concern than any of the other summer tourist vehicles passing along I-77.

Remember your mission. Today's the Day.

He was seated in the driver's seat now, and waved an impatient hand toward the back of the van. "I know, I know."

Do you have everything you'll need?

"Not everything."

The sacrificial instrument?

"The gun?"

The gun. It's back in the apartment, isn't it?

"Yeah."

You'll have to go back there and get it, won't you?

"Uh-huh."

Well, do it. And be careful. They're watching.

He nodded.

They're watching. They're watching...

Rankins maneuvered the van out of the space he had occupied for more than eight hours and drove back toward Massillon.

At ten minutes to six, Dr. Russell Marino followed his last patient out of an examining room. He stopped by at the staff lounge and said to Maharos and Vandergrift, "I'll dictate some notes and be ready to leave in fifteen minutes."

During the day, Maharos and Vandergrift had taken turns walking out of the office and surveying the surrounding area. The building occupied by the orthopaedic surgeons, was one of several small look-alike professional buildings on the street. On their walks, neither Maharos or Vandergrift had seen anyone or anything unusual. Yet, Vandergrift told Maharos she had the feeling that they were being watched. He shrugged. "I never discount a woman's intuition, but my signals tell me we're striking out."

"You don't think he'll make a move?"

"I don't know *what* to think at this point. We've still got a long way to go to get through the day."

He reflected that all but one of the previous murders had occurred after dark. In early July, that would be past nine o'clock.

At six-fifteen, they walked to their cars in the parking lot. Vandergrift rode in the BMW with Marino. Maharos followed them to the house.

Kim Marino passed the platter to Maharos. "Finish the rest of this. Chicken cacciatore is no good left over."

He held up a palm. "Thanks. It's delicious. But I can't eat another mouthful. I've already had three helpings."

Marino said, "Where'd your partner disappear to?"

"She's checking the house."

"Again?"

"That's why we're here."

Vandergrift came back into the dining room and sat down. For the third time that evening she had checked the doors and windows from basement to attic to make sure they had not been tampered with. She wore the same outfit she'd had since morning, but her blouse was no longer tucked in. Under it, her service revolver, in a narrow belt holster, was discreetly covered.

Maharos had never seen her so nervous. "Everything locked up?"

"Tighter than Fort Knox."

DEAD END

They were drinking coffee when Dr. Marino said, "I brought home some work. If you'll excuse me, I'll go up to my study and dictate some reports."

Vandergrift said. "Would it disturb you if I went with you? I promise I'll keep my mouth shut."

"Come on along."

Maharos said, "I'll wander around the house." He spoke softly into the walkie-talkie he carried. "All secure inside. How about you?"

The voice from the surveillance van came over the speaker, "All quiet."

Maharos carefully examined every door and window. Houdini would not have been able to pierce the defense they had set up. But Maharos was worried.

Ike Show sat in the kitchen of Rankins' Massillon apartment facing a window. The view from the second floor apartment, gave him a clear look at the alley behind the building. Directly below him was a back door to the building which Clemens had checked and found to be locked. Anyone who wanted to use the back door would have to approach it from the alley. There was even a spotlight mounted over the door to be turned on after dark. In plain view was the row of garages that lined the alley. He could also see a half block down Fern, the street that ran along the north side of the building.

It was only five-thirty. Still a lot of daylight left.

Show sat with the chair tilted, balanced on its two back legs. His feet were propped on the window sill. In one hand he held the walkie-talkie, in the other, a porn novel in paperback.

The scratchy sound of the two-way radio speaker interrupted his reading. "Unit One. Suspicious person approaching your building."

"Ten-four."

For the fifth time since he had been in the apartment, the surveillance team downstairs had called in a "suspicious person" sighting.

A few moments later, "All clear." Again.

These dumb shitheads were nervous as fifteen year-old-kids in a whorehouse. "Come on, you guys. Knock it off."

Downstairs in Warner's apartment, Clemens said to his partner, "That prick is getting on my nerves."

Conrad said, "Fuck him. I'm gonna call what I see."

Show had insisted that only one person, himself, was needed in Rankins' apartment. He had sent Clemens downstairs. Told him if two people were needed anywhere, it should be in Warner's apartment. When Clemens had objected Show said, "You ever been staked-out?"

"This is my second."

"Look, I been on so fuckin' many a these things I got one eye shaped like a keyhole. If this guy shows, which I doubt, the only way he's gonna get upstairs is from downstairs. Don't it make sense to have two guys downstairs, where you can innercep' no matter which door the guy uses?"

Clemens had said, "I wasn't at the briefing this morning, but seems to me—"

"Well I *was* at the briefing, so don't sweat it."

Clemens wasn't entirely convinced but he wasn't secure enough to question the more experienced man's judgment.

Now Show was calling on his walkie-talkie. "Hey. I'm gettin' hungry. How about picking up a hamburger and a Coke for me."

Clemens said, "Want relief?"

"Nah. I'll stay here. Bring it up."

Clemens clicked off. "Bastard treats us like flunkies, 'Bring it up.' I oughta tell him blow it up his ass."

Conrad said, "I'll go. I'm getting hungry myself. Want something?"

Clemens shook his head. "I'll go when you get back."

Carrying a paper sack with Show's burger and coke, Joe Conrad walked into the apartment house vestibule. He unlocked the inner door with the key Warner had given him, and walked up the flight of stairs. At the door to Rankins' apartment, he pressed the doorbell. He heard the deadbolt slide. Show opened the door, took the sack and peered into it.

He nodded. Conrad noticed that he didn't offer a word of thanks. "Did I get it right?"

Show recognized the sarcastic tone. He looked into Conrad's face. "Somethin' crawl up your ass?"

"Fuck you, Show." Conrad turned and heard the door slam behind him. He stopped for a moment at the head of the stairs, listening for the deadbolt to click into place. This time he heard nothing, shrugged and continued downstairs.

Rankins parked the van on Fern Street, a block from his apartment building. By walking close to the houses that faced Fern, he could not see the window of his kitchen, nor could he be seen from there—until he reached the alley that ran behind his building. When he crossed the alley, a distance of twenty feet, he would be in the open.

As he approached the alley, his kitchen window came into view. His heart pounded. Someone was in the apartment He watched the person walk to the window, peer out in his direction and disappear from view. Had he been spotted? Rankins stood still, his sweaty hands balled into fists. Like a cornered animal, he sensed that he would be less conspicuous motionless. He heard the front vestibule door slam and a moment later, a man wearing a flowered sport shirt appeared at the corner of the apartment building. Rankins tensed, ready to run back to the van.

You're not backing out now. You're too close to getting it all. You can do it. Do it!

He watched, not moving, not blinking, not breathing, as the man in the loud shirt kept walking along Bridges, away from where he stood and continued east. Upstairs, the figure again appeared at the window, his back turned.

Rankins took a deep breath and sprinted across the alley.

In the upstairs apartment, Show was taking his sandwich and Coke container out of the Wendy's paper sack. Another boring, fucking stakeout that would end up a big zero. At least he wasn't going to be hungry.

Rankins was at the back door; key in his hand. The same key that opened the inner vestibule at the front door, also unlocked the back door. In seconds, he was inside.

He stood for a moment on a small landing just inside the back door, then crept silently down the stairs to the basement. In the dark he felt his way, along a row of storage lockers, in the direction of a second stairway which led to a door to the inner lobby. His hands touched a railing and he knew he had found it. The door at the top of the staircase unlocked with the same key he had used to open the back door. From the inner lobby, Rankins passed the door to Warner's apartment, quietly went up the carpeted staircase to the second floor.

Rankins stood outside his apartment and put his ear to the door but heard nothing.

He carefully put his key in the upper keyhole, hoping to minimize the noise of the sliding deadbolt by turning it slowly. But the key would not turn. The deadbolt wasn't locked! The second latch, a simple spring lock above the doorknob responded noiselessly to his key. He turned the knob and slowly cracked open the door. Peering inside, he could make out the back of a man seated in the kitchen, facing the window. One hand held a sandwich, the other a large soft drink container, a straw stuck out of the top.

Rankins bent low and moved into the living room. The slight squeak of his rubber-soled shoes on the uncarpeted hardwood floor, was obscured by the slurp of the soft drink passing through the straw in the man's mouth.

Rankins crept toward the kitchen. Now he was at the doorway between the living room and the kitchen. His body still in the living room, Rankins reached around the doorjamb, his fingers groping toward a rack of knives mounted on a magnetic plate. Noiselessly, he removed the largest knife, an eight-inch blade. He gripped the handle until his knuckles were white. Now, Rankins told himself. Do it now. He started moving into the kitchen, feeling as though the tension inside him would burst out The man in the chair chewed noisily.

Slowly—he moved a millimeter at a time. Now he was three feet behind his prey. Now two feet.

"UNIT ONE. SUSPICIOUS PERSON APPROACHING."

THIRTY-THREE

THE SUDDEN BLARE of the speaker made Rankins jump back into the living room.

Every muscle taut, he watched as the man in the kitchen picked up the walkie-talkie from the table. "What is it now, some kid on a bicycle?"

"Show, it's a man getting out of a blue Honda in front of the building."

The man put down the walkie-talkie, went back to chewing on his sandwich. A few moments later, the tinny voice came through the speaker again. "Cancel the suspicious person alert. It's a guy going next door."

Rankins watched the man they called Show speak into the radio-phone. "Listen, I'm eating. Don't bother me unless you see some dude walking up the front steps with an assault rifle, you hear?"

He slammed the radio-phone on the table and went back to his hamburger.

Rankins drew the knife across the man's neck and watched the mouthful of food he had just swallowed drop through the slit in his throat that extended from one ear to the other. The wad of hamburger dropped from the opening in his esophagus and plopped to his chest before landing in his lap. His eyelids flew open and his eyes turned up until only the whites were exposed. A double jet of crimson pulsed out of his neck and splattered the window he was facing. His hands clawed at the air, and in slow motion he toppled from the chair, landing with a thud on his side on the kitchen floor.

Rankins carried the knife to the sink. He rinsed it and dried it as though he were cleaning up after a meal. As he walked back to the bedroom, he barely glanced at the body that writhed in terminal agony. He carried with him a thin-bladed screw driver that he had taken from a kitchen cabinet drawer.

At the bedroom closet he knelt and, with the screw driver, pried up a floorboard. Reaching into the space below the floor, he retrieved the small semi-automatic pistol and placed it his trouser pocket.

He left the apartment building the same way he had entered. As he walked down Fern toward his parked van, he turned, glanced up at the kitchen window, now streaked with red rivulets.

Clemens said, "Maybe there's something wrong with his radio?"

"Nah," said Conrad. "I'll bet the prick is just being stubborn. Plus he doesn't want me reminding him that he still owes me for his lunch."

"Jesus, it's been over an hour since we heard from him."

"Let's wait another fifteen minutes. If he doesn't answer I'll go up. Probably wake the bastard." Conrad leaned back in the chair, laced his hands behind his head. "So, anyway, this broad is comin' onto me like I'm fuckin' Prince or someone. . ."

Vandergrift put down the magazine she was reading and folded her hands in her lap. Across the room, Dr. Marino was talking into his dictating machine, several charts spread out on the desk in front of him. He stopped and glanced over at Vandergrift. "Bored?"

"Huh? Oh, I'm just thinking."

"Here, want something to read while you're waiting?" He picked a manila folder from his desk. "I brought home Rankins' records. Thought I might go over them. So far, I haven't had the chance."

Vandergrift shrugged. "Okay, but is it all right if I interrupt you for questions? I probably won't make much out of the medical terminology."

"I don't think you'll have trouble understanding it. Mostly these reports are in straightforward English. Maybe a little jargon. Sure, yell if you get stuck."

She reached forward to take the chart. He said, "Of course, this is confidential doctor-patient material, but under the circumstances. . ."

She smiled and raised her right hand. "I swear it won't go any further than this room—unless it turns out to be juicy, in which case I'll only tell the rest of the guys on my shift."

Marino went back to his dictating, and Vandergrift started to read the records.

The first several pages of typed and dated notations labeled "Initial History and Physical Exam," related the onset of Rankins' back problem to the lifting injury he sustained while working at the feed store. His treatment by Dr. Long in New Philadelphia was summarized and followed by the progression of symptoms leading to his first visit to Dr. Marino's office. The description of the physical exam included terms Vandergrift did not understand, but she could figure out their meanings from the context.

The next page was a report headed "Stark Medical Imaging Laboratory." She skimmed over the details of the MRI scan, focused her attention on the conclusion: "Probable herniated nucleus pulposus, L4-5, left with compression of nerve root."

"What's a 'nucleus pulposus'?"

Marino said, "That's the disk between two vertebrae. Actually, it's the central part of the disk, the softest part and is the part that ruptures."

"I see."

The sheet headed, "Report of Operation" was replete with medical terms. Apparently, the ruptured nucleus pulposus had been removed, but the details of the operation were beyond Vandergrift. In the final paragraph, the patient "left the OR in stable condition." She smiled as she pictured the patient walking out of the operating room, waving goodbye.

A discharge summary from St. Agnes Hospital repeated, in abbreviated form, Rankins' condition on admission, and confirmed that the herniated disk was found at the time of surgery which was performed without complication.

A paragraph in the summary caught Vandergrift's attention. She read it through twice, finally glanced up at Marino. "What's a p-h-i-m-o-s-i-s?"

His brow furrowed. "A what?"

She repeated the spelling.

"Oh, a *phimosis*. That's an inflammation of the foreskin over the head of the penis. Where the hell did you get that term?"

She pointed at the record. "In here. It says, 'The patient's postoperative course was complicated by development of a phimosis. The patient was seen in consultation by a urologist, who performed a dorsal slit relieving the constricted foreskin. This was followed by a circumcision two days later.'"

Marino held out his hand. "Let me see that."

She passed him the chart open at the page she had read. He turned a few pages scanning quickly. Still reading the record, he said, "I had forgotten all about that. Sure, Rankins had some difficulty urinating after the operation, which is not that unusual. He was catheterized and probably got the phimosis from all the manipulation."

"So the catheter caused it?"

Marino became defensive. "Well, it was uncleanliness on his part that really caused it. He didn't clean the space between the head of his penis and the foreskin over it. The catheterization was a factor, of course."

Vandergrift said, "What's a 'dorsal slit'?"

"It's a little operation that slits the foreskin over the head of the penis. Like opening the seam of a dress to make more room."

"Ouch!"

"Under local anesthesia, of course."

"Of course. Then he was circumcised to prevent it from happening again, I guess."

Marino grinned. "Congratulations. You're eligible for your degree—A.A.D."

"A.A.D.?"

"Also A Doctor."

Vandergrift laughed. "By the way, who was the urologist who did all this?"

Marino referred to the pages in front of him, "Hal Schneider —Dr. Harold Schneider."

"Did Rankins have much contact—" The phone on Marino's desk rang. Vandergrift stopped in midsentence, but the surgeon made no move. After the ringing stopped, he explained. "Kim would have picked it up downstairs. I signed out to my partner so there shouldn't be any medical calls tonight. Sometimes people will call me at home, and it's difficult for me to tell them I'm not on call."

Maharos entered without knocking. The grim look on his face spoke of trouble. Quietly he said, "He got Show."

THIRTY-FOUR

VANDERGRIFT LOOKED PUZZLED. "Show?"
"The Vice detective they assigned to us."
"My God! What happened?"
Maharos relayed the details he had gotten from Cassidy in the communications center, who had been advised of the homicide by Clemens at the Massillon stakeout. "It means Rankins is on the loose and he's still in the area. No doubt of it now."
Vandergrift was gazing at a blank spot on the wall behind Marino's desk. Maharos caught her far away look. "Something?"
Slowly she turned to face her partner. "I wonder if we're guarding the right person."
Maharos cocked his head, waited for her to continue.
"I've just been going over Dr. Marino's record of Rankins." She repeated the story about the phimosis and the subsequent operations to correct it.
Dr. Marino broke in. "Wait a minute." He leafed rapidly through the chart. "Yeah, here it is." He looked up. "I don't know why I didn't think of this before. The last time I saw Rankins for a follow-up, his back was okay, but he looked more depressed than usual. He said something about losing his manhood. I was quite sure the back operation hadn't caused him to become impotent. But just to be certain I sent him back to Dr. Schneider. Hal ran some tests and told me that the guy had *always* been impotent. I remember Hal telling me that even after he reassured Rankins that none of the operations had caused his impotence, he didn't seem convinced. He wanted to blame *someone*."

Maharos and Vandergrift exchanged glances. Maharos' mind was racing. Loss of his manhood! A motive? You've got it!

"Where is Dr. Schneider?"

Marino said, "Probably at home."

"Can you get him on the phone?"

Marino pulled a thin book from a shelf alongside his desk. Rapidly he flipped the pages. "I've got his home number. He jotted the number on a pad, picked up the phone and punched in some digits. He sat for a few seconds, the phone cradled at his shoulder. "Naomi?. . .Hi. Russ Marino. Can I talk to Hal?. . .Where?. . .St. Agnes?. . .He went there directly from the office?" Marino glanced at his watch. "It's after nine. You mean he hasn't been home yet?. . .No, that's all right. I'll see if I can reach him at the hospital. Thanks."

He disconnected the call without removing the receiver from his shoulder and immediately punched in more numbers. While waiting to be connected, he looked up at the officers. "He had an emergency at St. Agnes. His wife thinks he's still in surgery."

Maharos fidgeted. Vandergrift held up crossed fingers.

Marino was speaking into the phone. "Dr. Schneider, please, this is Dr. Marino. . .What time did he sign out?. . .Try the OR anyway."

He glanced up at Maharos. "He signed out of the hospital at eight-ten. . . OR?. . .Is Dr. Schneider still there?. . .I see. Thanks." He shook his head.

Maharos flicked the switch on the walkie-talkie he held. "I want one of you in here, stat. The other remain in place."

"Ten-four."

He turned to Marino. "Get back to Dr. Schneider's wife.. Ask her what car her husband was driving and the license number. If he has a car phone, get the number."

Marino punched the phone keypad. While he waited for the connection he said, "I know he drives a fairly new white Cadillac Seville. He has a vanity license plate, 'PP DOC'."

Vandergrift's brows went up. "How would you remember his licen— Oh, he's a urologist, right? Real cutesy."

DEAD END

Marino's call to Schneider's home was connected. "Naomi, Russ again. Was Hal driving his Caddy?. . .Uh-huh. Does he have a car phone?. . .Great. What's the number?. . .Uh-huh. . .Oh, you did. When did you try last?. . ."

He put his hand over the mouthpiece. "She tried to call him on the car phone and got no answer, twice." He spoke into the phone. "No, he wasn't at the hospital. . .Yeah, probably on his way. Well I'm anxious to reach him. If—When he comes home, please have him call me right away. I'm home." He started to hang up, kept the receiver to his ear, listening. "What time was that?. . .Okay, thanks." He hung up, turned to Maharos. "She thought she heard the automatic garage door open and close around eight-thirty. When Hal didn't come into the house, Naomi looked into the garage, saw the Caddy wasn't there, decided she had been mistaken."

Maharos grabbed the phone. He punched in the number of the communications center at Stark County Sheriff's Office and waited while his call was connected. "Cassidy?. . .Get the sheriff's helicopter in the air. I want the pilot to cruise I-77. Start south of Canton for about twenty miles, then proceed north. He's to look for a white Cadillac Seville. Ohio tags: PP DOC. Got that?. . .Next, call highway patrol. Have them alert all units. The car we're looking for is probably on I-77. If they spot it, have them trail it along with the 'copter. Have them hold fire, repeat, hold fire. Either the driver or the passenger is our perp, Wiliams The other is a hostage. Right now we don't know which is which. Wiliams is armed and extremely dangerous. Vandergrift and I are leaving Dr. Marino's and we're heading for I-77. Keep in touch with my car. The sheriff's surveillance team will keep cover on the Marinos. Got all that?" He listened for a few moments, hung up and gestured with his chin for Vandergrift to follow as he sprinted for the stairs. He called over his shoulder to Marino, "Keep trying the car phone. If you get him, advise my man— Les Cassidy at Stark County Sheriff's office." He was already out of the front door and headed for his car, Vandergrift a step behind.

State Highway Patrol Officer Chuck Schulte in car 86 was parked on the right shoulder of I-77 just past the Portage Street entrance ramp. Elbow resting on the open window frame, he monitored the northbound traffic. Just past nine on a Tuesday evening, there were relatively few cars. The sun had set an hour before. He looked up at the sky. Rain was predicted for the next day. It was already muggy.

He glanced at his watch, calculated how long before he would head for the barn. Miller time. Sandy digging in the refrigerator for his beer. Cold sweat on the outside of the can, the icy fluid on his tongue.

The static of the two-way radio speaker broke into Schulte's thoughts. "All units I-77. On the lookout for a late model white Cadillac Seville. Ohio tags: PPDOC, repeat Peter-peter-dog-otto-cat. Suspect is armed and dangerous. Hostage aboard. Trail and report but do not, repeat, do not fire. Air search will assist."

Schulte acknowledged into his dashboard microphone.

He did not have long to wait. The ninth car to pass after the call was a white Cadillac traveling in the number two lane at an unhurried pace. The highway patrolman almost missed it., because a semi traveling in the right lane, passed Schulte at the same time. He spoke into the microphone as his patrol car pulled onto the road. His eyes were fixed on the Cadillac's red taillights two cars ahead as he reported his location. With Cassidy's acknowledgment came the caution—no flasher, no siren.

Twenty miles to the north, in the Akron area, State Highway Patrol Officer Ham Fisher in Car 92 was cruising south on I-77. He heard Schulte report a visual on the Caddy. He went on full burner, racing to meet Schulte and the car he trailed.

Dr. Harold Schneider lay face down on the floor behind the driver's seat. His hands, bound tightly behind his back, were already numb. His feet were bound at the ankles and a rag was tied across his mouth. He had no idea how long he had been there. When he'd first regained consciousness, the bumpiness of the road and the occasional stop and start of the car told him they were traveling on city streets. Some time later the ride became smooth, the car no longer made stops. This could only mean a highway.

Who had done this to him? Why? The urologist vaguely remembered getting out of the car in his garage, then coming to tied up on the car floor. He wasn't even sure whether he had been knocked out or if he had fainted., although the back of his head was tender where it rested on the floor.

Schneider tried to yell. His cries, muffled by the gag, were met with silence from whoever was in the driver's seat. He'd strained his neck to try to see over the back of the front seat, but finally had given up. Schneider knew he was in trouble. Had he been robbed? When he could think more clearly, he realized that this was not a simple robbery. He was being taken somewhere, kidnapped. *Kidnapped?* That only happened in Europe and the Middle East.

Schneider recognized the irregular, racing pulse at his temples. Paroxysmal atrial fibrillation. It had come on several times since his heart attack four years ago. Each time it had been successfully treated with medication. He wondered if his heart would survive the current assault. Did he have chest pain when he got out of the car? He couldn't remember, but was encouraged that he felt none now.

The car phone buzzed for the second time since Schneider had regained consciousness. Whoever was in the front paid no attention and the calling party rang off.

He rolled to his side until his back came to rest against the bottom of the backseat. Wiggling his fingers to try to regain some feeling, he touched an object on the floor behind him. Something that moved, but he couldn't recognize it by feel. He touched it again and again—a soft material intermeshed with something that could be metal. Suddenly, he knew what it was. An umbrella. He always kept one in the back of his car, and it usually fell off the seat, ending up on the floor. He was now quite certain that he was in his own car.

With his fingers, Schneider grasped one of the metal ribs of the umbrella. He bent it back and forth. Each movement caused him to wince as the cord cut into his skin. Finally, he felt the metal rib break. He could feel the sharpness of the jagged edges. Tediously, he worked a fragment of rib loose from the fabric that surrounded it. The piece was about four inches long. He now had something—a tool? A weapon? He tried to manipulate the fragment so that the sharp end could be pressed upward into the cord around his wrists. Maybe he could weaken the strands, break the goddam cord. Working the metallic segment with his fingers just increased the numbness. Finally, the piece of wire fell out of his grasp. He groped the carpet with his fingers and managed to find it, but when he tried to pick it up, it rolled away and he could not find it again.

The car phone buzzed a third time. Naomi is trying to reach me, he thought. Maybe she'll realize something is wrong and report me missing.

At the wheel of the Olds, Vandergrift drove along the surface streets of Canton at speeds up to sixty miles an hour from the Marino home in the northeast part of the city, west toward I-77. The emergency light sent a few cars scurrying to the side, but others ignored it, forcing her to slow down. The traffic became heavier as they approached the business section. As they approached the interstate, she slowed and asked Maharos in the shotgun seat, manning the two-way radio. "What's your guess, north or south?"

So far, Schneider's car had not been sighted.

Maharos threw an imaginary coin in the air and looked at the back of his hand. "Try south."

They had reached the top of the southbound entrance to I-77, when Cassidy's voice came on the speaker. "Maharos. We have a location for your suspect. Northbound I-77, now four miles north of Portage Street ramp. Highway Patrol car is trailing."

Northbound. His guess was wrong.

Maharos acknowledged while Vandergrift spun the car around on the shoulder, and with her finger pressing the horn button, sped down the ramp they had just come up.

"Look out!" Maharos shouted as a car came up the ramp directly at them. Vandergrift swerved to the side, avoiding by inches a collision. The eyes of the woman driving the other

DEAD END

car were saucer-wide, her mouth gaped. At the bottom of the ramp, Vandergrift drove to the northbound side and in a moment was back on the interstate, headed in the right direction.

Maharos yelled into the mike, "Give me a location on the Caddy."

Cassidy said, "They're about fourteen miles ahead of your position. Just passing the airport. Speed fifty-five."

"Tell Highway Patrol we'll be with him in ten minutes. Have him pursue but don't make a threatening move."

On the floor of his own car, Schneider could not recall ever being so uncomfortable—even lying in coronary care attached to monitors. Then, at least, he could call for painkillers.

The Cadillac slowed and his body slid toward the right door as the vehicle made a turn. A moment later, he was rolled against the back of the front seat. The car seemed to be going downhill, then leveled off. The roadway was no longer smooth.

In the highway patrol car, Officer Schulte reported that the Cadillac was turning off I-77 and headed east on State Route 619. He was following, a hundred yards behind.

Fisher's patrol car, streaking south, was approaching the state route 619 exit on the opposite side of the highway when he heard Schulte's radio report.. He swerved into the exit lane and sped down the ramp. At the bottom of the ramp, he turned east, the direction Schulte had reported the Caddy was headed. Twenty yards ahead of him was the bottom of the exit ramp down which Schulte was speeding, past the triangular "Yield" sign. Fisher saw Schulte's car as a blur out of the corner of his eye. Too late to avoid the sideswipe collision at the bottom of the ramp. Both racing patrol cars teetered on two wheels for a second before falling over on their sides like the covers of an open book. Both vehicles skidded on their doors along the asphalt for another thirty feet, then coming to a stop, blocking the entire width of the roadway.

The silence of the night was broken only by crickets in the surrounding fields and the hum of the cars on the highway behind.

Schulte opened his eyes, thinking he'd been asleep, dreaming. Why was he gripping a steering wheel? Lying on his side in the dark? Last thing he could remember was seeing another car out of the corner of his vision. His head ached and something wet dripped onto his lips. He tried moving an arm, then the other, each leg in turn. Everything moved. He looked up, saw stars in a black sky.

Gotta get out of here. Schulte moved toward the opening above his head, bumped against glass. A window. He found the crank alongside his thigh, turned it and saw the window open. He strained to pull himself up, but was bound by something that dug into his shoulder. A moment later he realized that his shoulder harness was still buckled, and he groped at his side until he found the buckle, snapped it open. It took all the effort he could muster to pull himself up and out of the car window. He slid to the ground and lay for a moment. When he forced himself to stand, the earth beneath his feet spun and he had to hold the side of his overturned car to keep from falling. When the dizziness eased, he spotted the other car. He stumbled to it and peered down into the front seat. The form slumped against the opposite door moved slightly and moaned.. He glanced down the darkened roadway ahead. The car Schulte had been trailing was out of sight.

THIRTY-FIVE

WITH VANDERGRIFT HUNCHED forward in the driver's seat, the Olds raced along I-77 at ninety miles an hour.

They were level with the Akron-Canton Airport when Cassidy's voice came over the speaker. "Maharos. Caddy has turned off on State Route 619. Appears headed east."

Maharos said, "That's the next exit, just up ahead."

Vandergrift nodded and veered into the right lane.

Cassidy again. "As of five minutes ago state patrol car 86 was trailing the Caddy, state patrol car 92 approaching on the interstate from the other direction. Now we have no contact with either."

A hundred yards ahead, lights illuminating the exit ramp to 619 appeared. Vandergrift slowed to sixty and started down the ramp. Halfway down, the headlight beam picked up a figure in the middle of the road, waving both hands in the air. She jammed the brake to the floor while she turned the wheel sharply to the left. The car skidded to a stop, a foot from the overturned patrol cars.

Maharos stared at the wrecks, then shifted his gaze to the highway patrol officer hobbling toward him, hatless, a trickle of blood running from his forehead to his chin. He leaned out of the window. "You all right?"

The state officer glanced at the red blinking light on the roof of the Olds. "Just shook up. I'm Schulte. The other guy is still in his car. I don't know how badly hurt he is yet."

Maharos and Vandergrift started to get out of the car to help. Schulte held the door on Maharos' side keeping it from opening. "Look, we've just been down a few minutes. Why don't you go after the Caddy—you should be able to pick him up. Just call in for some help. I'm worried about Fisher in the other car and my radio's out."

Vandergrift said. "Will do."

She swung the car over on the shoulder, drove through a roadside ditch and came back on the pavement beyond the wrecks.

Maharos was telling Cassidy about the state officers who were down, when the beat of helicopter rotor blades emerged overhead and a searchlight beam illuminated the road. Over the noise of the beating rotor blades, he shouted into the mike, "The bird is here. Tell him to cruise ahead and pick up the Caddy."

Rankins spotted the dirt road and turned onto it. In the distance he heard a terrible noise that drew closer. They were chasing him from overhead. A helicopter. Why couldn't they leave him alone. Couldn't they see, he had to do this? It was the only way. He was about to get his manhood back. He shut off his headlights and slowly drove on in the dark. The ruts in the unpaved lane served as tracks for the car wheels, guiding the Cadillac along. All he had to do was hold the steering wheel lightly to keep it from going into the underbrush.

He stopped the car, turned off the engine. Too dark to make out landmarks, but he knew he was close to where he had stashed the motorcycle. He remained seated in the car as the overhead noise came closer. A searchlight beam swept slowly from one side of the road to the other. For a few moments the engine noise seemed to be hovering directly overhead, but the searchlight beam missed the white car. The helicopter passed on, its engine noise gradually ebbing.

Rankins got out of the car, looked up at the sky for a silent moment. A warm feeling surged over him. Delicious. It was the same feeling he'd had with each of the others, but stronger this time, much stronger. He closed his eyes to savor it, then reached down and felt his crotch.

On the floor in the back, Schneider had felt the car stop. The throbbing at his temples became more intense. The sound of the helicopter engine came closer. Oh, God. Please. Please. As the motor sound moved off, grew fainter, he tried to cry out. No, come back. Please, come back. His eyes stung with tears, he felt them roll down his cheeks.

Maharos and Vandergrift listened to Cassidy relaying reports from the helicopter which, so far, had not spotted the Cadillac. They drove slowly, surveying both sides of the road.

Vandergrift said, "He can't have gone much farther than this. If he's not on the main road, there's got to be a turnoff." Her right hand was on the steering wheel. With the left she manipulated the car's searchlight, sweeping its beam over the road, from one side to the other. Maharos watched the aircraft's searchlight beam in the distance, saw that it was starting back toward them. Like a huge paint brush, it had been sweeping back and forth. Now it remained fixed on the right-hand side of the road, shining directly down.

Rankins stood alongside the Cadillac. They were not going to stop him now. Not when he was so close. He blinked to shut out the blazing white light that suddenly enveloped him.. He glanced up, moved toward the back car door. He had waited so long. He knew what he had to do. Nothing else mattered.

"GOT 'EM!"

Cassidy's voice boomed through the speaker in the Olds.

Vandergrift gunned the engine, speeding the car toward the helicopter's light. Maharos spotted the entrance to the dirt road, shouted to Vandergrift. She slammed on the brakes, the car skidding to a halt. Judging by their distance from the searchlight beam, Maharos estimated that the Cadillac was about two hundred yards into the woods. The beam was not moving. He reasoned that the Cadillac had stopped, the spot marked by the searchlight's beam.

In the helicopter, a sheriff's deputy sat next to the pilot. He knew that below him a man was being held hostage, but peering down through the tree branches, he saw only one person. He raised a bullhorn to his mouth and aimed it at the ground. "PUT YOUR HANDS ON THE HOOD AND DON'T MOVE."

Rankins heard the voice coming from the helicopter. What was the son of a bitch yelling for? He was busy. Didn't want to be bothered by no voice in the sky. He opened the back door. The prick doctor was lying on his back, his bound-up feet just inside the door frame. This one was no different from the others. The fright in their eyes like that of the cats he'd strangled as a kid. Muffled cries came through the gag, partially drowned out by the noise of the helicopter engine. Pearl-like beads of sweat shimmered on the doctor's bald head. Rankins took from his trouser pocket the twenty-five caliber handgun and stepped into the car just beyond the doctor's bound feet.

Schneider raised his head from the floor of the car. For the first time, he looked at the man who had tied him hand and foot and kidnapped him. Had he seen him somewhere before? A gun in his hand! Each heartbeat sent a pang of pain surging through his chest and left arm. He knew he was about to die. Adrenaline surged through his body and, as though the lower part of his body were detached from the rest of him, he felt his knees draw up to protect his exposed chest and belly. Then, like a leaping giant bullfrog, he let his legs shoot out and his feet crashed into the man's upper belly, sending him flying out of the car. Schneider could no longer see him, but over the noise of the helicopter he heard gasping sounds as the man fought to get air back into his lungs.

Finally Rankins was able to breath, slowly climbed to his feet. This one was a fighter. He had to be careful. He walked around to the other side of the car and opened the back door. Now he was staring down into the doctor's face, gazing down into his eyes, wide open in fright. He was almost there. Almost. He placed the muzzle against the doctor's forehead and tightened his finger on the trigger.

Turn him over!

Rankins turned his head, looked around. "What?"
Turn him over!
He nodded once, understanding. It had to be done correctly, ritually.

Lying on his back, Schneider knew he was already dead. Hadn't he seen the gun muzzle at his forehead, the man's finger on the trigger? Couldn't understand why he was still able to watch as the man came at him from the other side of the car, toward his head. Saw him tuck the pistol in his belt and felt himself grasped by the shoulders. Trying to turn him over? No, he might be dead but he was not going to let this happen. He struggled until the man stopped trying. Watched him back out of the car and bend down to pick up something from the ground. Saw him raise his arm, something in his hand. Saw him start to bring it down.

Rankins watched the doctor's body as it twitched for a few seconds, then lay still. Blood poured from a deep forehead gash where the rock had hit him, but his chest moved, he was breathing. Good. That's not how he must die. He grabbed the doctor's shoulders, pulled him out of the car and rolled him over so that he lay face down in the dirt road next to the car.

Vandergrift and Maharos left the Olds parked at the entrance to the dirt roadway. Maharos grabbed a flashlight from its dashboard clip. With guns drawn, they ran down the dirt road in the direction of the helicopter's beam, Maharos playing the flashlight beam on the rutted roadway. Fifty yards into the woods, the roadway took a turn. Past the bend they could see the Cadillac one hundred yards ahead. As they ran, they saw Rankins' raised arm suddenly come crashing down.

"FREEZE. POLICE."

They shouted almost in unison as they ran crouched, one on either side of the narrow dirt roadway, their guns pointing toward the sky. Now Rankins was pulling a form out of the car without even looking in their direction.

Rankins straddled the doctor's body, loosened the man's collar, then gently placed his finger tips on the bony prominence at the base of his neck. Yes, there it was. The first thoracic. Above that the seventh cervical. Now. He marked his place with the tip of his index finger and with the other hand slowly brought the muzzle of his gun toward it.

Maharos was now directly behind Rankins, a foot from his head, his extended hands holding his service revolver in front of him. "DROP IT NOW!"

Maharos waited one second, watched as Rankins continued in slow motion to position the muzzle of his gun at the back of the man's neck. For the second time in his life, Maharos squeezed the trigger of his gun while it was aimed at a person. The back of Rankins' skull suddenly disappeared.

Maharos remained frozen, his gun extended in firing position. Rankins slowly fell forward on top of the unconscious doctor. For a moment there was no further movement, then Rankins' right leg began to twitch violently. Maharos counted silently as the leg jerked—two, three, four, five, six, seven times. Then lay still in the dirt road.

THIRTY-SIX

VANDERGRIFT ALMOST FELL backward out of her chair as flames shot halfway to the ceiling from the *sagan-aki*, a goat cheese flambé, the waitress was holding.

"Oompah!"

Maharos and the Sussmans shouted in unison with a dozen other diners in the Athenian Restaurant.

Marc Sussman guffawed. "Karen, you're going to have to learn to get used to these fireworks when you eat in a Greek restaurant."

She shook her head slowly. "I hate to wait around and see what comes out of the *dolmas* Al ordered for me."

It was two weeks following the chase down I-77 after Rankins. A few days later, Maharos had called Marc Sussman to invite him and his wife, Annabelle, to dinner. "I owe you one for your help on the case. You called it."

"You mean the heptamaniac. Yeah, I read the gruesome report in the paper. Are you still on administrative leave?"

"No. They gave me back my gun."

"You feel okay?"

"You asking if I need a session on your couch?"

"Don't be a macho wiseass. I happen to know that inside that hairy chest there beats a heart."

Maharos said, "No, really, I'm feeling fine now. I *did* have a couple of bad nights afterward, but I convinced myself that I had no choice. I gave Rankins a chance. It was either him or Dr. Schneider."

"How is Pee-pee Doc?"

"Except for a row of stitches that make his head look like a National League baseball, he's all right."

Sussman said, "Last time I talked to you, you were cursing because you'd been subpoenaed to appear as a witness in the trial of that decorator in Canton—the one who'd been arrested for killing his lover. What ever became of that?"

"Yeah, Lance Harwood. The charges were dropped on the basis of evidence that Rankins had killed Burnstein. There was another guy too, Roy Young, who was being held in New Philly. They had booked him for killing Hamberger. Of course, they let him go.

"I'm sure I don't have to tell you that it's rough being an executioner, but—"

Sussman said, "I know what you mean, Al. It resolved a lot of problems. You know, of course, that Rankins probably would never have gone to trial. With his background, he'd have ended up back in Oakwood or another institution for a few years. Then—well, who knows?"

"You're probably right, even though there was no question that he had killed the eight people—six on his list and one bonus plus that bastard Show on the stakeout. We had collected a file full of evidence. Incidentally, we got a match on the blue fibers from his sweater, also on his shoe prints with those we found at a couple of the murder scenes."

"I'd love to write a paper on Rankins for one of the psych journals. You know, a guy who's impotent, paranoid-schizophrenic, heptamaniacal—and does serial murders."

"Would it help your paper if I told you that he also had dandruff and athlete's foot?"

Sussman chuckled. "I guess you're over your depression."

"Seriously Marc, I know the guy had scrambled eggs for brains—although he was not stupid. But you've always told us that most psychotics are not dangerous. What made this one different?"

"I can give you an answer, although I can't vouch for its accuracy. My theory is that he thought he was getting instructions from someone in the Bible."

"Voices?"

"Uh-huh. Schizophrenics have auditory hallucinations at times. Some of his testimony at the preliminary hearing on the disappearance and presumed death of his landlady strongly suggest that he was hearing voices in his head."

"That's still not a reason to kill someone."

"Of course not. But we know that he was impotent, had been all his life, probably on an inherited hormonal basis. Give someone with paranoid-schizophrenia an idea that his failure to get an erection is due to something like an operation on his genitals—for example, the circumcision—and you've got what, in his mind, is a reason to kill. In this case, the doctor who performed the circumcision became a potential victim, and so did anyone else in any way connected.

"Notice that all the victims were male, except for Abelson's paramour. We're quite sure that she wasn't an *intended* victim. Rankins probably had some weird idea that the sexuality of the men he killed would be transferred to him if he took their lives. In that case he would see his victims as sacrificial."

"One thing that had us puzzled was his using a different gun for each of the killings. We wondered why. He put his signature on each of the victims by shooting them in the same place, so he wasn't trying to fool us on ballistics."

Sussman said, "Of course, we'll never know. But my guess is that the voices in his head told him that he had to use a new sacrificial instrument for each one."

"Speaking of sacrificial instruments, we never did find the guns he used."

"They're probably at the bottom of a lake—maybe several lakes."

Maharos said, "You guys have an answer for everything."

"Ask and ye shall receive. How about a little therapy?"

"No thanks. I'm handling it all right. But thanks for the offer."

Now, seated in the Greek restaurant, Annabelle Sussman said, "Karen, have you ever had this lemon soup before?"

"Never. I've been missing a treat."

Marc Sussman said, "You've been hanging out with Alexander the Great for over a month and he hasn't introduced you to *gyros* and *spanakopita* either?"

"Do hot dogs and hamburgers count?"

Sussman threw up his hands. "For the next occasion I'm going to give you a copy of the *Joy Of Greek Cooking*."

Vandergrift dropped her gaze and examined some crumbs on the tablecloth. Annabelle Sussman looked from Vandergrift to Maharos. A suppressed smile touched the corners of Maharos' mouth.

Annabelle said, "It'll make a great wedding present."

Vandergrift's face turned pink.

Marc Sussman spread a glob of cheese on a piece of *pita* bread. "Isn't that just like a woman? For God's sake, Annabelle, just because they look at each other like a couple of lovesick school kids it doesn't mean they're picking out silverware patterns."

Maharos put his hand over Karen's. "Well, we're not ready to make an announcement, but Karen has put in for a transfer to the Mahoning County Sheriff's Department."

Sussman smiled, nodded his head slowly. "There's real romance for you. Whether they get married, depends on a clerk in some bureau finding the right stamp—what are you staring at, Al?"

Maharos had a grin on his face. He pointed his fork at Sussman. "Hey, did you know you chew each mouthful seven times?"